ELVIRA CHAN

The State of Us

Elvira Chan [signature]

Trish, thank you so much for supporting my novel and taking an interest in it. I can't wait to hear what you think and hope you love the story and characters as much as I do.
Happy reading! ♡

Copyright © 2023 by Elvira Chan

All rights reserved. No part of this publication may be reproduced, stored or transmitted in any form or by any means, electronic, mechanical, photocopying, recording, scanning, or otherwise without written permission from the publisher. It is illegal to copy this book, post it to a website, or distribute it by any other means without permission.

This novel is entirely a work of fiction. The names, characters and incidents portrayed in it are the work of the author's imagination. Any resemblance to actual persons, living or dead, events or localities is entirely coincidental.

Designations used by companies to distinguish their products are often claimed as trademarks. All brand names and product names used in this book and on its cover are trade names, service marks, trademarks and registered trademarks of their respective owners. The publishers and the book are not associated with any product or vendor mentioned in this book. None of the companies referenced within the book have endorsed the book.

© 2023 Elvira Chan. All rights reserved.

First edition

Cover art by Flavia Chan

"Love is so short, forgetting is so long."

Pablo Neruda

Contents

Acknowledgement	ii
Chapter 1	1
Chapter 2	8
Chapter 3	18
Chapter 4	31
Chapter 5	45
Chapter 6	54
Chapter 7	71
Chapter 8	86
Chapter 9	101
Chapter 10	113
Chapter 11	132
Chapter 12	144
Chapter 13	155
Chapter 14	180
Chapter 15	194
About the Author	215

Acknowledgement

With heartfelt thanks to the people in my life who have encouraged and supported me in every way possible. Thank you to my mother, who is the strongest and most thoughtful person I know. You offer an endless supply of unsolicited advice, delicious home-cooked meals, and unconditional love, and I feel lucky to have you as my biggest support. Special thanks to my sister, Flavia, for illustrating the cover of this book and creating something that perfectly captures the heart of this story. To my brilliant family, thank you for your love, support, and generosity. To my partner, thank you for your encouragement, sense of humor, and cake supply while I edited this book a thousand times and brought it up in every conversation. Your love and support mean the world to me. To my friends, thank you for all the joy, strength, and memories you bring into my life. Thank you for having me in your life. I am grateful for you in more ways than I possibly know how to say. Last but not least, for anyone who has ever been in a long-distance relationship or picked up this book, here's to you. Thank you for giving *The State of Us* a chance to be as special to you as it is to me.

Chapter 1

Autumn came quickly for Seattle that year. The smell of damp leaves being ground into the pavement by car tires and riding boots was fresh in the air. It had been pouring rain the night Olivia's father called in November. It had rained so hard that every drop sounded like a pebble thrown against her bedroom window, with the streets below washed clean. Her father had called to ask if she would fly to New York so he could see her in January.

New York was on the opposite side of the country from where Olivia lived with her mother. Olivia had decided long ago that Seattle was a dreary place in comparison to sparkling New York City, and a fresh beginning with her dad in January seemed as good a time as any.

It had been a long time since she last saw him, and if not for the occasional text or generic birthday card he sent, he would have been no different from a stranger to her. For years, she wondered if she'd see him again or if their relationship would consist only of short phone calls and polite texts for the rest of her life.

But something felt different this time.

Something good was going to happen. She could feel it.

It was a chance to close the gap between what she wished for and what she knew to be the reality, and she wasn't going to let it slip away.

Olivia's father preferred the world in a muted haze, with stiff drinks and a night at the casino as an antidote to numb the unforgiving blows he had been dealt all his life. He'd arrive home at odd hours, making up implausible stories to explain his absence and worsening temper, his tired eyes darting around, searching for something Olivia couldn't see.

Those memories and those nights were the grey ones to her. There was no color or celebration or joy in any of them. There was no light in them.

Those grey memories were cold and hard and sharp, just like glass.

But sometimes, just sometimes, the memories were colorful.

One sweltering afternoon in September, back when she was just a child, her dad had driven them down to the beach after school ended one day. They sat in the blinding sunshine, sharing green tea and cherry ice cream cones while they watched seagulls do their acrobatic dives and somersaults above the grey and blue waves.

Olivia's small palms had gone sticky with melted ice cream and gold sand spilled into their shoes even as they tried very hard to avoid it. Her dad brought a plastic bag full of stale breadcrumbs and Olivia threw fistfuls of them into the sky like confetti while the seagulls and pigeons feasted at their feet. Olivia and her dad ran across the golden hills of sand as their footprints trailed their route like a treasure map.

She remembered how hard she had laughed that day and how *good* things used to be.

It was hard to say just when everything came apart for them.

One little snag seemed to undo everything over time, all the tiny moments where her parents' relationship had unraveled in front of her like the threads on a cheap sweater until it all came undone.

Eventually, her father left Seattle's dimming glow and traded it for the glittering towers that made up New York City, leaving behind everything and everyone that ever mattered, including the two people that would have bet their all on him the way he bet his all on red or black at the roulette table.

* * *

As Olivia left campus and waited at the university bus stop, the pavement shone from the sheen of the rain, apartment windows and headlights glowed in the darkness like phantom eyes, and the leaves on the streets had been softened by the relentless drizzle of autumn rain.

CHAPTER 1

The stuffy lecture hall had been warm and dry, and the comforting drone of her professor's voice had almost lulled her to sleep. The sound of clicking laptop keys mimicked the sound of the rain outside and she found her mind drifting lazily away to other things.

What would her father think if he saw her now as a young woman, someone who was educated and talented, someone who would make him proud and was so full of potential? Maybe he would finally see her differently now that she didn't need him to take care of her in any way, now that she wasn't a child or a liability any longer.

All the way home, she thought about how much trouble her dad had already caused in the past and how much uncertainty those memories stirred up now in her heart. The proposition of leaving for New York to visit him had resulted in weeks of fighting with her mother. Eventually, they both grew tired of it and opted for silence instead. The silence had been a necessary break from the fighting, but it didn't bring either of them peace. Olivia and her mother had never been close by any means, but weeks had already passed and the silence stubbornly remained. Olivia just wished that her mother could see her point of view.

She still cared about her father.

At least, she must *still* care a little if she keeps so many details and memories of him close to her heart. Her dad was far from perfect, but he was still a hero figure to her in some twisted way.

Olivia closed the front door quietly behind her when she got home and shook the snowflakes out of her hair, hoping their stony-faced resident landlord wasn't snooping around as usual. He always seemed to stick his nose in their business, constantly giving Olivia and her mom a hard time about one thing or another. His hobbies included nitpicking over everything, trudging noisily around on the second floor where he lived, and waking Olivia up in the middle of the night with his hacking cough from smoking one too many cigarettes on the upstairs balcony.

But the house was quiet as Olivia entered the living room, the indoor heat warming her cheeks and melting the snowflakes that had collected on her clothes. She looked over at their pale imitation of a Christmas tree as it blinked tiredly at her from a corner with its dimming bulbs, casting unearthly shades of red and green on the walls.

It was especially hard not to think about her dad during the holidays. She was too old to believe in dragons and fairies, but nobody seemed to question a belief in miracles. Miracles seemed just as improbable as little cottages with dwarfs living inside and witches with poisoned red apples.

It had been a Christmas tradition for Olivia and her dad to make hot chocolate from scratch together, filling up their favorite mugs and topping them with the biggest marshmallows they could find. He'd always use the good cocoa from a specialty store, not the cheap packets from the drugstore with the granules that never seemed to fully dissolve, and he always remembered to use Olivia's favorite mug with the gold stars—the one she had picked out during a road trip to Los Angeles when she was five.

The two of them would sip their cares away every Christmas in front of the fireplace while the rest of the family talked and laughed in the kitchen. It was by the fireplace where she would witness magic with him. Her dad always said that if she closed her eyes and counted to one hundred, there was a chance she would see one of Santa's elves when she opened her eyes again. And she always saw the elves.

Or at least, she was *pretty* sure she did.

As Olivia got older, she still played along whenever her dad pointed out a little man in green and red or claimed that he saw a pointy ear sticking out from behind a fireplace log.

When he left for New York, Olivia never saw the dancing elves again.

She wasn't sure if she had ever seen them at all.

Drawing herself back to the present and away from the long-gone memories, Olivia shrugged off her jacket and took a look around the house. It was quiet, save for the incessant ticking of the clock mounted on the wall and her footsteps. There was something a little melancholy about a house so silent during the holidays.

As she started to head down the hallway to her bedroom, a shadowy figure slumped on the couch began to move. Olivia swallowed her fear and twisted around to face the phantom, only to find her mother sitting silently there,

CHAPTER 1

her fingers twisted into a nervous knot in her lap. It was strange to see her in one place as still as a statue when she was usually flitting about and chattering endlessly like a nervous bird.

She was the older and more worried version of Olivia. They both had the same dark hair and deep almond eyes, the same petite build, and comparable features. It sometimes seemed like their looks were the only real commonality they shared besides the blood running through their veins.

"Oh, good. You're home. I was beginning to worry." Her mother sat up, unclasping her hands and leaning forward expectantly. "Did you get a chance to think everything over for January?"

Her tone was light and harmless to the untrained ear, but Olivia could tell there was a hidden meaning beneath her words. Olivia lightly folded her coat over one arm and perched carefully on the edge of the couch. "Think about what?"

Her mother waved her hand in the air as if dismissing something insignificant. "About flying to New York in January to see *him*," she said, almost spitting out the last word. "It's going to be stressful for you to fly to him right after your exams. And the airports are insane during the holidays anyway. You've only traveled by yourself once or twice, Olivia. I just worry." She paused. "I don't think you should see him."

"Don't do this," Olivia groaned, shifting away from her mother and feeling the familiar flames of disappointment licking at her. "This is the first time Dad has ever asked me to be in New York with him and I might never get the chance to do it again. I'll only be there for a week and you know as well as I do that schoolwork and traveling alone is *not* the issue." She stared at her mother. "Do you really expect me to avoid him for the rest of my life?"

"He could be someone completely different from what you expect or want. I think you're getting your hopes up."

Olivia didn't respond.

"I just have a bad feeling about this whole thing." Her mother leaned back on the couch as if the very idea itself exhausted her. "Your dad's never asked to see you before. Ever. And now, making you fly out in the middle of winter to see him like it's some cozy family reunion all of a sudden? Ridiculous.

Your schedule and needs clearly aren't at the top of his priority list, not that it's a surprise. Nothing's a priority to your dad except his own happiness."

They were just words, but the pain Olivia felt twisting around her heart was evidence that they still cut deep. Her plan was unraveling very quickly in front of her and the thought of having to tell her dad that she couldn't visit filled her heart with both disappointment and fear, though she couldn't explain why she felt that last emotion along with the first. Her dad wasn't a monster. There wasn't anything to fear.

"Well, I want to go." Olivia didn't look at her mother as she spoke. "It's not too much to ask for, Mom. It's *one* visit. And maybe he's no longer the villain you've convinced yourself he is? You said it yourself that you barely know him anymore. So much time has already gone by. Maybe Dad really wants to make amends. After all, the holidays are about family and peace and goodwill and all that jazz, right? There's no better time if you ask me." She paused. "Not that you would."

Her mother bristled, pressing her lips together into a hard line, the loaded conversation eating at her from the inside out. Faith was a valuable quality, but life wasn't often known for dealing the most favorable cards. Being blindly optimistic and naive would only lead to self-destruction in the long run, and she was painfully aware of this fact.

"The holidays should be spent with family, yes. But he chose not to be a part of our family, Olivia. He chose to lie, he chose to take advantage of us, and he ultimately chose to leave."

"But he's choosing something different now, isn't he?"

"You don't know *anything* about him. It's naive to think that he'll change who he is for you. He wasn't here for this family when it mattered most, and he certainly doesn't deserve to have you when it's convenient for him. He has to live out the consequences of his choices, with or without us."

"You don't know who he's become, Mom."

"And *you* do?" Her mother's voice was hard, but then a look of softness passed over her face a second later as she huffed out a resigned breath. "Olivia, all I'm saying is that he isn't someone you should have high hopes for. I don't want you to be disappointed. We were a family once, but he decided one day

CHAPTER 1

that he didn't want it anymore. He was never cut out to be a good father or a good husband. Even if you go to New York, things are not going to be the same."

It was true. Things weren't going to be the same again. Things were never perfect or warm in the first place, but Olivia wanted it all still. It used to make her feel incomplete and different as a kid when everybody had stories about family vacations or asked Olivia why her dad never went to their school plays in the evening or parent-teacher conferences or even just picked her up from school.

She knew her mother tried her best to fill the gaps that her father left, but there always seemed to be a raw and jagged piece of her life where her dad used to be that just couldn't be smoothed over.

But she couldn't sit and twiddle her thumbs anymore and run away from the truth.

All her life, she wanted to know the reason why he left the way he did, and why he didn't love her the way she loved him. Even if she didn't get those answers from her father, she would at least get to start over with him.

Olivia breathed out slowly, surprised at the strength in her voice when she spoke again. "I know you're not going to approve of this, but I hope you can forgive me." She took a breath. "I already booked the flight."

She got off the couch and started to walk down the hall to her room, pushing away the image of her mother staring at her from the couch, her expression one of disappointment and defeat.

Chapter 2

Outside, the bitter chill of late December swept unforgivingly through the city of Seattle. Passersby wrapped snugly in their plaid scarves and winter coats dashed by in a rush, though some entered the restaurant where Olivia worked with rosy cheeks and a sigh of relief at the sight of warm tea and hot food. The murmur of conversation was at an easy pace throughout the room and the clinking of knives and forks against plates was reassuring and familiar.

The restaurant was familiar and comforting to Olivia as well, but for different reasons. From the sound of the barista grinding the coffee beans to the familiar smell of the sweet potato soup with coconut milk simmering in the kitchen, the busyness of the restaurant environment kept her mind off everything else.

The chefs were absorbed in their tasks of slicing, tossing, scrubbing, mixing, and plating, but they still took the time to grant Olivia a warm smile and a quick wave when she came in. Olivia smoothed her dark hair into a neat knot and rolled up the sleeves of her white oxford shirt, mentally preparing herself for the rush of hungry lunch customers. From the looks of the kitchen and the number of patrons already seated at multiple tables, it was going to be a busy shift. Olivia swept into the kitchen to grab some laminated menus, nearly bumping into her coworker, Ingrid, who was leaning against the counter with her head in her hands.

"Ing, are you alright?" Olivia touched her shoulder.

At the sound of her voice, Ingrid looked up in surprise and smiled. "Oh! Good morning, Liv, dear," she said, pulling Olivia into a small hug. "I'm fine, just got a terrible migraine this morning, but that's nothing to write home about. I get them all the time. I'll be fit as a fiddle once my shift is over."

"You sure?"

"I'm sure." Ingrid gave Olivia's arm a reassuring squeeze before hoisting a tray of dirty dishes up on her shoulder with practiced swiftness and ease. "Don't worry about me."

"If you say so, but make sure you take care of yourself."

"You're beginning to sound like me when I talk to Sophie." Ingrid shot her a smile as she walked away, a real one that crinkled up her eyes and broadened her cheeks. Ingrid's four-year-old daughter, Sophie, was pretty much a regular at the restaurant, often sitting alone at one of the empty tables near the back while Ingrid waited tables late into the night. Olivia and the other waitresses would sneak Sophie warm milk and apple pie while she colored and daydreamed and read books. Ingrid loved her to bits and would do anything and everything to keep her happy and safe.

A part of Olivia hurt when she thought about her own mother and all the distance that had come between them since the night they argued about going to New York. There had been so much uncomfortable silence and evening meals that consisted of sitting at opposite ends of the table, each with their phone or a magazine propped in front of them while they ate in silence. During the day, Olivia attended classes while her mother worked and it gave them some space to breathe before coming home, but it didn't fix anything at the heart of it.

Space gave them clarity, but it didn't give them peace or closure. The silence between them felt heavier and heavier with each passing day, and it killed Olivia to leave for New York like that.

She sighed and shook the thought out of her head. Instead, she began to pile plates with steaming cuts of seasoned beef and roasted russet potatoes on an empty tray. Work was a welcome distraction despite its demanding pace—there was no thinking, there was just doing, and the entire morning and afternoon passed by in a familiar haze. Customers seemed to be in a grand mood, with uproarious bouts of laughter interspersing the sound of ice clinking against glasses and forks scraping against plates. There were only a handful of people left in the restaurant by late afternoon, including a group of elderly women chatting idly over their Turkish coffees and a couple deep in conversation while they shared a piece of chocolate cherry cake.

Olivia leaned against the counter and massaged her shoulders gently to get rid of the stiffness there, her gaze absentmindedly landing on one of the new hires. He had as many smart remarks coming out of his mouth as there were freckles splattered across his fair-skinned face, and he was clearing a table that Olivia had the misfortune of serving that afternoon.

He stood in front of the table littered with half-eaten plates, crumpled napkins full of dissected sandwiches, and used teabags and sugar packets tossed on the floor, looking as if his soul had just left his body.

"Some people don't deserve to go to restaurants," he grumbled. "There are decent humans and then there are assholes that leave wet, snotty napkins and soggy cake on the table and have crumbs all over the carpet like it's a damn frat house. This is the human spectrum."

Olivia laughed. "You forgot to add people who say they have a gluten allergy and then come here to eat our famous flatbread pizzas to the list."

She was relieved to see him roll his eyes and smile, even as he begrudgingly cleared away the restaurant crime scene at table twenty-nine.

* * *

The bus windows on the way back home were streaked with salt and snow, and the blanket of cold pressed down on the city heavily that evening. The house was both empty *and* frigid when Olivia got home, and she silently cursed her landlord for not raising the thermostat in the dead of winter. Keeping her coat around her shoulders, she took out a pot of leftover vegetable soup from the fridge and popped it in the microwave.

It was a little lonely without her mother around the house that night. Olivia was leaving for New York soon, and although the two of them had agreed to put aside their disagreement for a moment to make dinner plans before she left, her mother had to work late that night.

As the slow hum of the microwave worked its magic, Olivia went to her

CHAPTER 2

room and eyed her suitcase in the corner that was ready to go. She popped open her bedside drawer and took out her journal, thinking she'd write on the plane and during the trip itself. As she did so, she saw a little white envelope at the bottom of the drawer that she had long forgotten about. Flipping it open, she saw photographs she had rescued from the trash years ago after her parents had separated. Her mother had tossed them out one night, so Olivia had picked through the photographs like a miner digging for gold, kneeling by the trash bin and carefully cleaning them off one by one.

They were memories of happier times. There were photos of her parents standing together at Coney Island with its striped tents and colorful Wonder Wheel spinning in the background, photos of their travels across several states, and even ones from ordinary backyard barbecues and of them sharing a soda on the boardwalk on a normal Tuesday night.

Olivia flipped to the last two photos in the envelope, which also happened to be her favorite ones. The first was taken when she was just a few weeks old, swathed in a blushing pink blanket with only her dark eyes and rosy cheeks visible from underneath a knit beanie, her parents smiling at the camera and leaning affectionately into one another.

Her parents had smiled like it was the best day of their lives, and maybe it had been.

The second photo was of her dad. It had been taken at her parents' wedding, two years before Olivia was born. He looked handsome and excited in his dark suit with his hair slicked to the side, an eager and slightly mischievous grin on his face as he looked somewhere just out of frame. Olivia always liked to think that her dad was looking at her mom, standing somewhere just behind the photographer in all her bridal glory.

Olivia held the photos for a moment longer, then carefully put them back inside the drawer. There were only a few days left until her flight on New Year's Eve.

It was going to be a new beginning.

She could feel it in her bones.

* * *

The weather was awful the night of her flight, with fat flakes of snow sticking to the windshield as quickly as the wipers could brush them away.

The taxi driver would look up at the sky and mumble about the horrible weather every few minutes, his eyes flicking to the slick roads and the piles of dirty snow pushed into dark hills on both sides. The snowflakes that streaked across Olivia's window in violent flurries made her nervous, but she prayed that she would make it to the airport on time anyway.

Her flight was on schedule when she last checked, but when she was met with the sight of unhappy passengers after the security checkpoint, her stomach clenched. Olivia forced herself to continue walking until she found her gate, even as the familiar feeling of anxiety started to constrict her throat.

She made her way to a ticket agent who looked like they were debating on a career change as more irritated passengers gathered in line. "I think my flight is delayed due to the weather conditions, but could you please double-check?" Olivia asked, slipping her boarding pass across the counter to the agent, her heart thumping with equal parts anxiety and blind hope.

"I'm afraid all flights are either delayed or canceled for tonight. Flight 1219 to New York is going to be delayed until tomorrow morning." The agent pushed the boarding pass back across the counter to Olivia with a rehearsed smile that was free of true empathy. "I'm terribly sorry."

"What time will it be leaving?"

"If everything goes accordingly, the next available flight for New York will be taking off at 7:15 a.m. tomorrow once the weather clears up."

Olivia's stomach twisted as she dragged her suitcase away from the counter, weighing her options. Her fingertips instinctively reached for her phone in her coat pocket.

Home was just ten digits away, just a call to the taxi company.

But going back home felt like giving up, like taking another step backward.

Her fingers tightened around her phone. Sucking in a deep breath, she looked beyond the sky-high windows of the airport, watching the powdery snow come down, burying everything in mountains of white. There was nothing she could do, so she wandered over to an empty seat by the departure gates, everyone else absorbed by the news, their phone, a conversation, or a

CHAPTER 2

glossy magazine. She hadn't eaten much that night before leaving for the airport, and hunger was beginning to gnaw at her stomach now.

The airport was crowded and noisy and she could hear strangers getting all bent out of shape at the check-in counter over one thing or another. Olivia squeezed her eyes shut and sank into the seat, the familiar waves of anxiety beginning to rise. Her face was starting to feel warm and breathing was beginning to feel almost impossible, and if she didn't find some way to reel herself back in, she'd be having a full-blown panic attack at the airport, and the thought of it made things a hundred times worse.

She was so lost in her thoughts that it took her several seconds to realize that somebody was tapping her on the shoulder. Olivia opened her eyes and peered behind her to see a stranger sitting there. "I was wondering if you were alright," he said, cocking his head. The corners of his mouth turned up in a kind smile.

Olivia released her death grip on the armrest. "I could be better, not going to lie."

"Yeah, kind of looks that way. Anything I can do to help?"

Olivia shook her head slowly, not wanting the lightheaded feeling to get worse. "Not really." She paused. "Well, maybe you can sit with me for a bit? I could use a distraction."

The stranger laughed, his brown eyes crinkling at the corners. "If there's anything I'm good at, it's being a distraction. Or a wise guy." He paused, pretending to think. "Depends on who you ask, but my mom would vouch for the latter."

A laugh bubbled from Olivia's throat. "Okay, I'll ask her if I ever see her, but for now, think you can be a distraction instead?"

"Sure." He walked over to her side and took a seat. "All you have to do is ask."

* * *

The past year had been different from anything Jamie had ever experienced.

It was a year of packing up everything he knew, a year of letting go of control for once. His grandfather had gotten so sick, and it broke Jamie's heart to see him bedridden and unable to move without feeling pain when he was usually so jubilant and armed with bad puns and a big hug for anyone and everyone around him.

It had been a unanimous decision for his family to fly back and forth from New York to Texas to take care of him, but they decided to take a hiatus from their home in New York and just stay in Texas for a year. His grandfather had gotten ill to the point of potentially meeting his maker any day, and Jamie didn't have the heart to be away when it happened. Staying in Texas with his grandfather was the easiest decision he ever made.

The whole flight to Texas last year, his parents had been quiet. While Jamie didn't ask, he knew they shared the unsinkable feeling that everything would change.

And things *did* change.

Their days and nights revolved around taking care of a dying man, and the grief and helplessness that came with it was obvious.

One morning, Jamie woke up and just knew he had to be somewhere else. He couldn't take another day watching his grandfather fade away. There was just the feeling that he needed to go someplace where his grandfather wasn't dying, someplace where his grandfather wasn't slowly coming undone in the worst way possible. Seattle was where his grandfather and grandmother had spent many of their years before they retired, and although Jamie couldn't bring his grandfather back there, maybe there was a way for him to bring Seattle *to* him. It was the place where his grandfather fell in love and the place where he once worked, walked the streets, ate the food, and breathed the air. And Jamie desperately wanted to hold on to that.

Seattle felt like home in some ways to him too. The ivory snow made the red-orange buildings look like Christmas ornaments littered across the city. The glassy marina and its docked ships floated like diligent guards in the evening while the deserted wheel by Elliott Bay glowed in shades of romantic fuchsia every night. It was a breath of fresh air to be somewhere else, after feeling stuck and suffocated for so many months in Texas. There was nothing left for his family to do now. They simply had to see Jamie's

CHAPTER 2

grandfather go, which was going to be any day now.

So, he didn't mind leaving Seattle a little later than he intended due to the weather. He rather enjoyed watching the snow collect outside, the little tufts of white cotton cascading down like a gentle veil. Other times, it was a relentless shower of glistening specks, but it was all beautiful to him. It reminded him of the winters back home in New York. A canceled flight on New Year's Eve seemed like the worst way to start the year for everyone else at the airport, but Jamie was almost grateful for the prolonged pause from his reality.

But then he saw her.

A twenty-something woman stood alone at the counter with dark brown hair and round eyes that sparkled. She was pretty, he concluded, but her features were all distorted by worry as she eventually walked toward him and the empty seats, dropping tiredly into one. She gripped the armrests so hard that her knuckles turned white and had her eyes squeezed shut as if blocking out the world.

Jamie wasn't usually one to poke his nose into other people's problems unless they asked him to, but a little voice pushed him to do it that night.

So, he did.

And now, after sitting with her for several minutes, her breathing was slow and even again and her cheeks seemed to have a little bit of color back in them.

Finally, she opened her eyes and looked at Jamie, slowly exhaling.

"Thanks a lot for sitting with me. Anxiety's a bitch and it pops up at the worst times," she chuckled. "But I'm also stuck at the airport and starving, so that's probably enough reason."

"You're welcome. I don't know if I can do anything about the flight or being stuck here overnight, but this might help with the hunger pangs." Jamie pulled out a large Tootsie Roll log, the familiar white, brown, and red wrapping glinting underneath the bright airport lights. It was his favorite—it was a portable chocolate milkshake wrapped in wax paper, a blend of cocoa and fresh cream. "Just don't blame me if you end up getting a sugar crash later."

He unwrapped it, broke off a piece, and offered it to her.

"Thanks, but no thanks. Tootsie Rolls were the only candy my parents would buy when I was a kid, and I can't say they've grown on me. I used to pay my friend a few dollars to bring over an assortment of gummy worms and caramels instead and we'd hide out and eat them all up in my room. She was my candy dealer."

Jamie snorted. "I can't believe you don't appreciate the finery that is a Tootsie Roll. Did you know that they were Frank Sinatra's favorite candy? He was buried with them alongside a bottle of Jack Daniels and some cigarettes." He popped the candy into his mouth and chewed thoughtfully. "According to Google."

"If you have a sweet tooth, you'll have to try the red velvet cake from Sugar Bakery here in Seattle."

"Are you from here?" He peered at her, his eyes narrowed with curiosity.

"Born and raised, but it's not true what they say about us."

"Oh, no? What's that?"

She rolled her eyes, smiling. "It's not true that we're all seafood-loving, passive-aggressive, introverted hippies that personally know someone who made an appearance on *Grey's Anatomy*."

"I just wanted to hear it straight from the source."

Olivia nudged him. "What about *you*? Coming or going?"

"Going. Back to Texas." He smiled. "You know the basics. Acres of barren desert, more tumbleweed than humans, gun-toting cowboys riding horses through the city streets."

"Sounds fascinating."

Jamie chuckled. "I'm pulling your leg, but it's a great place. My grandparents retired there as soon as they got the chance. They never wanted to visit us in New York with all its chaos."

"You're from New York? Ah, I'm actually headed there tonight." She turned so that she could fully face him. He had nice eyes, and his smile was kind. "Well, I *was*. Before my flight got delayed."

"Well, you've got yourself a tour guide if you ever need one." He pointed at himself.

CHAPTER 2

"I'll have to check out your reviews first. I won't settle for less than five stars."

"You won't find anything higher than a three, I'm afraid."

They shared a laugh, but it was cut short as their eyes drifted to the massive swirls of snow that billowed across the tarmac at that moment. Piles of sparkling snow had already collected on top of the airplanes as more fell from the grey sky.

"It's my first time seeing all this snow again since I moved. I used to complain about the cold back in New York, but it's home. It still makes me feel like a kid growing up in the big city whenever I see it." Jamie grinned, shaking his head at the memory before turning to look at Olivia. Her dark eyes were inquisitive and warm and vibrant and all at once, he found himself getting a little lost in them. Suddenly, he stood up.

"Well, we're going to be stuck in this storm all night. If you're not going to fill up on Tootsie Rolls, want to see what else this airport has to offer? Now that we're basically best friends after our five-second conversation, I can't let you starve."

Olivia looked up at him, the airport lights brightening her eyes enough that Jamie could see all the flecks of hazel he hadn't noticed before. "I'm with you."

Chapter 3

Every restaurant and coffee shop was crammed with impatient travelers that night as the winter storm showed its worst. Icy bursts of wind and sleet somersaulted across the tarmac outside and the howl of the wind was loud enough to be heard from behind the glass.

But Jamie and Olivia paid it no mind from where they sat inside a cozy coffee shop, the smell of baked goods and lattes a welcome distraction.

"Bet you're happy to see this." Jamie set a tray on the table that was full of warm chocolate croissants, hot coffee, and sandwiches with side salads.

Olivia leaned forward to take a look. "Ooh, chocolate and carbs. My favorite food groups."

"Hate to break it to you, but chocolate isn't a food group."

"Depends who you ask." She reached for the coffee, savoring its heat between her hands. "For now, coffee first."

"You'll appreciate it even more in New York. If you don't have coffee there, you're never gonna make it through the day." He paused, leaning forward and resting his hands lightly around his own cup. "Are you going to visit family there?"

Olivia nodded but didn't offer any details, feeling defensive and private. She knew it was a normal question to ask, but she didn't need to tell a stranger about her life story. She had been holding it in for so long that if she started talking about it now, she was afraid she wouldn't be able to stop. What would happen then?

To her relief, Jamie didn't press for details and only nodded politely, moving on to tell her a story instead. His uncle back in New York had planned a cross-country road trip to eat each state's most famous dish, and while there were fifty different dishes for him to try, he only got to number thirteen before stopping and declaring the deep-dish pizza in Illinois as the winner.

"That was only partially the reason he stopped. He also gained fifteen pounds and ended up getting really sick from eating some undercooked lobster from Maine. Anyway, enough about him." Jamie picked up one of the chocolate croissants and waved it. "Do you save the best for last?"

Olivia smiled, grateful for the distracting story and question. He really *was* good at distracting her from her thoughts. "Nope, I usually eat my dessert first. You know, in case the world ends right this second, at least I'm spending my last moment alive eating a chocolate croissant instead of a crumbly meatloaf or something. You have to enjoy the good things first."

To her surprise, Jamie laughed. He had a bright, warm laugh that she liked very much. "Then you might want to get started on your croissant. With the way the snow is coming down, who knows if we're getting a tomorrow?"

She gave him a small roll of her eyes and bit into the flaky pastry. "I guarantee you this isn't the end."

"No? You promise?"

"I promise."

* * *

Jamie flipped a postcard over, put it back, then spun the rack around again, slowly this time. He glanced over at Olivia, who was flipping through a home decor magazine next to him, and then glanced at the cashier who was drumming their fingers on the countertop at the front and looking bored out of their mind.

"Not to sound dense, but why postcards?" Jamie asked. "It's not like I have anyone to write and send them to."

"Well, you never know." Olivia looked up from her magazine. "It might be nice to have a reminder of where you've been one day. You know, the things you've seen and heard, the people you met along the way." She glanced up at him, surprised to find that his eyes were already focused on her. Feeling suddenly shy, she snapped her magazine shut and busied herself putting it back on the rack. "I mean, you don't *have* to get one, but when I used to travel with my parents as a kid, it was a must-buy souvenir. I have dozens of blank ones from all different states by now."

Jamie held a postcard up for her to see. "Now that you put it that way, what do you think?"

"I think—" Her eyes flicked to the postcard depicting a gorgeous view of the city skyline at night with the Space Needle glittering mysteriously in the background and snowflakes drifting down from the purple sky. "I think it's perfect." She plucked it from his fingertips and slid it across the counter to the cashier. "We'll take this one."

Jamie smiled, happy that she approved. He hadn't been feeling like himself for quite some time since his grandfather got sick, but he was beginning to feel like his old self again just by being near her.

In just a few hours, he would be on his way back to Texas and reality. His grandfather's harsh coughs and milky eyes, the strong smell of antiseptics that reminded him of hospitals and doctors and disease, and his parents always casting worried glances at each other day in and day out. The thought of it made his heart sink and a part of him longed to sit and watch the snow pile up forever, to stop thinking about what was inevitable.

Maybe if he sat for long enough, the snow would bury the Seattle airport and he wouldn't have to go back and face facts, but he knew that was crazy talk. He wasn't a child anymore and he needed to be there for his grandfather, no matter how difficult it would be. Jamie was so lost in thought that he didn't even realize Olivia was studying him with those big eyes of hers, her head cocked to the side with curiosity.

"You okay?" She reached out and touched his arm.

"Yeah, of course. Just thinking about home." Jamie cleared his throat and then busied himself by tucking the postcard into his bag. It wasn't a complete lie. He *was* thinking about home, in a way.

Olivia nodded. "Well, it's been fun. I guess we should get going."

Jamie nodded politely. "Yeah, I guess we should."

For a few seconds, they stood there in awkward silence until Jamie started

CHAPTER 3

laughing.

"What's so funny?"

"It's just that there's nowhere *to* go right now, at least not with that storm outside." He gestured to the windows, where it was still a living nightmare beyond them.

"Guess I'm stuck with you then." Olivia shrugged, her smile suggesting she was more than okay with that condition.

* * *

11:59 p.m.

Times Square beamed down at Jamie and Olivia in all its neon brilliance from mounted television screens as the final seconds of the year ticked away.

Strangers around the airport crowded closer, their tired eyes shining with optimism and excitement for the first time that night.

"Let's go watch the ball drop." Jamie led her over to the closest television screen, his shoulder touching hers as they stood together.

Olivia wondered how many times he had gone to Times Square to celebrate the beginning of a new year. Was he one of the loud ones or did he hang back to admire the spectacle from afar? She wondered if he had ever kissed anybody there.

She stole a glance at Jamie, then looked away. *Probably.*

He was attractive and charismatic and sweet. He was funny, too. There had probably been a dozen people back in New York who sobbed into their silk handkerchiefs the day he left.

Olivia shook the silly thought out of her head as the two of them joined the crowd and stared at the golden numbers and colored sparks on the screen, the final moments of the year ticking away, one by one. She was pressed so close to him that she could feel the rhythm of his breath.

"Five! Four! Three! Two!" The crowd counted down together as the final seconds of the year fell away.

It was strange how she was supposed to be on a plane right then that was taking her to New York and her dad, but here she was instead, ending the year with someone she only met a few hours ago.

"One!" The crowd in Times Square cheered and clapped. Confetti rained down on the crowd from the television screen as colorful pyrotechnics lit up the sky. The city glittered as music played triumphantly in the background. Olivia watched as strangers on the screen shared a kiss, cheered for a fresh start, and grabbed at the fistfuls of confetti that rained down like colored snow.

She saw Jamie lean down in what she thought was going to be a very presumptuous kiss. To her surprise, he shouted, "Happy New Year! Did you make a wish?"

"A wish?" She furrowed her brows. "I thought people made resolutions, not wishes."

Jamie shrugged and cracked a smile. "Can't hurt on the one day we're supposed to get a fresh start."

Olivia turned away from him for a moment so he wouldn't see her shutting her eyes and making one. Maybe he was right about the stars aligning for just a moment.

It couldn't hurt to wish.

* * *

12:29 a.m.

"Favorite movie quote?" She scrolled down the list of questions on her phone.

"There are way too many good ones out there, but mine is probably from Yoda in *Star Wars*. You know, the one about trying."

"How could I not know? First job?"

Jamie leaned back to rest his head against the wall. "I used to loan my parents money from my weekly allowance with a 50% interest rate." He chuckled. "I was nine. Clearly, I was an investment banker in the making. But if we're being serious about a *real* job, then a grocery store clerk."

"Look at *you*. Already gypping people long before you knew better. When I was nine, I was stabbing my hands raw with thorns from picking blueberries

CHAPTER 3

for just two dollars a bucket at a local blueberry farm." Olivia reached into the huge bag of Twizzlers sitting between them and took one out, nibbling thoughtfully at the end as she skimmed the other questions on the list. "Okay, next. Favorite director?"

"Tim Burton."

"Good choice. *The Nightmare Before Christmas* is my all-time favorite childhood movie. Go-to order?"

"Chicken tenders."

"Chicken tenders?" Olivia's eyes bugged out at him.

Jamie shrugged. "Whether they're from McDonald's or a restaurant with a Michelin star, I'll take it. Chicken tenders, I'm telling you. You can't go wrong with 'em."

"So how many times have you gone to a five-star restaurant and requested their finest chicken tenders?"

"Next question." Jamie laughed, took two more Twizzlers out of the bag, and passed one to her.

"Worst date mishap?"

Jamie leaned over her shoulder to squint at the screen. "Is that question on the list or are you just trying to get me to talk about my love life?"

"It's here!" Olivia jabbed insistently at the screen. "Blame whoever wrote this list for being nosy."

"Okay, okay." He groaned. "Freshman year, I was at a friend's house party one night and I brought this girl I was into. All my friends were egging me on to make a move, so I went to get her a drink. She and I were flirting and drinking but then halfway through our conversation, I was suddenly on the floor with a black eye."

"Jesus. What happened?"

"Her ex was at the same party that night and saw us together. I didn't even see it coming. The worst part was that she ended up going home with him, too."

"Yikes. Did you at least get to throw a punch back?"

"Oh no, you don't." He lunged for the phone, laughing. "We agreed. Only five questions each turn."

23

"Not answering *is* an answer, just so you know."

Jamie rolled his eyes and smiled.

* * *

3:07 a.m.

The other stranded passengers slept in hushed silence while some stayed at nearby hotels for the night. A few courageous souls even decided to brave the remainder of the storm and went home.

Jamie and Olivia had staked out a perfect spot right in front of some enormous windows in a back corner of the airport that most people never ventured to. It offered a clear view of the outside world swathed in snow, and the echoes of the airport faded away into silence where they were sitting. They had been watching the snow outside for a while now, and the relentless shower of white was hypnotic.

Olivia must have fallen asleep at some point, but everything came back into clear focus a few moments later. Lifting her head, she realized with mounting humiliation that she had fallen asleep on Jamie's shoulder and there was now an obvious damp spot on his sweater.

"I'm so sorry, let me clean that for you." She leaned back for a better look at the damage and dabbed hurriedly at his shirt with a paper napkin she fished from her pocket, her cheeks growing warm as she avoided Jamie's gaze.

"Don't worry about it. You seemed pretty tired, and I didn't want to wake you." He laughed and gently moved her hand away. "I have at least a week's worth of clothes with me in my suitcase anyway. You caught me at a good time." He unzipped his suitcase, pulled out another sweater, and waved it at her. "See? No harm done."

"Watching the snow come down must have lulled me right to sleep," she said, stifling a little yawn with the back of her hand. "I'll have a lot more energy once I get to New York."

"Well, you'll have to enjoy it for me. I miss the place more than I thought I would."

"I'll try to. I'm going to see my dad there and I have no idea what that's

CHAPTER 3

going to be like. I've always wanted to visit New York, but I always associated it with him, and I kind of hate that. I'm placing so much importance on the place and person and tying them together." Olivia laughed quietly, surprised that she was even talking about it in the first place. "It sounds kind of stupid saying this out loud, but it's easier talking to you about this than my friends and family back home. You don't know me, and we'll probably never see each other again, so it feels like less of a big deal." She paused. "Anyway, I'm just nervous about seeing him again. We didn't have a great relationship after my parents split and I haven't seen him in years."

"I don't think divorce is ever going to be a walk in the park. You know, back when I was a kid, whenever I had a bad day or was stressed about something, my grandpa would say that there was something better waiting for us on the other side, that all the hard things I persevere through in life will give me wisdom and gratitude. He always told me that gratitude was the key to happiness and that always stuck with me."

"He sounds like a great grandfather."

"He was." Jamie flinched at how he automatically said it in the past tense. "Well, he still *is*. Things are just different now, that's all." He offered a sad smile, thinking about how his grandfather was now only a pale imitation of the man he was before he became ill. Still, it didn't change the fact that he taught Jamie everything he knew and had been a shining example of unconditional love. No matter how much time they had left together, his lessons and love would always remain. Jamie caught Olivia's gaze, soft and kind without judgment, and he knew right then that he could tell her the truth about his grandfather dying.

"Well, now that we're on the topic, it's why I decided to come to Seattle. It's my grandfather. He's—" Jamie let out a breath, swallowing over the lump that was forming in his throat. "Well, he's dying. Maybe it wasn't the bravest thing to do, but it took this trip for me to face the truth. And the truth is that he can't be saved. I feel like shit because I'm a palliative care nurse and I've taken care of so many people. I stayed by their side, making sure they got the best care possible so that their physical and emotional health wasn't deteriorating too quickly, and eased the whole healing process for them and their families. But now that it's my own grandfather, I can't even seem to face the truth. What kind of coward am I to do that?"

Olivia reached over to give his arm a reassuring squeeze.

"A part of me wanted to grieve the loss of him without showing my parents how I felt. It's better they think I'm selfish than to be breaking down every single moment in front of them. I mean, the only reason they wanted me to be in Texas was because they thought I could handle everything like he was just another patient." He looked at Olivia, his voice cracking. "But he's my grandpa."

"What did your parents say about you going away for a few days?"

"Not much," he sighed. "I think they're just coping by pretending nothing's wrong." A small smile graced his lips. "My grandma was born and raised in Seattle, but she and my grandpa didn't come back to visit often after retiring to Texas. I figured he'd enjoy seeing some pictures and videos of familiar places again. He loved my grandma more than anything and they made some great memories here."

A few minutes of silence dragged by before either of them spoke again.

"Sometimes, we need to get away so that we can come back stronger, and that's okay," Olivia gently pointed out. "You're still facing it and coping in the best way you know how. You're right about your grandpa not being another patient. How could he be? Maybe it doesn't mean much coming from me, but if you ask me, I think you're incredibly brave."

"You do?"

"Definitely."

Jamie smiled. He had to admit that he did feel a little braver right then. Olivia stretched out her legs and leaned back to rest her head against the wall, steadying herself. "You know, I've only mentioned half the truth too," she confessed. "My parents separated and it was a whole thing, yes, but my father also struggled with addiction and that was really hard for all of us. It's been three years since I last saw him and I feel this giant pressure to be someone he can be proud of. Maybe I don't need to prove myself to him, but I feel inferior or unimportant in some way, like I need his approval as my dad even after all this time."

CHAPTER 3

She could hear the strain in her voice as she spoke, but once those words were out in the open and hanging between them, she found it rather relieving. There was none of the shame and embarrassment and inadequacy she used to feel. There was just a satisfying emptiness, like finally dumping all the weight that she had been carrying for years. She had shared it with somebody else and they hadn't tried to mend it. Jamie didn't fill the silence with pity or scrutiny—he just listened. And it felt good to have somebody listen for once.

"Sometimes, the hardest part is even acknowledging that there *is* something wrong with our family," he said, his dark eyes studying hers. "Whether it's because of pride or shame or any other reason. I think you're incredibly brave for wanting to rebuild your relationship with your dad. It doesn't sound like it'll be easy, but I think you'll be okay. You seem like a very courageous, caring, and intelligent person, and if you give it your best, then you've already done everything you could possibly do. The rest is up to them. You've got this."

He nudged her shoulder gently with his, and Olivia finally cracked a smile. Jamie's words sank gently into the space she usually reserved for her wounds, somewhere safe and hidden and deep. Olivia took a shuddering breath and then nodded, letting his encouragement settle over the wounds and soften them.

She was going to be okay.

* * *

6:13 a.m.

It was nearly dawn.

They had listened to comedy podcasts and Bruce Springsteen together over tangled earbuds, eaten an entire bag of Twizzlers, and shared so many stories that it was hard to know where one ended and the other began. Olivia found herself barely caring about her delayed flight and the snowstorm outside at this point, or the drowsiness that was finally settling in her bones after their long, long night.

It didn't take much to realize that it was because of meeting Jamie.

Meeting someone new was always like that. Things were exciting until they weren't anymore. Olivia found herself wondering if this was how her parents felt once upon a time, back when things were good. At some point, they had been each other's favorite and it had been enough to make them promise forever to each other. Until it *wasn't* enough. Until the other person became a source of resentment and their love turned mundane and all of the extraordinary things that brought them together in the first place were no longer special or beautiful anymore. Flowers were made to bloom and die and the sunniest of skies turned grey eventually.

It was just how the world worked.

"Do you believe in the saying that everything happens for a reason?" Olivia punctured the silence with her voice, taking a sip of the iced tea from the vending machine that had long since turned warm in its can. "I think I might."

"Why's that?" Jamie's voice was soft in the early morning.

"It's easy to write off bad things happening as rotten luck and wrong decisions, but whenever something good happens, people always say that it was meant to be, like happiness and good times are a guarantee. I like to believe that the universe knows what it's doing, even when we're wading through the mud. It kind of gives me a sense of peace." She paused to fold her legs up underneath her, then shrugged. "Maybe things are already written out for us."

Jamie smiled, unable to deny that meeting her felt a little fateful when she put it that way. They could have easily missed meeting each other if he decided to sit at a different departure gate or if she had chosen another day to fly to New York, if it hadn't been snowing so hard that night, or even if one of them had been in a slightly different place at a slightly different time.

"So, you think that meeting certain people is also meant to be?" he asked, his tone lighthearted.

"Well, I hope so." Olivia paused, her eyes sweeping across his face. "I'm really glad I met you."

"Me too." Jamie turned to look at her from where he was sitting, noticing for the hundredth time that night how pretty her features were.

CHAPTER 3

Her dark hair fell over her shoulders in a sleek wave and her eyes shone with the reflection of the snow glistening from the pavement outside. Everything was so peaceful and muted around them, with the airport more secluded and private during the early morning hours without the incessant rush of people catching their flights and the sound of luggage being dragged hastily across the airport floors.

It felt like being in their own little world.

Suddenly, he started laughing.

"What's so funny?" Olivia watched as he tried unsuccessfully to stifle his laughter from behind a fist. His laugh was warm and good-natured and before too long, Olivia found herself following suit, her eyes crumpling up at the corners until her snickers turned into genuine bouts of laughter. The two of them laughed so hard that tears sprang to their eyes. Their laughing fit eventually wound down after several minutes, and they both wiped at the tears running down their cheeks, both of them still smiling ridiculously at each other.

"It's just this whole crazy night," Jamie explained at last. "Everything was looking to be a lost cause and then I meet you out of nowhere. This whole night felt like catching up with an old friend and I just found myself wishing that I had more time to get to know you." The moonlight reflecting off the snow outside turned Olivia's skin incandescent. Once again, Jamie found himself wanting to reach out to touch her face. "And I still do."

"Do you?" Her eyes trailed to Jamie's mouth just a few inches from hers.

"You bet I do."

With his dark hair and bronzed skin and his warm eyes and charming smile, there was no denying that Jamie was attractive in many, many ways. Still, they'd be leaving soon and heading off in different directions. It was pointless to start anything now.

Despite the warning siren traveling through her head telling her she was thinking like a crazy person, she had to admit it had been a long time since she felt a spark just like the one she felt with Jamie.

Even if only in her wildest dreams, she wanted more with him. More time, more conversations, more everything.

Olivia couldn't tell if it was her imagination playing tricks or not, but they seemed to be sitting closer together than she remembered. The silence stretched between them, and the hush of the fallen snow and the dormant airplanes outside seemed dreamlike. It was as if the whole world suddenly stopped just to see what would happen next.

Jamie's gaze trailed to her lips and then back up to her eyes as if asking for permission. He was so close that she could make out all the shades of brown in his eyes as he blinked at her, the space between them but an inch. She held her breath and waited as he brought his mouth close to hers, and then closer still.

At last, he kissed her. Hesitantly at first, and then with certainty.

His mouth was soft and the kiss deepened as they both melted into it. Olivia couldn't say for sure when they finally stopped, but by the time they pulled apart and returned their gaze to the glittering tarmac and resting planes, the sky was a little lighter.

It was one of those nights where two people could start as perfect strangers and end up as something a little more.

Chapter 4

"Well, this is it." Olivia fidgeted with the boarding pass in her hand as the two of them stopped before her gate. "Thanks for walking me here."

"No problem, my flight isn't for another hour. It's the least I can do." He paused, scrunching his nose. "You know, I didn't catch your name. I never asked."

"It's Olivia."

"I'm Jamie." He held out his hand and she shook it. The line between formality and familiarity was already a little blurred between them.

"Here." She pressed a small piece of paper with her name and number into his hand. "If you get stranded at another airport, call me for moral support."

Jamie laughed. "Something tells me it won't be as memorable as last night."

"Maybe just a tad less entertaining." She held her thumb and forefinger just a fraction apart before dropping her hand. "Okay, I'm going to get going before something *else* prevents me from leaving this airport."

Jamie nodded, taking a small step closer. "Have a safe flight." He smiled shyly, and Olivia pulled him into a quick hug, surprising herself.

"Goodbye, Jamie." She felt his arms tighten around her for a moment before letting go. "I'll see you around."

"I really hope so."

A final boarding announcement rang through the intercom as she disappeared into the crowd at last and away from Jamie's sight, taking with her the previous night.

* * *

The airplane lifted itself seamlessly into the sky at long last, leaving Seattle behind.
Olivia leaned back in her seat and rested her forehead against the window, looking out at the city that was growing smaller and smaller beneath her. The soft morning light warmed her eyelids and cast a red glow beneath them, lulling her to sleep. Before she completely succumbed to unconsciousness, Jamie crossed her mind once more. She thought about the way his warm skin and dark hair shone underneath the airport lights and his laugh whenever she said something funny. She found herself replaying the way he had kissed her, too. That was her favorite part, honestly.
But before she could reminisce any further, she was already fast asleep.

Blinking the sleep from her eyes a few hours later, Olivia woke to a mass of butterflies fluttering nervously around in her stomach as the plane began its slow descent into New York.
Before too long, she was at the arrivals gate. Beyond the airport's sliding glass doors, the sleet-colored city and its eternal traffic beckoned to her. In just a few minutes, she would be seeing her father again.
Olivia pulled out her phone to call him but heard her name instead; her father was just a few feet away and he was waving at her. "Olivia, I'm over here!"
She took a step forward, raising her hand in a tentative wave, barely recognizing him at first. She self-consciously tucked her hair behind her ears and forced herself to smile as she closed the distance between them. His eyes had crinkles at the corners that were a little deeper now, and his previously greying hair was now the glossy and impossible black only achievable from a trip to the salon. Everything about him seemed new and sharper, from his fresh white shirt to his piercing smile that would have done any toothpaste company proud. He didn't look like the man who used to stumble home intoxicated, slurring his words and reeking of liquor before passing out on the couch in his rumpled work clothes.

CHAPTER 4

When Olivia reached him, he pulled her into a hug, his strong arms wrapping around her and supporting her in a way she never felt before. She let herself be held, burying her face in his chest and breathing in his old familiar scent. "Hi, Dad," she murmured. "It's good to see you."

"How are you, kid?"

"A lot better now." She smiled up at him, finding it to be true.

New York suddenly felt a whole lot more like home.

* * *

The coffee shop just a few minutes from the airport was as busy as ever, but the grey skies had significantly cleared up by the time Olivia and her father sat down inside. It felt a lot more electric than Seattle, where things were slower and she knew it like the back of her hand. In New York, she knew absolutely nothing and no one and it was equally terrifying and exciting.

Olivia could feel her father studying her from across the table, his cup of coffee untouched and turning cold. A part of her felt ashamed wondering about his sobriety right then when she had only been with him for a moment. The last thing she wanted was to push him away by scrutinizing him.

Her father wrapped his fingers tightly around his coffee. "How's your tea?"

"It's great." She took a big mouthful. "It's a nice place here. Thanks for bringing me."

Her father relaxed a little in his seat and gave her a lopsided smile that didn't quite reach his eyes. "Anything for my daughter. I want you to be comfortable while you're here." He took a small sip of his coffee, grimaced, then pushed it to the side. "How's your mother doing?"

"Good. Still as stubborn as ever."

"Still her usual self, I see." He chuckled.

"She's working a lot more lately and staying busy with her projects and hobbies. She's taken up painting again, Dad. I haven't seen her do that in a long time."

"There's a lot about her that you don't know." Her father clasped his hands together on the table, looking out into the distance for a moment before turning back to his daughter. "Staying busy with work and hobbies, or staying busy with someone else?"

"Just work and hobbies, Dad." She laughed uncomfortably.

"Ah. Well, I don't expect you to be an open book anytime soon, but if you're talking about hobbies, one of her favorite hobbies has to be telling the folks in Seattle about what a pathetic alcoholic I was. She's why I left, but you already know that."

Olivia didn't know how to respond, so she didn't.

To people who didn't know him, he was such a charismatic and ambitious man that the idea of him being a subpar father and husband seemed inconceivable.

Just as Olivia's thoughts began to drift back to how things used to be, he abruptly stood up and extended a hand to her. "You must be tired. Let's go back home and get you settled in."

* * *

The two of them had Chinese takeout for dinner at his apartment that night. Their awkwardness melted away little by little as they ate their spicy tofu and chow mein with stir-fried vegetables swimming in a delicious sauce, and finished it off with crispy fortune cookies that held vague premonitions.

It was their first dinner together in years.

After spending most of the day at crowded airports and in the hustle and bustle of the city, Olivia was grateful for the peace and quiet of the apartment.

After dinner, he retreated to his home office to get some work done, so Olivia made herself comfortable on the couch and dialed home. Her mother's voicemail on the other end made Olivia wish that she could apologize. She was likely still at work, but Olivia figured she'd give it a try and call anyway. There had never been so much silence between them for so long.

The rain began to fall harder now, ticking against the glass in staccato.

Olivia hung up. A moment later, her phone lit up with a notification.

It was a text message from an unknown number.

Just got back home a few hours ago, but I miss Seattle already. I keep thinking

CHAPTER 4

about you, it read.

She sat up a little straighter and read the message again before lowering her phone. It was Jamie. She rested her thumbs over the screen, thinking hard about what to say. Suddenly, she heard her father clearing his throat loudly from the other side of the room.

"Jesus! You scared me, Dad. I was just—" She paused. Was that a green liquor bottle he was holding?

She squinted.

No, it was a carton of matcha ice cream.

"Sorry, didn't mean to make you jump." Her father raised his eyebrows and walked over to the couch to sit with her, peeling back the lid and spooning the ice cream into bowls. "Dessert?"

"Thanks, I could use some." Olivia took the bowl and smiled, grateful. She took a couple of bites, aware of his gaze. "Why are you looking at me like that?"

He shook his head. "You just look more like your mother every day. Feels like I'm staring at her from years ago," he admitted, pulling his gaze out the window to the falling rain at last.

He looked a little wistful when he said it, but his expression had changed by the time he turned back to face her, and a part of Olivia wondered if maybe she had imagined it.

"Well," she said, "I've always heard that we look alike."

"You're her spitting image. The older you get, the more I get déjà vu."

Her father reached over and threaded his fingers through her hair in a playful tousle, a smile finally breaking upon his face. "Olivia, I just wanted you to know that I'm really happy you could make it," he said. "I know I haven't always been there for you, but trust me when I say that I really tried to be. You know that I love you, right?"

He put his bowl of ice cream down on the table in front of them. The rain streaked across the glass behind them, the dark sky thickening as rain poured from the clouds.

"I know." There wasn't much else that Olivia could say, so she reached over and touched his hand. "I'm just happy we get to do this. Me being here, having dinner with you, and then getting to sit and talk? It means the world to me."

"Okay." Her father relaxed, his expression softening. "That's all I wanted you to know."

* * *

The next morning, Olivia woke to hazy winter sunlight streaming in through the curtains and the sound of busy traffic. Her phone was still next to her pillow where she had left it the night before when she stayed up for hours to message Jamie. It was the first time they got the chance to talk again since parting ways at the airport.

She smiled lazily now, sitting up at last. The unmistakable scent of breakfast was in the air and her stomach gurgled its approval. She slid out from underneath the covers and padded barefoot toward the kitchen. Her father was standing by the stove with his back to her, humming to himself while still in bed-rumpled pajamas and sporting messy hair for the first time. Olivia tucked the image of him away in her heart, then walked over to the kitchen table and took a seat.

"Good morning," she said, stifling a yawn.

Her father turned and smiled. "Well, look who's finally up. It's almost noon, but I don't blame you for needing a little extra sleep after your flight." He brought over two plates of toast drizzled with golden maple syrup and sliced bananas on top. "Eat up. We're going to do a little sightseeing today. The Brooklyn Bridge awaits," he said.

Olivia smiled and cut off a piece of the toast, but paused when she brought the fork to her mouth. "Dad, I can't eat peanuts."

Her father looked up, his expression one of slight irritation. "Why not? I never pegged you for a picky eater."

"No, I'm allergic," she replied flatly, gesturing to the peanut butter drizzled across the pancakes.

His eyes widened. "Jesus Christ, since when did you become allergic to *peanuts*?"

CHAPTER 4

"Just recently," she lied, taking a sip of her water and shrugging nonchalantly. She had been mildly allergic to peanuts since she was in the third grade, but there was no way she was telling him that just to make him feel bad.

"Ah, that's what I thought." He waved a finger at her, then cracked open his fridge door. "I know my daughter better than that. You were never allergic to anything when you were a kid. Anyway, let me make you some eggs and toast."

"Sounds great." He was trying, and that was all that mattered.

The dreary weather even disappeared for a glorious few hours that afternoon, seemingly just for them. The Brooklyn Bridge stretched into the distance and the sun painted the city in gold while the two of them walked in silence, both of them lost in their respective thoughts. It was nice just being together. It was a simple pleasure, something Olivia wanted to cherish every second of. She walked with her arm looped through her father's, the two of them suspended hundreds of feet above the navy water below as they crossed the famous bridge together.

Her mother had been wrong about him. In some ways, he *had* changed.

They reached the middle of the bridge and Olivia stopped to take in the view from above, the wind whipping mercilessly through her hair. There was something poetic about the bridge and all, with their past behind them and their future up ahead.

"Dad, can I ask you something?"

"Shoot."

"Do you feel more at home here?"

Her father laughed, the sound of it swallowed up by the wind as it rolled easily across the dark water. "When I change my mind, I change my path," he explained, shrugging his shoulders. "Everybody does it. Seattle just wasn't doing it for me anymore, and a man shouldn't feel lousy for wanting something different."

"And what did you want to be different?"

"Am I being interrogated now?" He laughed again, but it sounded strained. "I just wanted something different from what I had in Seattle. My life back there wasn't for me. I know that now."

"I get it." Olivia wrapped her arms tighter around herself, keeping her head down. What he had in Seattle was his family. "So, you're happier now?"

"I am."

"Good. That's all I want for you, Dad. I hope you know that I never wanted us to drift apart or to become strangers. Whatever problems you had with Mom are between you and her and I get that. Even after all this time, I still wish the best for you. All I want is for you to be okay and for us to have a relationship." She paused. "A better one."

Her father pulled her into a hug from the side. "I get you. Well, no time like the present. Where do you want to start?"

* * *

When Olivia got back to the apartment that night, her first and only thought was to wind down with a night of mindless television and a hot shower. Her father said he'd return in an hour and went out to get some grocery items.

The rushing hot water and steam washed the day away as Olivia thought about potential plans for the evening. When he came back, they could play some board games and try the strawberry cheesecake she bought earlier that afternoon. He always did have a competitive side and a sweet tooth, so there was no way it could go sour.

She stepped out of the shower, reaching for a towel on the rack, and felt nothing. Huffing out a breath, Olivia padded over to the sink cabinet and threw it open.

No towels.

Shivering a little, she pulled on her clothes and threw open the linen cabinet in the hallway.

It was empty as well.

Frustrated, Olivia made her way down the hall to her room, her damp skin soaking through the fabric of her sweater and pants.

She passed by her father's bedroom and paused at the sliver of light that leaked from the door being cracked open an inch, beckoning to her. Despite

CHAPTER 4

wanting to respect his privacy, something nudged her to go inside. Olivia walked over to a large dresser near her father's bed, justifying to herself that she was just looking for a clean towel and nothing more.

She had never been inside his room before, but it somehow made her feel closer to him. Olivia lay down on his bed, pressing her face into his pillow. Aside from the interruption of her thumping heart, all was quiet. For some reason, she found herself tearing up.

If only things could have been different.

Olivia sat up, feeling foolish and childish, and wiped roughly at her tears. *Stupid. What was there to cry about?*

As she did so, she knocked a photo frame off his bedside table, watching as it tumbled to the carpet. Olivia reached over to pick it up, but when she saw the photo, she felt her blood run cold.

It was a photo of her father with his arm around a woman she had never seen before, the two of them looking stupidly happy at some beach somewhere.

Olivia quickly put the picture back on his dresser, as if touching it physically burned her. She had to leave the apartment or else she'd be sick.

But she still needed to find a damn towel. Frustrated, Olivia stalked over to his dresser and threw it open, surprised to hear the sound of clinking glass.

She peered into the drawer. There was the unmistakable shine of glass at the very bottom, underneath some folded clothes. Olivia reached down and closed her fingers around something cold and hard. It was a liquor bottle. She pulled out a second. Then a third and fourth. She didn't stop until she had emptied the entire drawer. Drinking had been a problem for her father long before the separation.

Maybe it still was.

For what seemed like an eternity, Olivia stared at the bottles sitting in a row on the carpet. They brought her back to a time when the sight and smell of liquor made her feel sick, made her feel small and helpless.

When she heard the apartment door open, she quickly stuffed the bottles back in the drawer and ran out of his room and back to her own, throwing herself underneath the covers like she was a kid again. Everything was getting so complicated and questions flew through her mind so quickly that they made her dizzy.

Frustrated and more confused than ever, Olivia squeezed her eyes shut and willed herself to go to sleep. If she could just sleep the week away, she would be back in Seattle and this nightmare would be over soon enough.

As the week wore on, her father stayed later at the office in the evenings and started going to bed earlier, too. When he wasn't holed up with his spread of papers or ordering takeout for dinner instead of cooking, he would sleep. Something was wrong, and even though he kept saying it was because Olivia was leaving soon, she had a feeling it was something deeper. If her father knew anything about her being in his room the other night, he wasn't letting on.

And that was what hurt most of all.

Olivia almost wished that they could both stop playing pretend just to keep the peace and admit that things were never going to be the same again.

* * *

For her last night in New York, the two of them went to a nice restaurant to celebrate. Olivia had chosen it, thinking that it would be a good way to end the week together. But now, she was eating her honey-glazed salmon in awkward silence and finding it funny how the restaurant food seemed tasteless that night even though it was a popular spot.

As they ate, her father ordered one whiskey after the other, drinking them as quickly as they were being put down. After his third glass was emptied in a matter of seconds, Olivia set her knife and fork down, her tone firm as she said, "I think you've had enough tonight, Dad."

He looked at her over the rim of his glass and laughed loudly. Almost too loud. "Christ, you sound like your mother."

"Do I?"

He nodded, then changed the topic. "How are classes? What are you studying again?"

CHAPTER 4

"Journalism."

"Journalism?" he repeated, the word sounding almost dirty the way he said it. He picked up his glass of whiskey and was about to take a drink when he realized it was nearly empty. "You're going to write for a living? And you're actually paying money for it?" A laugh erupted from his mouth. "Are you going to build a career writing for tabloid magazines and obituaries in the papers or something?"

"Maybe." Olivia stabbed at her food. "It's what got me into university in the first place. I got a scholarship *because* of my writing."

Her father raised his eyebrows. "Okay. And what do you do now for work?"

Olivia wondered why it even mattered. "Well, I'm working part-time at this restaurant downtown to save up some money for after graduation. It's not much, but—"

"So, you're a waitress."

"I am."

"I see." He shrugged. "I'm just surprised. I thought you had more ambition than that."

"Look, let's just talk about something else. I don't want to spend my last night explaining myself to you."

Her father stared at her from across the table, silent as he picked up his glass and swallowed the last mouthful of amber liquid. "I don't appreciate the attitude, Olivia. I'm just looking out for you," he said, his tone indignant. "You know I love you." A drop of whiskey fell onto the white tablecloth, spreading like a dark sun across the snowy fabric.

"I know you do." The lie came easily.

* * *

For the rest of dinner, Olivia stared out the restaurant window and nibbled at her tasteless salmon. Her father had seemed distracted all week, but the last straw was him going back to drinking heavily in front of her when he had promised he was sober.

There was no laughter and there were no stories to share that night.

Deep down, Olivia sensed his unease. She felt like some alien that had invaded his planet, something that he welcomed only out of civility and due diligence. But now, the party was over and the truth was out. He was not the person she had hoped he would be.

And that was her fault.

When they got back to his apartment much later that night, her father retreated to his room and disappeared inside. The whiskey at the restaurant made his head spin and the only thing that would help was another glass to end the night. Sighing, he went to fetch one of the bottles from his drawer. He didn't drink often anymore, but it had been stressful to try to be this perfect father figure when he knew he was far from it. Even if he didn't drink much anymore, he didn't want Olivia to find the bottles he kept for entertainment and to cope with lousy days at work and make assumptions.

His head was pounding and the room was looking a little fuzzy, but it wouldn't hurt to have just one more. As he moved to close the door, he caught sight of something sticking out from underneath his bed.

He moved closer and pulled it out. It was a bottle of brandy.

Hands shaking, he opened up his drawer and peered inside. The bottles were slightly out of order, but he knew enough to know what had happened. He clenched his fist, taking in a shuddering breath as he got up from the chair and wrenched open his room door. With every step he took down the hallway toward Olivia, he felt his disgust and resentment grow.

When he saw her, he let out a humorless chuckle, gripping the bottle of brandy so hard that his knuckles turned white. She was sitting on her bed, looking innocent in her pajamas and reading a book, but he knew better.

"Dad, what is it?" She set her book down and looked over at him.

"You went through my things." His voice was raspy with anger as he pointed to the bottle of brandy. "I invite you into my home and you thank me by going through my things."

Anxiety, shame, and humiliation gnawed at Olivia. "I'm sorry."

Her father took a step into the room, his stride unsteady. He pointed at her. "No, *I'm* sorry. I'm sorry I ever brought you back. I shouldn't have brought

CHAPTER 4

you here. You only wanted to come here to prove a point to yourself. Now you've done it."

"Dad, I didn't come here to prove anything," she said, each word slow and deliberate as they left her lips. "I shouldn't have gone through your things, and I'm sorry. Just let me know how I can fix this."

"*Fix it?* What the hell is there to fix?" he shouted. "There's nothing to fix!" He took a step closer to Olivia, swaying as the liquor finally hit him. Something inside of him was breaking and it was too late to go back. He pointed at her, shaking with anger. "I knew it," he said, his face turning red. "I knew you were here for the wrong reasons."

"I shouldn't have gone into your room, but I didn't know I'd end up finding those liquor bottles. It was an accident."

"Don't make excuses," he snarled. "And don't you *dare* turn this around on me, Olivia."

"I'm not."

"Why don't you just say what you mean?" He took another step closer. "Tell me that you're ashamed of your deadbeat dad and how disappointed you are that I'm not the superhero dad you made me out to be. Tell me how all the shit your mother said about me was right on the money. Say it!"

Before Olivia could answer, he hurled the bottle of brandy at the wall behind her in one swift motion, the glass shattering upon impact and spraying liquor across the room in a golden arch. Olivia cried out as little pinpricks of blood bloomed like roses on her skin, the shards cutting clean through. Everything in the room spun as her father grabbed her roughly by the shoulders, his face in hers as he screamed and cussed. She couldn't even remember much of anything he said, but the next thing she knew, she was on the floor and her face was stinging.

Forcing air into her lungs, Olivia stood up and forced her legs to move. She ran past him, out of the room, and then out of his apartment. Her heart was in her throat as she jabbed at the elevator button, panic choking her.

When the doors finally opened after what felt like an eternity, she rushed in, pressed her back against the elevator wall and slid down, her legs finally buckling. Her breaths came in ragged gasps and her ears rang as she squeezed her eyes shut.

She had no idea how long she sat on that dirty elevator floor, but it certainly felt like forever.

And forever was a long enough time for Olivia to realize that the pain hadn't come from her injuries that night.

It came from a broken heart.

Chapter 5

Back home in Seattle, the streetlights seemed to twinkle ten times as brightly. Olivia was sitting with Ingrid at one of the empty restaurant tables where they worked, long after it had closed to the public.

"Everything I thought I knew was wrong," Olivia said, wrapping her hands around her steaming mug of chai. "He's even worse than I remember."

"I still don't know why you won't talk to somebody about it. It's one thing to get angry, but to hit you because he didn't know how to deal with it?" Ingrid made a noise in the back of her throat. "What a coward."

Olivia's fingers stretched subconsciously to touch the bandages on her legs. The cuts from the glass shards had mostly healed, but there were some things that Band-Aids and Polysporin couldn't fix. The shame and disappointment that had burrowed into her bones stayed, even after coming home from New York and leaving it all behind. "He didn't hit me," she responded, her voice dull.

"Abuse is abuse. Throwing that bottle at the wall behind you? What if it hit you? What then?"

"I just feel like an idiot. I shouldn't have gone."

Ingrid looked at Olivia from across the table, a smile softening her face. "I know it was far from what you expected, but you're back home now. You're safe."

Olivia stared out the restaurant window. The snow outside had a purplish tinge to it from the fading evening light. "At least I won't have my hopes up again."

"There's nothing wrong with being hopeful. We should wish for the best, but we should also prepare for the worst. It's a good piece of advice, isn't it?"

"It is." Olivia returned her gaze to her friend and plastered on a smile. "Anyway, let's talk about something else. I've been driving myself crazy thinking about New York and everything that happened."

"Let me get us some more scones first. You take all the time you need tonight, okay?" Ingrid patted the back of Olivia's hand before leaving the table.

As Olivia took another sip of tea, still buried in her thoughts, her phone lit up with a notification from Jamie. He had texted her multiple times that week asking how her trip went, and though she never responded, the truth was that she hadn't stopped thinking about him.

But she was afraid to want more, because wanting anything led to expectations, and expectations led to disappointment more often than not.

So she was done wanting anything.

* * *

It was past midnight in Austin, Texas, where Jamie found himself wide awake and staring at the ceiling. He played with the postcard he got at the Seattle airport nearly a week ago, flipping it between his fingers as he thought about Olivia. She hadn't spoken to him much, but he couldn't stop thinking about her. They had one good conversation at the beginning of their trip after parting ways, but she withdrew more and more and talked less and less until there was only silence. She was probably busy making up for lost time with her father and had a million other things to do other than spend time texting some stranger she met at the airport.

Jamie sighed, wishing he knew what she was doing and wondering if he'd ever see her again, but maybe it didn't matter.

It was just a single day with her, after all.

Still, he wanted more.

Earlier that week, when Jamie got back home to his grandfather, the older man seemed more animated than he had been in a long time, asking for

CHAPTER 5

every detail and smiling over every photo Jamie had taken. It had been so long since Jamie got to see his grandfather so lively. He could barely say more than four words most times when the pain got to be too much, but that day, his grandfather had laughed and smiled and made jokes, poring over Jamie's photos from Seattle and talking fondly about living and working there before finally retiring to Texas with Jamie's late grandmother.

Everything felt so great that Jamie started talking about meeting Olivia too, but stopped himself when he realized that his grandfather could see right through him, his milky eyes sparkling with curiosity.

His grandfather's smile was warm when he spoke again. "Well? Are you going to see her again?" He had leaned back in his armchair, the sunlight casting him in a halo of white.

Jamie had laughed with uncertainty and rubbed the back of his neck. "Well, I don't know. She's probably forgotten all about me by now."

A knowing smile lit up his grandfather's face. "Ah, but if a single day was unforgettable to you, imagine what many more days together could bring. I know that look in your eyes, Jamie. You want to know how this story ends."

"Well, maybe we'll end up meeting again and fall madly in love and elope in Vegas one day," he teased, "but right now, I'm just happy to spend time here. Just you and me."

His grandfather chuckled and patted his hand lightly. "Well, I'm flattered that you're interested in spending time with an old man like me instead of the very interesting and beautiful girl you just told me about."

The clouds had parted at that moment to reveal golden swaths of sunlight, and the two of them sat together there for many more hours until his grandfather eventually fell asleep in his armchair. Jamie stayed, watching the way his grandfather's chest rose and fell so peacefully, the scent of cigar smoke and aftershave familiar and heartbreaking all at once. A part of Jamie was worried that his grandfather would cease to exist the minute he walked away, so he didn't. All afternoon, he stayed right there by his grandfather's side until he fell asleep as well.

But now, alone in his bedroom, Jamie pulled himself away from the conversation earlier that day and sat up, knowing he wouldn't be able to sleep. He wasn't tired at all. The little postcard on his bedside table reflected the lamp's soft glow, reminding him of Seattle and snow and New Year's Eve and that special someone.

Especially that someone. And he didn't want to let her slip away.

* * *

Several weeks passed before the two of them spoke again.

It was on a February evening right before the long weekend, and it was already dark out by the time Olivia's seminar was over. As the other students left the lecture hall, Olivia's professor waited patiently at the front for her. He resembled a kindly storybook wizard with his blindingly white hair, round glasses, and collection of unusual-looking ties and shirts. All his students loved him, but no one more than Olivia.

She hoisted her backpack onto her shoulder and flashed a smile at him, ready to finally have a nice, hot meal at home and some time to herself. "Thanks for the extra help during office hours the other day. No matter how busy you are over the years, you always somehow find the time."

"That's what I'm here for." He humbly waved the compliment away. "Whenever you enroll in one of my courses, I just know it's going to be a good one. And if I'm not careful, you might end up replacing me one day. You've got a good head on your shoulders, Olivia."

"Thanks. It means a lot to hear that."

Her professor crossed his arms, chewing on the inside of his cheek, looking thoughtfully at her. "You know, I've been meaning to talk to you about an opportunity that I think you'll be very interested in."

"What is it?"

"I have a good friend in the industry who's looking for someone to take under her wing and to help her out for quite some time. It's a paid internship position for the fall semester, and I think you'd be a perfect fit for it. It'll have a little bit of everything you love. There's writing, editing, interviews, current events, storytelling, news…" He waved his hand around in the air. "I could go on and on."

CHAPTER 5

"Do you mind if I ask who's looking?" Her curiosity was piqued.

"Not at all." He opened his desk drawer and dug out a business card and handed it to Olivia. "I assume you're familiar with Marcia Browning?"

"CEO of The Seattle Tribune?"

"The one and only." Her professor nodded, a humble smile on his face. "Well, we kept in touch over the years and she told me that she's been on the lookout for a fresh face, someone with talent. I hope you don't mind, but I put in a good word for you and she's hoping to get in touch with you. You're a very promising candidate and I know you'll make us proud."

"I don't even know what to say."

"Say you'll think about it." Her professor smiled warmly at her, his thick glasses balanced on the tip of his nose. "It will be lots of time and effort if you should decide to take the opportunity, but you'll be learning the ropes and working alongside some of the most influential people in media that I know of. You have a gift, Olivia. Just promise me you won't waste it. I want you to be successful and to go after anything you set your mind to."

"Thank you so much for everything." Olivia gave his arm a squeeze, her heart nearly beating out of her chest. "Thank you, thank you!"

"You're very welcome, Olivia." Her professor smiled and shook his finger at her. "I have a great feeling about this, I'm telling you. You'll see."

All the way home on the bus, she kept going over their conversation.

Marcia Browning was going to take someone under her wing and *she* was a potential candidate. Marcia had covered some of the biggest stories in Seattle and beyond, published several bestselling books, and was at the top of her game in the industry. If Olivia got to work at The Seattle Tribune, there would be no more grueling months of pitching articles to the local papers only to have them end up on the last page or in the rejected pile.

Things were finally starting to look up.

She pulled out her phone and texted a couple of her closest friends and her mom the good news. As she scrolled through her text history, she saw Jamie's name and stopped. Their last conversation was from nearly a month ago, and it was her fault that there was silence now. She hadn't responded to any of his texts, not since everything with her dad went downhill. The trip had been such a disaster and anything related to it made her want to break out in hives.

But if she were to be honest, Jamie was probably the one good thing that came out of the trip.

She chewed her lip, her thumb hovering uncertainly over his name. She missed hearing his stories and having someone to talk to, but it had already been so long.

Any chance of even being friends was probably long gone.

Olivia pocketed her phone, unsettled by her sudden urge to hear his voice again.

* * *

Her mother was working late again that night, so the first thing on Olivia's mind when she got home was to make them both a nice dinner.

She rolled up her sleeves and put some music on, humming in the kitchen as she prepared the ingredients to make some pesto pasta with grilled chicken and cherry tomatoes. For dessert, roasted sweet potatoes with cinnamon and butter would hit the spot.

As she cooked, she kept glancing at her phone, hoping it would light up with a notification again. Just one more time. She'd say something back this time.

Olivia leaned over the counter and brushed her hair out of her eyes, huffing out a resigned breath because there was no denying it to herself.

She wanted to talk to him.

There was a bit of fear and pride, but then she remembered what Ingrid had said at the restaurant. Hope wasn't a bad thing. And maybe it was time to be a little hopeful again.

She paced around the kitchen as she dialed his number, her heart thudding as she waited.

"Hello?" Jamie's voice came through a few seconds later.

Olivia hung up without saying anything.

CHAPTER 5

When Jamie called back, she picked up, wanting to sink right into the floor and disappear. "Oh, hi, sorry about that. It was an accident, I didn't mean to call you."

"Oh, was it?" She heard Jamie laugh on the other end. "Way to break my heart. I was pretty excited to see you calling, to be honest. Thought maybe you got yourself stuck at another airport and needed some company."

"Ha, not tonight." Olivia walked over to the couch and sank into it. "Tonight is all about being at home and celebrating and relaxing. I received some pretty exciting news today and I'm still on cloud nine."

"What's got you so stoked?"

"Well, I have this professor that I've taken courses with since my first year in uni. And today after class, he pulled me aside and told me about how The Seattle Tribune has been looking for someone to fill a seat, and guess what?" She paused. "He put in a good word for me. Jamie, this means I might get to do what I love for a change. It's the foot in the door that I've been looking for."

"I don't think your prof would have done that if he wasn't blown away by you," Jamie said, his voice rising with excitement. "Man, I'm really happy for you. I hope you've got plans to go out and celebrate tonight."

"Eh, not really. Just dinner for one tonight since my mom's working late. What about you?"

A chuckle escaped Jamie's lips. "Tonight? I've got an exciting dinner date with my grandfather's cat, Fuji. She doesn't seem to appreciate canned tuna by candlelight."

"If your dinner date goes south, there's always room for one more here."

"If there's dessert involved, then count me in. We can make a night of it. I'll bring the Dom Pérignon."

"I can guarantee dessert, but you'll have to fly over here for it. Chef Olivia doesn't do delivery."

"Worth it. Totally affordable, if you ask me."

The two of them shared a small laugh and Olivia pressed the phone closer to her ear, not wanting to miss a single word he was going to say next. It had been a little while since she felt this way about somebody. It was so

51

comfortable talking to him that it felt like no time at all had passed since they were stuck at the airport together. "Not to change the subject," she said, "but I have a confession to make."

"I'm all ears."

"Okay, I'll admit it. I wanted to call you. I mean, I *did* call you, but then I got nervous and hung up and it was because I felt really bad about going MIA for so long, and it was all because of this big mess that happened with my dad in New York when I went and—" She sucked in a breath, aware that she was rambling. "Sorry, I don't know why I'm going a million miles a minute."

"Hey, it's okay." Jamie's voice was soft and reassuring on the other end of the line. "I know what a big deal it was to visit him and I'm so sorry you got the short end of the stick on that trip. I don't know what happened, but if you ever want to talk about it, I'm here. Whether it's been a couple of weeks or a couple of months, I'm just happy to hear from you, okay?"

"Okay. Thanks." Olivia relaxed a little, grateful that he didn't hate her at the very least. "How's your grandpa doing?"

"He's doing the best he can, but he's sleeping a lot more lately and has trouble staying awake for more than a couple of hours. The amount of medication he's taking right now is crazy." Jamie sighed, and even that somehow sounded sadder than usual. "We've got another nurse coming by twice a day to check on him, but she's not feeling too optimistic about things and neither are my parents. I always knew it was coming, but I just never thought it'd happen so soon. But then again, I'm never going to be prepared to lose him, no matter how much time has passed."

"It's never going to be easy losing someone you love. I'm so sorry, Jamie."

"Don't be. I always knew it would end this way. And you've already been the greatest support to me, listening to all of this."

"Well, that's what friends are for. I'm just happy you trust me enough to tell me any of that."

"Whoa, wait. Back up, back up," Jamie laughed. "Friends? I thought we were more than friends at this point."

Olivia's cheeks reddened. "I mean, I didn't—"

"I'm just pulling your leg," Jamie laughed, the warmth of it breaking through

CHAPTER 5

their tough conversation. "But in all honesty, I'd love to talk to you again. If it's okay, can I call you again tomorrow?"

"Tomorrow?" She wanted him to, and there was no sense lying to herself anymore. "It's a date."

Chapter 6

It was a Tuesday night in late April when Jamie's grandfather passed away. The last of winter was finally melting away and flowers were just beginning to bloom again in the gardens and parks. It felt unfair that his grandfather left just when the world outside was at its liveliest and everything was blossoming and healthy and vibrant.

Even though Jamie had worked with many people who suffered from terminal illnesses and constant pain and grief, it was nothing like the pain and grief that he felt during those final nights when Jamie just sat in his grandfather's room, unable to do or change anything. He watched his grandfather take labored breaths, his eyelids fluttering as if struggling to open one last time. When Jamie held his clammy hands, he could still see the old scars he got from working so much when he was younger, a reminder of how much he had sacrificed for the family all those years ago.

On the day of the funeral on Sunday, it stormed.

Whenever it stormed, his grandfather used to ask Jamie to keep him company and sit outside on the porch, taking in the sounds of the rain together. He'd put on some Sinatra and close his eyes, a smile on his face as the rain washed everything else away.

Now, the rain only made Jamie feel lonely.

He wore a black suit and tie that morning and new leather shoes. If not for the funeral, he would have curled up on his grandfather's bed in his old shirt and shorts, all alone. The last thing he wanted was a big crowd and to accept six different homemade casseroles from friends and family.

CHAPTER 6

While his parents got ready downstairs, Jamie went to his grandfather's room and cracked open the door, stepping inside with trepidation. It was already emptier with some of his belongings carefully packed up to be given away to charity or for storage. His grandfather's scent was already disappearing from the place, that familiar mixture of mint and clean soap fading away into nothing. The half-completed crossword puzzles still sat on his bedside table with a few missing words here and there, and it nearly killed Jamie to think that they would never be finished now. Fuji, his grandfather's caramel-colored cat, poked her head into the room and sat next to Jamie, her eyes wet and sad as she peered up at him as if asking where her owner had gone.

He still hadn't cried much that morning, if at all. He just kept his head down during the funeral, staring at his shiny leather shoes while the minister spoke about God and death and life at the front. Even while reading his eulogy, Jamie remained calm and composed, stuffing his emotions down. He told everyone about what a great man his grandfather had been while a collage of photos and Bible verses flashed behind him on a screen. Then they played a few of his grandfather's favorite Sinatra songs, folks said their final goodbyes and dropped roses into the casket, and refreshments were served.

The whole time, people squeezed Jamie's shoulder and gave him hugs and talked about what a wonderful grandson he was, never noticing that his fists were clenched so hard they were turning as white as the flowers adorning the wooden pews.

The last to leave that evening, Jamie walked up to the casket by himself, the sound of his footsteps echoing the whole time. He looked down into the casket, surprised at the wonderful job that the mortician had done. His grandfather had on his favorite brown suit with his eyes gently closed and his chest was still. He looked at peace.

Jamie reached into his pocket and emerged with a wrapped Tootsie Roll in his palm. "Give Sinatra my best when you get up there, Grandpa," he whispered, tucking the candy into his grandfather's suit jacket pocket.

No one loved Sinatra and Tootsie Rolls more than him, even in death.

THE STATE OF US

* * *

"You're really going to stay in Texas for a while?"

"Yeah, for a little bit." Jamie sighed on the other end of the line, rubbing a hand across his face. "Once we figure everything out here, it's back to New York for us, I'm sure. But if it's okay with you, I could use your company for tonight."

"You don't even have to ask. How are you holding up?" Olivia sank into the couch, her brows furrowed as she held the phone to her ear. She and Jamie had been calling nearly every day, but that day, she knew he needed her more than ever. "Did you get a chance to eat yet? It's already past dinnertime over there."

"Not really, but I'm not hungry, thanks for asking. You have no idea how many times I've walked into my grandfather's room today only to remember that he's gone."

"I'm sorry."

"My parents are already talking about selling the house and packing up the rest of his things. It's my mom's coping mechanism to just keep moving so she can forget that her dad died." He huffed out a breath, unsure of why he was suddenly getting emotional. "Sometimes, I think I can hear his voice, but it's hard to know if I'm remembering it correctly anymore. I keep wondering what I would have said or done differently, but that's the thing about goodbyes. There will forever be an unfinished conversation. Just things you want to say, but can't. Not anymore."

"You really loved him, Jamie. I'm sure he knew that. And if you feel like you need to talk again, you know that I'll be here."

"Thanks," he replied. "I'm going to figure things out with my parents and see what they need, then I'm going to take some time for myself. Maybe I'll go back to Seattle or something."

The two of them shared a sad laugh, but Olivia couldn't help but wonder if she'd ever really see him again. "Just take care of yourself for me, okay? Get some food, then get some sleep. I'll be up all night working on a paper for class, but call me anytime." She paused. "Okay?"

CHAPTER 6

Jamie breathed out, his voice softening. "You're right, I'll try to get some rest." He paused. "And Olivia?"

"Yeah?"

"Thanks for checking up on me all day. My friends back in New York are worried about me being by myself here, but I'm glad I've got you looking out for me, too."

"I care about you."

The corners of Jamie's lips tipped up in a small smile. He pressed the phone closer to his ear. "You know," he said, "I care about you, too. I wish I could see you again. Even if it means getting stranded at the airport again, it'd be worth it."

"Very funny."

They hung up and Olivia fell back onto her bed, his words still echoing inside her head.

* * *

Bright and early the next day, she entered a looming building with her portfolio of writing samples and resume, feeling more hopeful than she had in ages, her heart beating wild and free. The elevator doors opened to the spacious twentieth floor that was home to The Seattle Tribune and Olivia stepped inside, taking in all the sights and sounds.

Almost immediately, Olivia found who she was looking for.

Marcia Browning stood on the far side talking animatedly to one of her employees, her presence strong and warm at the same time. She had handled some of the biggest stories the Seattle networks and papers had ever seen, without ever breaking a sweat in front of those who doubted her. Not only was she in charge, but she was also in demand. There was something in Marcia's focused gaze that made it very clear she was aware of that fact.

She turned her head and saw Olivia, who gave a polite wave and smile, and with just a few confident strides, Marcia was standing in front of her with her hand outstretched. "Olivia, it's good to finally meet you. I'm Marcia Browning, CEO of The Seattle Tribune. I've heard wonderful things about you and I'm looking forward to getting to know you." She gestured to a door down the hall. "Why don't we head into my office for some privacy?"

Olivia shook her hand firmly and nodded, following the older woman into a very tastefully decorated corner office. Everything in that space seemed deliberate, even the empty coffee mug sitting on the edge of her desk. The sunlight that morning seemed to hit everything at the perfect angle as well, bathing them all in a warm pool of gold.

Olivia took a seat, sinking into the plush material of the chair and glancing out the big windows at the bustling city streets sandwiched between enormous skyscrapers. Marcia took a seat behind her desk and smiled, her teeth flashing white against her dark skin as she studied the younger woman seated before her.

"Before I begin to ask any questions and look over your portfolio, I want to preface our meeting with something that I tell everyone I work with here at The Seattle Tribune." Marcia clasped her manicured hands together. "All writers, whether they're journalists, novelists, poets, or playwrights, have one thing in common." She paused for emphasis. "The willingness to grow into their voices."

"And what does that look like?"

"Well, it's essential to have the ability to push ourselves beyond our limited thinking and to take on different roles and mindsets to see other people's perspectives freely. We need to do that when we cover a range of topics and stories, even if they may be difficult or foreign to us. But it's also equally important to stay true to our own voice, to continue to shape it and bring our unique perspective when our work calls for it."

Marcia's voice had a natural pull to it, drawing those who were listening in with the gravity of her words as she spoke.

Olivia nodded. "That makes sense."

"One more thing," Marcia added, taking off her glasses and clicking her tongue. "Thick skin. It's important. The stories we cover aren't going to be a walk in the park most of the time. You're going to see, hear, and write about some gritty things, and it's easy to feel disheartened by everything out there." She leaned forward, the smell of her expensive Yves Saint Laurent perfume wafting through the air. "The good news is that we get to champion the truth. We get to make a difference with what we write and put out into the world. So, put out something good. See the tough stuff, change the pattern."

The two women locked eyes, an unspoken understanding passing between them.

Marcia leaned back in her seat and grinned, stretching her lips up in an encouraging grin. "But we're here to talk about *you* today. So, why don't I let you take the lead and tell me about yourself?"

It was the winning question. Even though she was nervous, she had nothing to lose, so Olivia took a deep breath and began to speak.

An hour later, she texted Jamie.

I got the position! I'm going to start in a few weeks. Can't wait, she wrote.

Congratulations, he texted back. *I knew you had it in you.* A few seconds later, another message from him popped up. *I know this is out of the blue, but how would you feel about coming to Texas for a few days?*

Olivia sucked in a breath. She wanted to see him, but she didn't have the money. Between her job at the restaurant and the occasional articles she got paid for to be published, there wasn't much left after tuition, rent, and bills.

It sounds like a great idea on paper, but I don't know if I can, she wrote back.

Jamie called her immediately.

"Look, I know it's a lot to ask," he said, almost as soon as she picked up. "Flights and hotel costs are insane, and I know you've got a lot going on in life right now, but I don't mind waiting a little longer if that means I get to see you. The truth is ... I want more with you, Olivia. I know I'm rambling right now but damn it, I have to say it." He laughed nervously, then continued. "I've been thinking about you ever since we met at the airport in Seattle. And I know we don't live in the same place and all, but I'm not asking for that. All I want is time to know you better and to see if what we felt at the airport was real. Because it felt real to *me*."

So, he felt it too.

"Jamie, I know what you mean. And I felt it too," she said, making her way to an empty bench and sitting down. The air was sweet and warm where she sat by the water, and she breathed it in deeply now, trying to relax. "But the problem is I don't know if I can."

"Why not?"

"Because I can't afford it," she said flatly.

"I can cover the cost of the flight and the hotel if that's everything keeping you from me."

"You and your doctor money," she teased.

"I'm not a doctor, just—"

"A palliative care nurse. I know, I know," she laughed. "Look, I'll tell you what. I'll think about it. But is it a good time to see you? I mean, with everything going on with your family right now and you guys moving back to New York soon."

"I wouldn't ask you if it wasn't the right time, I promise. Just let me know and I'll make it work."

"If you say so."

They hung up and Olivia squeezed her eyes shut, a stupid grin stretching across her face. It was insanity. Or maybe hope.

Probably both.

Starting a long-distance relationship was something she never really thought about. It seemed like a really bad idea. All the long months of waiting to see the other person, the missed opportunities, long and expensive flights, the days and nights of longing, and the big question mark about the future that plagued every long-distance relationship.

Olivia walked, deep in thought about what it meant for them, ignoring the hustle and bustle of Seattle. She passed by buildings and restaurants and shops and people, everything a kaleidoscope of color and movement as she went back in time to when she met Jamie. There was something there.

But was it enough?

And New York. Eventually, he was going to go back there. The thought of being in New York again made her shudder, and it seemed ironic that the two people she felt most curious and hopeful about had decided to make it their home. Olivia's entire life was in Seattle, and though she told herself that it was reckless and impulsive, a part of her ached to go see him. She had never felt that way about anybody else, so maybe it meant something. Everything in her life was usually so structured and sensible, and this trip would mean doing something completely different.

By the time Olivia started to make her way to the bus stop to get home, the skies were the color of orange sherbet and it was past dinnertime. A young couple passed by, clearly newly in love as they talked and laughed and leaned against one another as if they couldn't stand to even be an inch apart, and she found herself wondering what it would feel like to have that again.

She had loved before like most twenty-somethings, but this time felt different. She was losing track of time and focus when it came to Jamie, and even if it meant unanswered questions and leaps of faith, she wanted more, too.

When she got home, the sky was already a blue so dark that it looked nearly black. The velvet sky had stars scattered in its folds and white moths circulated her porch lights, welcoming her back. Olivia got to her room, closed the door and fell back on the bed, her mind dizzy with possibility.

She was falling in love, she was sure of it.

And for the first time, it wasn't completely terrifying to lose control.

* * *

It rained for an entire week in Texas while Jamie waited for Olivia's decision. It was the kind of heavy rain that sounded like the entire world was going to wash away into the storm drains.

His family had cleaned his grandfather's house, packed away most of his things, and started playing with the idea of selling the house at last. He knew it would be hard, and it was agonizing knowing that his grandfather's life in that house would eventually boil down to paperwork, closing costs, and offer negotiations, but it meant the start of a new chapter for his family.

His mother was finally ready to part ways with the past. She went into Jamie's room one night and sat on the bed, looking a little nervous as she fluffed her hair and smoothed her dress, avoiding Jamie's eyes.

"Well, honey, I've finally decided that it's time to sell the house," she had said, her voice brightening a little as if finding strength in her choice. "And before you say anything, I want you to know that I love this house and I love your grandpa more than anything in the world, but this house isn't anything without him in it."

"I know." Jamie had reached over and threaded his fingers through hers. "I feel the same."

"I think it's time we moved back to New York, where we can really use the support of our family and friends and tie up all the loose ends there. We've been away from New York for far too long, and I feel most like myself when I'm working and doing things in the city. I know you also made a big sacrifice leaving work and your life for so long to come here with us."

"Mom, don't say that. I would've done it even if you hadn't asked. He's my grandfather."

His mother had rested a hand against his cheek, her eyes wet. "Knowing your grandfather, he would have wanted us to continue doing what we were doing before he got sick."

It was true, and one of the things he knew his grandfather wanted for him was to be courageous in exploring what the future held, and to take in every opportunity with gratitude and curiosity. Especially when it came to love.

And if Olivia agreed to meet him in Texas, it would mean something new for the two of them, too. It had been four months since he last saw her face, and he wanted to be in the same room with her again, just talking and touching and laughing.

At twenty-four, Jamie had experienced more than his fair share of relationships, but there was something special about the way Olivia made him feel, something he never experienced before. It was clear even after that very first night at the airport. After that, every time he came across that little postcard they had picked out together, he would remember.

And he would miss her.

They were already doing everything that lovers usually did, like calling and texting throughout the day, talking about their past and future hopes, and sharing jokes that were only funny to the two of them.

By the end of the rain-drenched week, she had sent him a message with

CHAPTER 6

just six words that would change everything.

I have made up my mind.

* * *

"You can't be serious about Texas." Olivia's mother shook her head as the two of them walked to the parking lot behind the restaurant. They had dinner together and things had been going so well that Olivia made the mistake of bringing it up. "You barely know this guy."

It had been a few days since Olivia decided to fly to Jamie and give a long-distance relationship a shot. But now, it did feel a little bit like a potential rerun of her flying to New York to see her dad only to have it end up as a total disaster.

Olivia slid into the passenger seat and buckled herself in, hoping her calm demeanor would rub off from pure proximity. "Well, Jamie said they're going to sell the house and move back to New York soon. His dad owns a catering business and also dabbles a little in event planning, and his mom is a financial analyst. Jamie and I are really good friends now, and it'll be just a few days."

"And what's so horrible about your life that you have to leave Seattle every few months?" Her mother started the car, driving slowly out of the parking lot while her question marinated in the air between them.

"Nothing. There's nothing wrong with my life right now." Olivia glanced over at her mother, her brows furrowed. "I don't have to be in a bad spot to go and have some fun, and to make my own decisions. You want me to be honest with you, but you never accept the truths I have to say. What is it about Jamie that you don't approve of?"

"The problem isn't *Jamie*," her mother pointed out, stepping on the gas with more force than necessary as the light turned green. "I happen to think he's a decent guy. But the problem is that you're flying all over the country for someone you barely know and letting yourself get mixed up in something that's bound to end poorly."

Olivia picked at a loose thread on her pants, keeping her head down and her expression inscrutable. She knew it wouldn't be a piece of cake to be with Jamie and that it would take lots of planning, waiting, communication, and compromise.

Her mother looked over at her, a few strands of hair loosening from her bun and falling in tired tendrils around her face as she impatiently brushed them away. "Your degree, your job, and your future are the things that you should be focusing on right now," she said. "You've got so much going for you and I don't want you jeopardizing your future for one person. Relationships and people change, for better or worse. I just don't want you to make mistakes that you'll regret one day. I mean, look at what happened with me and your dad. We went through life's ups and downs together and he was *still* keeping things from me even while living together under the same roof." Her mother sighed. "And Jamie's in a different state. He could be a different person underneath all those idealistic seeds he's planting in your head."

"It's not like I'm throwing everything in my life away just because I met him," Olivia replied. The moon was as round and shiny as a persimmon that night, and she stared at it out the window, trying to stay calm and reasonable. "I'm still working hard to save money, graduate early, and have a decent career, Mom. I know we've been struggling with stability for a long time, even when Dad was around. But I don't plan on letting anyone get in my way of a better life."

Her mother pressed her lips together and frowned. "Do you love him?"

"I care about him."

"You care too much, Olivia. Look at how your dad was able to twist you around his finger for his own selfish reasons. Now you're doing the same thing with Jamie because it's all you know."

Olivia felt tears prick at her eyes, and she forced herself to breathe out and focus on something else in the distance. The tension between the two of them grew, and the beginning of a headache was surfacing for Olivia as tightness gripped the base of her skull.

"This has nothing to do with Dad. Not *everything* is a byproduct of our dysfunctional family. You tell me to stop obsessing over the past and trying to make things right, but I know that you see this family as a failure. You

CHAPTER 6

want to make sure that I don't make the same mistakes, but I am not *you*."

At a red light on an empty street, she got out of the car. It was quiet in their neighborhood at this time of night, stars were beginning to blink overhead, and it looked a lot more peaceful out there than inside the car.

She walked and walked for a very long time, lost in her thoughts until she found a park bench at the top of a hill and sat down, tilting her face up to the sky. Above her, the stars glittered and beneath her, the city lights sparkled like scattered diamonds.

Every few minutes, she'd hear a car driving down the street at the bottom of the hill, the sound of it reassuring. Olivia put her feet up on the bench and then lay down so that she was now facing the expansive sky. She had to stop going around in circles with her mother and grow up, and she had to see things without her rose-tinted glasses. But if she were to be honest, the worst part of it all wasn't even the pain of being let down by her dad—it was the fear of letting anyone else in.

It was all the walls that she had built up over time, the ones that kept her from ever truly being able to be herself because she learned that being herself wasn't enough to make people stay.

Sighing, she pressed her back deeper into the bench and closed her eyes, feeling her heartbeat slow down. Now, it was up to her to make things right, and she was going to fix things with her mother.

It took her twenty minutes to walk back home, and though it was late by then, she knew her mother would still be awake. She locked the door and stepped into the kitchen, not surprised to see her mother sitting alone on a stool by the island, cupping a mug of chamomile tea between her palms. She had changed out of her slacks and blouse into the pajamas that Olivia had gotten her for Christmas with the printed pugs on the front. In the dim light of the kitchen, her mother looked older and thinner than Olivia remembered, and the realization of it made her sad.

"How was your walk?" her mother asked, taking a small sip of the tea, her eyes downcast.

"It was fine." Olivia walked over to the island and took a seat next to her, not completely sure what to do. "I'm sorry ... for what I said to you earlier."

"I know."

"And I have something to confess, too."

Her mother cocked her head. "What about?"

Olivia swallowed around the knot in her throat, still keeping her head down. "About Dad," she said. "I lied about how bad things got in New York. I didn't want to tell you because I felt ashamed that you were right about him. And now, I'm scared that you'll be right about Jamie too." She sniffled and wiped at her nose, embarrassed that she was crying again.

"I know." Her mother rested her hand over hers and patted it.

"What do you mean?"

"I already knew. I don't know how, but I knew."

"Then why didn't you say anything?"

"Well, whatever happened has already happened. I didn't want you to feel worse about it. I figured if you were keeping it a secret, then it was for a reason."

Olivia laughed, feeling foolish. "I should've known."

"We all have to learn our own lessons, right? Maybe I've always been overprotective, but it's only because I want what's best for you. I know what it feels like to lose someone you think the world of." She reached over and put one arm around Olivia, which was an uncharacteristic move on her part, but they stayed like that for a few minutes, just leaning against one another. It was strange, but the longer they sat there together, the more Olivia realized that she wasn't the only one sitting in a dim kitchen with a bruised heart.

"So, what's going to happen now?" Olivia asked.

Her mother lifted her head off Olivia's shoulder, looking tired. "Well, we both know that there's nothing I can do to stop you once you've got your mind set on something. I realize that, sometimes, it's useless to tell people what they don't want to hear, so I won't do that anymore. I have to let you make your own decisions and live out their consequences, whether they're good or bad. But I want you to just promise me one thing."

"What is it?"

"Promise me that you'll be honest with yourself, always. The minute you start making excuses for someone else and lying to yourself, that's when you're in trouble. You're my daughter, and I know you better than you think I do. I know you see the best in the worst of people, but don't be blind to all of that just to keep the peace."

Olivia couldn't help but laugh a little. "That's very profound."

Her mother shrugged, took a small sip of her tea, and smiled. "What can I say? Mother knows best," she teased.

It was almost two in the morning by the time Olivia finally crawled into bed. She switched the light off and rested her head against her pillow, blinking against the darkness.

Despite everything that happened with her father in New York, she had a good feeling about things with Jamie. They had even called after her talk with her mother that night, and he had stayed for an hour just listening to her. There was no judgment, no fixing, no advice. All the ugly parts of herself that Olivia had stuffed down deep for so long finally came out, and it felt *good*. It felt amazing, even.

She let out a happy sigh and rolled over in bed, closing her eyes at last. A few minutes passed by, then she heard a noise. It sounded like voices, but they were all distorted.

And they were coming from somewhere within the house.

Olivia blinked, sitting up slowly. Her head felt heavy and her mouth felt as dry as cotton. Something was very, very wrong.

She craned her neck to listen, trying to figure out where the voices were coming from. They were only getting louder by the second, and she was surprised that nobody else had woken up. Olivia pulled her robe tighter around herself and padded out into the hallway in her bare feet, only taking a few steps before she felt a chill run down her spine.

She was back at their old house somehow, the one she lived in as a kid when her parents were still together, except everything was dilapidated and rotten. Ashes drifted down from a splintered ceiling and hazy trails of smoke drifted through the hallways, curling into shapes that looked like human fingers reaching for something she couldn't see. It was hard to see much of anything in the dark, and the whispering voices had disappeared so that there was only silence now.

Slowly, Olivia made her way down the hallway to the living room, where she could hear the crackling of a fire. As she rounded the corner, she noticed how even the orange and yellow shadows thrown by the flickering fire looked ominous instead of warm and inviting.

A strange rustling came from behind her and she looked down in time to see a scrawny rat with beady black eyes dash between her legs. Its limbs were too long and thin for a rat, jutting out painfully in a way that suggested its bones were too big for its body. She shuddered, feeling the rat's matted fur brush past against her ankles and then watched as it scurried behind something hidden deep in the shadows.

Olivia squinted, taking a small step forward.

All at once, everything went silent. The fire stopped crackling and her footsteps didn't make a sound as she moved toward the object, her heart in her throat the entire time. As she got nearer, she saw that it was a wooden casket. With her head pounding, she lifted the top and peered into its depths, watching as the darkness grew beneath her as if looking down into a well that had no bottom.

At first, there was just emptiness and darkness, but as her eyes adjusted and shapes began to form, she realized that she was looking down at what looked like a mountain of empty liquor bottles crusted with dirt and insects. As her gaze trailed down to the bottom, she could make out a figure sitting there.

With growing horror, Olivia realized that it was her father.

His clothes had filth and insects clinging to them, and his skin was pallid as he blinked up at her from the bottom. The gaping darkness was slowly closing in on him, the empty bottles disappearing as the blackness grew closer and closer. An acrid smell began to fill the air as thick, black tar surfaced on the ground where he was standing. Her father simply stood there, his lips stretching into a sinister smile as more tar burst from the ground, coating his clothes and skin in black. He didn't move, even as the liquid began to pull him down, the acidic and pungent aroma burning his eyes and throat. In a matter of seconds, the tar had filled his lungs and nose,

CHAPTER 6

and his head disappeared underneath the bubbling mass.

At last, a scream ripped free from Olivia's own throat as she lunged forward to try to save him, toppling right into the casket's depths herself.

The wind rushed against her face one last time as she fell, just before she landed directly in the scorching tar. The last thing she heard before her head disappeared underneath it was the sound of the casket lid slamming shut above her with deafening finality. Then there was nothing but the cold and the dark and the silence.

Olivia woke from the nightmare with a scream lodged in her throat, her skin prickling with sweat. She sat up and clutched at her neck, feeling like there was still tar stuck in her throat that was preventing her from breathing properly. Suddenly feeling nauseous, she forced herself to take deep breaths until the last wisps of the nightmare floated away into the darkness.

Lately, she had been getting nightmares several times a week. They weren't always so chilling, but they always made her feel helpless in some way.

She fumbled for her phone on the bedside table, glancing at the time.

It was nearly five in the morning.

Exhausted, she tossed her phone onto the sheets, still shaken from the awful nightmare as moonlight washed through the curtains. Despite everything, she still cared about her dad. She still wondered what he was up to and if he was doing better. In a lot of ways, she felt like he was a victim, too. And even if they never spoke or saw each other again, Olivia felt closer to him just understanding what he was going through from a distance.

In some ways, she was glad that she gave up hope after what happened in New York. There was no more pretending that he was someone different and that things would change. It was a bittersweet sense of acceptance, even if it came about in a really painful way.

Settling back into bed, she breathed in deeply and closed her eyes. In just one week, she'd see Jamie again, and soon after that, she'd be starting at The Seattle Tribune. There was going to be a lot going on for her over the next few months, and she was ready to transition to something new, something better. She could feel it in her bones that things were only going to look up from there.

They just had to.

Chapter 7

A week later, Olivia was standing at the arrivals gate at the airport in Austin, waiting for Jamie to pick her up. The airplane had been stuffy and cramped and smelled like dirty laundry, and an unhappy toddler howled miserably throughout the entire flight.

To keep herself busy, she had ordered an overpriced virgin cocktail to pair with her bag of complimentary trail mix and ate her sad little snack in silence. It wasn't any better off the plane, Olivia found out, fanning herself as she rolled her suitcase over to a row of empty seats. It was hot and humid in the airport too, even with her sundress and hair pulled up. Just as she was ready to take a seat, she felt a pair of arms wrap around her waist from behind, lifting her feet off the ground. "Welcome to Texas!" Jamie shouted, laughing as he spun her around.

As soon as her feet touched the ground again, she buried her face into Jamie's chest, too happy to speak. When she finally pulled back to look at him, he kissed her. It wasn't like their first kiss, which felt tentative. It was the kind of kiss that told her he knew exactly what he wanted, and it was her.

"Wow, hello to you too." She eyed him, smiling happily. "You look good."

He was wearing a cream-colored linen shirt that stood out in sharp contrast against his tan skin. There was a shadow of stubble along his jaw that made him look a little older, but his eyes still had that same youthful sparkle that she remembered so well.

Jamie laughed, reaching up and running a hand through his hair. "Let's be honest, I look more like burnt toast right now. I've been helping fix up my grandpa's house here and there with some smaller projects and gardening. We're going to sell the place soon, and I'm so glad I get to share it with you first." He smiled, producing a small bouquet of tulips shrouded in greenery from behind his back. "These are for you."

She let Jamie lead her out to the parking lot, his fingers intertwined with hers as they made their way through the crowd and out of the airport, together this time.

* * *

The wind whipped through their hair as Jamie sped down the highway with Bruce Springsteen crooning about hungry hearts on the radio.

The sun was suspended in a cloudless sky above them as they drove, and Olivia grinned as Austin lay open before them like a pop-up book, with colorful bars and turquoise lakes punctuating the plot of land every so often. From behind her sunglasses, she sneaked a glance over at Jamie in the driver's seat, singing along to the music while being sorely out of tune, making her laugh.

He turned to smile at her, taking her hand during an instrumental break and kissing the back of it. Olivia closed her eyes, taking a mental snapshot of Jamie with his sunglasses down over his nose, belting out a song at the top of his lungs with one hand resting comfortably on the steering wheel, as relaxed and happy as she'd ever seen him. She wanted to remember it forever.

After a quick stop for lunch, they were back at the house.

"Jamie, it looks *really* good." Olivia stepped out of the car, her eyes widening. "You guys did a great job with everything. It looks like something out of a home decor magazine."

The porch had a fresh coat of paint and plenty of comfortable chairs. It was a place of respite for reading, watching the sunset, or just sitting and dreaming about impossible things. Flowers bloomed brightly in the front yard and a hummingbird feeder hung delicately from a Texas redbud that took center stage in the yard.

CHAPTER 7

The two of them went into the house, where they were greeted with wood ceilings and warm lighting. Bright whites and soft blues gave the whole place an oceanic feel and a vase of flowers punctuated the calmer hues with its bright pink.

"You know, when we moved into our current place in Seattle, I didn't even repaint my room walls or decorate," she confessed, taking a seat near the counter. "It didn't feel like home, so I didn't want to bother. I somehow convinced myself that decorating or putting personal touches would mean I was putting my roots down there, so I promised myself I wouldn't. Kind of stupid, now that I think about it."

Jamie emerged with a pitcher of fresh sweet tea from the fridge and poured them both a glass. "I remember you telling me that. And it's not stupid." He took a seat next to her and put a hand on top of hers. "I might've done the same if my parents separated and we ended up moving."

She nodded, ready to change the subject. "Anyway, you promised me a grand tour. I'll take you up on that offer now."

"You don't mess around, do you?"

She took a sip of her tea and smirked. "Nope. A promise made is a promise kept."

"Look at you, all educated and quoting Aristotle."

"I didn't know it was Aristotle who said it, but thanks for giving me so much credit." Jamie started showing her around, but they stopped just before reaching his room. A piano sitting inside an adjacent room caught Olivia's eye and she moved toward it, drawing her fingers delicately over the ivory keys. "Do you play?"

Jamie moved next to her and pressed down on a key, the note echoing through the room. "I don't," he said. "It was my grandfather's piano. He used to teach piano, hoping I would pick it up." Olivia sat down on the piano bench and raised her hands to the keys, plucking out a gentle melody that filled the air. "What's that?"

"Chopin." Her fingers swept over the shiny keys, the music filling the room as she played from memory. After several minutes, she stopped and rested her hands in her lap, smiling contentedly as the last echoes of the notes faded away. "It's one of my favorites."

"Let me try." Jamie wiggled his fingers dramatically and sat down, and moments later, a Billy Joel song filled the air from memory.

Olivia gaped at him. "I thought you couldn't play piano!"

"I said I *didn't* play piano, I never said I *couldn't*. But I promise I'm boring from here on out. That's the only song I remember how to play when my grandpa taught me ages ago."

"Well, color me impressed." Her shoulder brushed his as she leaned in closer, her gaze flicking from his irises to his lips. He kissed her then, cupping the back of her neck and drawing her mouth to his, sending waves of warmth coursing through her body.

They kept kissing as he guided her backward to the couch, the afternoon sun washing over his skin and painting it gold as they moved across the room. Olivia let out a laugh as she fell back onto the couch, enjoying the way he was threading his fingers through her hair and dotting kisses along her neck the whole time. She smiled up at him and ran her thumb over his cheek, enjoying the way it felt just to touch him.

"I love you," he suddenly said. Olivia searched those brown eyes for a hint of dishonesty or malice, but there was none. The gorgeous absurdity of everything somehow made sense when they were together, and they both felt it. "And I'm so happy you're here. I know everything's a bit crazy for us right now, but I wouldn't want to do this with anyone else."

"I know." She tilted her chin up to meet his lips, holding him close. "I trust you."

* * *

That night, as she sat with Jamie and his family around the kitchen table laughing and talking over dinner, she thought of her mom. It had always been just the two of them. It was different sitting there as a family with everyone talking about their day and laughing over shared memories. In some ways, Olivia wondered if this was maybe a second chance to feel at home and to experience what other people got to when everyone was present

CHAPTER 7

in the family.

Meeting the parents was a relationship litmus test, but Jamie gave her hand a reassuring squeeze underneath the table every once in a while, reminding her that as long as her heart was in the right place, his parents didn't ask for much else.

Jamie's mother, a woman in her mid-fifties with short, chestnut-colored waves and a penchant for statement earrings, babbled endlessly throughout dinner, much to the amusement of everyone. His father, a well-dressed man with black frames and salt and pepper hair, was her quieter counterpart. He listened quietly to the conversation and enjoyed his food with a satisfied smile, only cracking a joke here and there to keep the mood jovial.

"Olivia, have some more of the paella." Jamie's mother gestured at the dish. "Jamie told us it was one of your favorites. He's been talking about you nonstop for the past few months, just so you're aware."

"Mom, please." Jamie laughed and pinched the bridge of his nose, shaking his head. "Don't scare her off already."

"By the way, Olivia, great choice for champagne. I'm impressed!" his father exclaimed, nodding with approval.

"Thanks, Mr. Reyes. I guess I just got lucky," Olivia replied. "I'm not much of a drinker myself."

"Please, just call me Samuel. I'm not as serious and ancient as I look, I promise."

"It's probably your thinning hair and wrinkles," his wife teased. "It's aging you, hon."

"I like to think they add character." Jamie's father winked and took another sip of champagne, the bubbles darting through the golden liquid like shooting stars. He turned to Olivia. "How are you liking Texas so far? Do you have any plans for tomorrow with Jamie?"

"You've all made me feel so welcome here. It's been a lot of fun," Olivia said, smiling at each of them. "Tomorrow, we're going to a museum and botanical garden. After that, Jamie said he'd take me to Houston sometime."

"Sounds like a great time." His mother smiled at them both. "Well, we're happy to see you two together at last. We won't be back in Texas for a long time, especially after we sell the house. It's great you decided to come by when you did."

"What do you like about our Jamie anyway? The kid's a goofy-looking one." His father said leaned over to poke his son in the ribs.

"I guess he takes after you," Olivia quipped, the retort sounding funnier in her head. Jamie's parents stared at her, their eyes widening in shock. "I'm sorry, I didn't mean it like that. I—"

His parents suddenly burst out laughing. "I like her very much already." His father wiped at the corners of his eyes. "She's got our sense of humor and can roll with the punches. Welcome to our crazy family, Olivia."

Jamie stood up, shaking his head. "Dessert, anyone?"

Everyone cheered.

* * *

"So, how was the interrogation?" Jamie asked, draping his jacket around Olivia's shoulders. He joined her on the porch swing in the backyard while a moth flew overhead in dazed circles against the May night sky.

Olivia slid over so she could lean her head on his shoulder. "I was armed with the right champagne choice and sense of humor, so I guess I passed. In all honesty, I like your parents. I feel comfortable and like I can be myself."

"You can always be yourself around me." He gave her hand a little squeeze. "And you made them so happy tonight. It's been a hard year for the whole family, but it's great that we get to create new memories here before selling the house and going back to New York for good."

The two of them rocked slowly on the porch swing as stars appeared like little lights overhead, flickering on in unison.

"Sometimes, I wish I had been more patient and spent more time with my mom and dad when we were all together," she confessed. "I had no idea that things would change so fast, and it makes me wish I had made some better memories, too. Seeing you with your family is bittersweet because it makes me wish I had that. Or at least appreciated it when I used to."

"Maybe you can't turn back time with your dad, but I think there's a lot

CHAPTER 7

of love between you and your mom, even now." Jamie nudged the swing forward with his foot on the ground. "Sometimes we just have to take a step back and see the bigger picture. Maybe the love you and your mom share shows up differently than you'd like and maybe you disagree more than agree, but that same love is there. It might not always seem like it, but it's there."

"You're going to make me cry." She laughed as tears pricked her eyes. "I mean it."

"Don't cry just yet," Jamie said, reaching into his pocket and smiling at her. "I have something that might cheer you up." He pulled out a little velvet pouch and pulled something delicate and shiny from it. "Since I can't be there with you all the time, this is a little something to remind you that distance won't change how I feel about you."

He moved closer and clasped something around her neck. She looked down at the silver necklace with surprise, noticing the little pendant in the shape of an origami paper airplane hanging from it.

"I love you, Liv. And I promise to try my best to make things work between us, even with the distance," Jamie said, sincerity causing his voice to waver. "You mean a lot to me and I want to make it to where you are. I'm going to do everything I can to keep you happy. I want to make that promise to you now, and I wanted to give you something to remember that promise by."

"Jamie, I don't need you to promise anything." She was nervous. "You know I hate when people make promises they can't keep."

"But I mean it. I wouldn't be saying this to you if I didn't mean every word. My Plan A is to give this long-distance relationship my best shot," he said, each word careful and deliberate. "I want to work hard at loving you the best I can, even when we're far apart. And I want to do everything possible to make you happy. If Plan A doesn't work out, there's always Plan B, Plan C, and maybe even Plan D. What I'm trying to tell you is that I wouldn't want to do this with anyone else. It's just you. Just you and me."

"I can't tell if that sounds more like insanity or love."

"Same thing, if you ask me," he chuckled. "But every time you wear your necklace, just know I'm thinking of you, too."

"Then I'll wear it every day." Olivia touched the pendant gently, reminded of the fact that they'd have to say goodbye in a matter of days. She paused, lost in thought for a moment. "You know what else is insane?"

"What?"

Olivia pulled her legs up underneath her on the porch swing, leaning back to look at the stars sprinkled like confetti in the sky. "I've been thinking about writing a book."

"No kidding? What's it going to be about?"

"I don't know yet, but I've got a few ideas."

"Just promise you'll let me be the first to read it."

"I don't know if I can promise that, but you'll be the first to know. Okay?"

"I can live with that." Jamie grinned at her. "Anyway, why don't we head back inside so you can get some rest?"

After showering and brushing her teeth that night, she curled up next to Jamie in the dark, the day on repeat in her mind. It was hard to believe she was in Texas with him and even harder to believe that something so wonderful came out of being stuck overnight at an airport four months ago.

Now, she was in a different state with someone who loved her, far away from everything and everyone back home. She turned to her side, resting a hand lightly on Jamie's chest and watching it rise with each of his breaths until it eventually lulled her to sleep.

In a matter of minutes, she was fast asleep, and it was the first time in weeks that Olivia slept through the night without having a single nightmare.

* * *

By the following Wednesday, she was already used to the way Jamie's singing would echo through the house when he showered and knew his breakfast order by heart at his favorite restaurant. She knew where to get the best crab-stuffed jalapeños in Austin and learned that she was surprisingly good at kayaking when they went to Lady Bird Lake.

There was his favorite linen shirt on the back of the chair by his desk, the same one he wore when he picked her up at the airport. She learned that he loved coffee any time of the day and was great at remembering the small details of every movie they watched. She taught him how to make jjamppong, a Korean-Chinese noodle soup that Olivia's mom always used to make, and read him passages from her notebook for story ideas. She'd be heading back home to Seattle very soon, and her time with him was dwindling to refolded dresses and packed toiletries in a suitcase, along with all the memories she had made with him in Austin.

Since it was their last morning together, she figured she could make breakfast for the whole family. It was just past seven in the morning, but she woke to an already empty spot next to her on the bed.

Olivia trudged to the bathroom, splashed some water on her face, and brushed her teeth, thinking about what they talked about the other night when it came to the distance. The thought of him going back home to New York filled her with equal parts trepidation and happiness. She was happy he would get to go home, to be back with all the people and places and things that he loved so much, but they were going to be on opposite sides of the country for an indefinite amount of time. She started moving down the stairs to the kitchen, still lost in thought when she heard her name.

"You should have told us about Olivia's background earlier." It was Jamie's mother speaking, and Olivia paused on the stairs to listen, hidden from their line of sight. "If her father struggled with addiction, you know there can be a genetic predisposition. I don't want you going down that road. Es un camino muy peligroso, no te vayas por ahí."

"Mom, I know you're stressed, but trust me when I say that there's nothing to worry about. "

"You bend over backward for the people you love and make excuses for them, Jamie. And who does that hurt in the end? Look at what happened between you and Emma."

"Mamá, no digas eso," Jamie said, his voice firm. "Things were different with me and Emma. And why does it matter if Olivia's background is a little different from ours? Estás pensando demasiado las cosas."

She clicked her tongue dismissively. "I'm not overthinking things, Jamie. You're an adult and I want you to make smart decisions. Our family makes good money, we have a reputable business and have everything at our fingertips. Why would you want to be involved with someone who will end up causing you problems? Es mucho para un hombre."

Olivia felt her heart squeeze and her face get hot. She felt ashamed and angry and wanted nothing more than to leave, but her feet felt glued to the stairs.

"I've heard enough," Jamie said, rubbing his face. "And Mom, please keep your voice down. Olivia's upstairs and I don't want her hearing this nonsense."

"You're around enough negativity and disease as it is, mi amor." His mother lowered her voice to a conspiratorial whisper. "You work in palliative care, for crying out loud. You don't want to see your own girlfriend suffer from liver disease or cancer due to some substance use disorder, do you?"

"Well, that's a bridge I'll cross when and if I get there," Jamie snapped.

At this point, Olivia had heard enough and was retreating up the stairs when Jamie rounded the corner of the living room, his eyebrows shooting straight up and his cheeks flushing with color when he saw her. The past week felt like such a big step forward for the two of them, and that morning felt like an enormous step back.

She watched as Jamie closed the bedroom door behind them, turning to face her at last. "You heard everything, didn't you?"

Olivia sat down on the bed and crossed her legs, patting the spot next to her, her eyes cold like a steel blade. He joined her, his lips pressed together in a grim line as the two of them sat in silence, watching dust mites float contentedly through the stream of sunlight by the bedroom window.

"We come from very different worlds, don't we?" Olivia asked. Her words came out quietly, but her voice was hard.

"I'm sorry you had to hear all that just now. It was my fault I told her." Jamie sighed and rubbed at his neck, avoiding her gaze. "But my mom's opinion of you and your dad doesn't matter. To be honest, it *shouldn't* matter. Why do you care so much about what other people think?"

"It matters to me what your parents think because I care about *you*. It's already hard enough with you moving back to New York and us being

CHAPTER 7

thousands of miles apart. I don't need people talking shit about me and my family on top of that. Do you get it?"

"I already told you," Jamie said, "it doesn't matter. It's not going to change my mind. My parents' expectations and values aren't my own. I mean, they've been big fans of Trump and the pro-life movement for as long as I can remember, but it doesn't mean I agree or stand behind them for that. It also doesn't make them bad people for thinking differently. It's the same thing with your dad. His problem with drinking and gambling is not *your* problem, right? And at the same time, it doesn't mean he's a bad person. That's what I've been trying to explain to my mom, but I don't know if you heard that part."

Olivia bent forward and put her face in her hands, wanting to scream. "Okay, your parents choosing to be fans of Trump is completely different from what my dad struggles with, which isn't always about *choice*. Don't even get me started on that right now." She flung her hands off her face, exasperated as she looked at Jamie. "And why are you turning this whole thing around on me when your mom is the one who thinks I'm going to end up in rehab or something?"

"Okay, you're right. I'm sorry, Liv, I just meant that it was never something that made me look at you any differently and I never would have told my parents if I knew they would judge you for it." He sighed and drew his hands through his hair in exasperation. "Can we just move on from this? I'm not saying things the way I want to right now."

"Okay, but before we do, can I ask you something?"

"What is it?"

"I heard your mom mention someone by the name of Emma, and how things ended badly between you two. What happened?" Olivia asked. By this point, she had shared with him much more than he had shared with her, and it felt like a good question to re-balance the scales.

She watched him get up and walk to the windows, the sunlight painting his skin as he stared out into the distance, not saying a word. After several moments, he simply shrugged and said, "It's just déjà vu, that's all. We don't talk anymore, but Emma and I were together for four years before she moved to London. Distance took its toll, and that was that."

"Then what made you want to try a long-distance relationship again?"

There was silence, then he turned around, a faraway look in his eyes. "Meeting you."

* * *

That afternoon, she borrowed Jamie's car and drove out past the suburbs and supermarkets and city lights, all the way out to an empty field that was several miles off the highway.

There was nothing but the land stretching out before her, and it was exactly what she needed. Even though she was leaving tomorrow morning and her time with Jamie was running short with just hours left, she needed to write. Her head was swimming with ideas and lines and dialogue, and everything that had happened during the last few months just came tumbling forward like a tsunami, drowning everything else out.

She parked the car and found a good spot near some trees that offered a sliver of relief from the Texas heat and began to write. The hours melted away as she filled the pages of her notebook, everything else in the world disappearing. She was in her zone, and there was nothing quite like getting swept away and pulled out to sea by the world and characters that she created.

By the time she walked back to the car, it was dark and stars were just beginning to blot the sky, but there was still one more thing she wanted to write about. Olivia kicked off her shoes and crossed her legs in the driver's seat, propping her notebook against the steering wheel.

She pressed her pen against the paper and wrote the first few sentences, the universal themes of love and loss creeping across the pages like phantoms. Writing felt a lot like therapy, with the good, the bad, and the ugly all coming out at once.

By the time she started the car and pulled out onto the highway again, she knew exactly what her book was going to be about.

* * *

CHAPTER 7

That night, neither of them could sleep.

It was extra warm that night, and the humidity settled over them like a thick, damp blanket in the dark. Jamie groaned and rolled onto his back, rubbing a hand tiredly down his face. "It's too hot to sleep." He glanced over at Olivia, who looked like she was suffering an equal amount, her cheeks as pink as lotuses as she desperately fanned herself with her hands. "Do you want to switch sides so you're closer to the fan?"

"No, it's fine." She sat up, piling her hair on top of her head to keep it off her neck. "I never sleep the night before a flight anyway."

"Don't remind me."

Olivia scooted closer and nudged him playfully. "Had enough of me yet?"

"Not even close." He sat up, his hair disheveled and sticking out in several directions. Olivia laughed and patted it down again. "I'm going to miss this. I wish I could just bring you with me to New York."

"Or you could come with me to Seattle."

"That's the plan." Jamie tapped the silver plane hanging from the end of Olivia's necklace, its wings gleaming in the low light. "Isn't it?"

"It is," she agreed. "And I'm sorry I took everything out on you earlier because of what your mom said. To be completely honest, I don't think it's ever going to be easy talking about my dad to anyone. I know how much it affected you when your grandpa passed away, but the kind of grief you feel from someone choosing to walk out on you is so different. It's a different kind of loss, one you don't get closure from. There's no funeral or eulogy, there's no explanation or apology. It's like you're just stuck as a kid mentally, waiting for someone to come along and make it all better."

"First of all," Jamie said, "you don't have to be sorry, because I know that what my mom said was messed up and I'm still going to apologize on her behalf. I don't know what got into her today. And second of all, you can always talk to me about things like this. I want to support you through it, even if we're not in the same place all the time. I remember how determined you were to get to your dad the first time I met you, and I could tell how important that trip was to you. Don't ever let that voice in your head tell you that you're not strong or courageous, because you're both. You went for it, even when there was no guarantee it would work out."

"I think I'm over it in a lot of ways, but the hurt will always be there when I dig deep enough," Olivia admitted, leaning her head on Jamie's shoulder. Her voice trembled, but she continued talking, pushing past all the walls she was so used to keeping up. "I just don't want to spend the rest of my life trying to prove my worth to him or wondering if he's proud of who I've become. There's so much going on in my life right now. *Good* things. I can't just focus on that one sore spot anymore."

Even if the drinking and distance went away, there was always going to be something keeping Olivia and her dad apart at the heart of it. It wasn't just his vice or the fact that he was in a different state that kept them in such different worlds. It was the fact that she was never going to be important to him, that she was never going to be someone he saw value in, even if she was his daughter. It was always going to hurt knowing that just existing and being his daughter wasn't enough, but she didn't want to feel worthless or like she was lacking something anymore.

"It sounds a lot like forgiveness to me," Jamie said. "I hope you can eventually forgive my mom for what she said."

"Already done." She patted his arm, gently laying back down in bed. "Anyway, I know it's going to be impossible, but we should get some sleep. We need to be at the airport in about two hours."

"Okay." Jamie joined her and lay down, his gaze still on her. "I don't know if I've said it enough lately, but I love you. We're gonna make this work and we're gonna figure everything else out together. I promise."

"If you say so."

"You know what I've been thinking lately? It's kind of a scary thought."

"What?" she asked.

"I keep thinking about how much I want to spend all my days with you, how much I want to always have you here with me."

"That sounds a lot like something you'd say in a proposal."

Jamie's laugh echoed in the room. "Well, you never know. Maybe one day, but for now, just trust me when I say that I'll make it to you as soon as I can, okay?"

CHAPTER 7

Olivia reached over and let her fingertips dance over his skin, tracing the curves of his face in the dark. She hated when people made promises liberally, tossing them out freely like confetti without ever having the drive or integrity to bring them to fruition. But here was an opportunity to really move forward, to work at something that had potential. Everything in the past was already out of her reach, and there was nothing she could do to change the outcome anymore.

While there was no proof, she had faith in what Jamie said he would do. She wanted to believe him more than anything.

"Okay," she said, laying down her internal armor at last. "I trust you."

Chapter 8

During her second week at The Seattle Tribune, she met Landon Parker. She had heard about him before and knew that he was the twenty-something nephew of Marcia Browning, the CEO. He had the charisma of a celebrity while also having the unspoiled good looks of someone who lived a very comfortable life. She later found out that it was a very accurate description.

It was a Friday morning and the energy in the office was unmatched. Luckily, things were a little calmer in the meeting room as Olivia waited for the other staff to take a seat. She played with the pen in her lap, feeling a bit like an imposter as everyone around her sipped their coffees and caught up on office gossip that she knew nothing about, only shooting her polite smiles, too focused on other things for the most part.

Her naiveté and youthful qualities were probably obvious to everyone else, but there was something about the challenge of proving herself that Olivia really enjoyed. It was a little intimidating to be around people who were experts in what they did, people who already earned their titles, eye-watering salaries, and accolades over the years. These were the people in the field that she would have given anything to learn from once upon a time, but she was sitting in the same room and getting to work alongside them now. Maybe one day, she would even be in the position to oversee a nervous intern herself and get to see how far she had come.

Just as she began to relax into her daydream, someone hovered next to her, close enough for Olivia to catch a whiff of their Tom Ford cologne. She tilted her head up to see who it was, only to make eye contact with a very attractive man. His pomaded hair gleamed underneath the lights as he moved to take a seat beside her, giving her an unobstructed view of his perfect features.

"I'm guessing nobody told you that you're sitting in my seat?" he asked her, his tone playful.

Olivia studied him. "Guess nobody did."

"Good to know you can take a joke." He grinned, then offered her his hand. "I'm Landon Parker, by the way." His gaze was so hypnotic and warm that it made her feel like she had been doused in liquid gold, and it suddenly made sense to Olivia why everyone had described him as the office Adonis. He moved so easily and assuredly in his body, like he believed that the world molded itself to suit him instead of the other way around.

"Olivia," she replied, shaking his hand with confidence. "The new intern."

Landon opened his laptop and signed in, scrolling through some emails as he spoke. "Marcia has very high standards for the kind of people she hires, so I'm betting you're pretty impressive. I'm kinda excited to see what you got."

"Stick around and you'll find out," she replied.

Landon was about to say something else, but the assignment editor, Dave, cleared his throat at the front of the room, silencing all conversation. Dave had a bad habit of slurping his coffee throughout meetings and constantly mopping his forehead with a handkerchief like he was aware of some impending disaster that nobody else was. But he was also very good at his job, so his quirks barely made a dent in his status of being irreplaceable to hires, both old and new.

"Okay, people, let's get this thing started!" he boomed, clapping his meaty hands together at the front of the room.

"Well, it was nice meeting you," Landon whispered to her, flashing a small smile as they both focused on Dave.

For a few minutes, Dave went around the room to ask for updates on current stories and to assign new ones.

When he got to Landon, he swiped a handkerchief across his forehead and took a big gulp of coffee before continuing. "Alright. Landon, you're handling the piece we talked about on Wednesday," he said. "You've got an interview over at Forster & Warren LLP with Shaun Grant, the managing partner, in an hour. You're going with Allison to shoot and I want there to be a heavy focus on the questions we discussed. I want numbers and quotes."

"You got it, chief." Landon saluted him with two fingers.

Dave turned his focus to Olivia. "You'll be going with Landon and Allison today to the law firm. You can sit and observe, take some notes, and see if there's anything they miss." He clapped his hands together, addressing the rest of the room. "Alright, that's it for this morning, folks! Grab some coffee, grab your things, and let's get going."

As the rest of the room collected their things and fell back into conversations, Olivia moved closer to Landon. "So, what's the story?" she asked.

"Stick with me and you'll find out," he replied, cramming his laptop in a leather messenger bag. He motioned for her to follow him. "A prestigious law firm might be just the place for a good one."

* * *

Allison, Landon, and Olivia arrived at Forster & Warren LLP after a short drive and were greeted by a shiny building with enough floors to reach the clouds.

The three of them entered the lobby and gave their names to the fresh-faced receptionist. Minutes later, they were in Shaun Grant's office exchanging pleasantries and being offered coffee and tea. He was a managing partner from the firm and had a habit of talking so fast that a successful rapping career seemed like a plausible backup. Shaun looked like he had been cut from marble and sculpted with precision, with the sharp planes of his jaw and his bright eyes catching the light from the office windows. Everything about him looked precise and formal.

After everyone had a cup of coffee and some scones, they got to work. Olivia sat to the side and took notes, trying to keep her composure when she learned that they were at the law firm to discuss alcohol use within legal professions, mainly to interview Shaun about his journey to sobriety and why he chose to incorporate assistance programs for employees who

CHAPTER 8

were struggling. It was humbling that even beneath the shiniest and most respectable exterior, there were grittier problems that most people could relate to.

"Reputations matter in the world of law," Shaun said. "The stress and high stakes are part of the package when it comes to legal professions, and drinking is very prevalent. Even if you're not drinking from stress, it could be from all the late nights and long days, the wealth and status, the secrecy. We deal with things that are both confidential and intricate, and alcohol use is, unfortunately, something that many people turn to in times of both stress and celebration."

Shaun shook his head, his smile a little sad as he set his coffee mug down. Landon checked the recording device sitting on the table between them and scribbled a few notes down on his notepad, his expression unreadable.

"Back when I was starting out, one of my mentors kept a couple bottles of expensive bourbon stashed away in his office," Shaun continued, his brows furrowing at the memory and breaking up an otherwise exquisite profile. "And they were always full, always ready for him after a long day or night. When he lost a case, he would drink. When he won a case, he would drink. Even when it was a perfectly normal day, he would drink. Deep down, I was aware of his drinking being overkill, but I almost saw it as an indication of success being so overloaded with cases and clients. Then the bottles of bourbon became symbolic of success and hard work to me. Everyone I knew was drinking regularly, and no one saw it as a problem. Years later, when I had the opportunity to become a law firm partner, *that* was when things came crashing down."

"What came crashing down?" Landon asked, leaning forward.

"Everything." Shaun's tone suggested that it was obvious, his eyes darkening as he went back to the memory. "I finally reached my goals, the ones I had set for myself so long ago. But I became reliant on alcohol like my mentor all those years ago. Everything else in my life derailed, including my family, my work, my health, and my happiness. All of it just seemed to slip away. I didn't mean for them to, but they did."

Olivia listened, her gaze never once straying from Shaun. Something like sadness spread itself across her chest. The more she heard from Shaun, the more she felt her heart soften toward her dad. Even some of the most successful practicing attorneys had struggled with the same thing he did, and it humbled her and humanized him when she accepted the fact that maybe he did the best he could at the time. It almost felt like a transcendental push from the universe for her to heal some more. She also didn't give enough credit to her mom for pushing through all of it back then, back when she had to keep everything afloat for the three of them.

She blinked, bringing herself back to the present moment. Right then, she was there to take notes about how Forster & Warren LLP, a very prestigious law firm, acknowledged the issue of addiction within their industry and successfully incorporated workplace assistance programs that benefited hundreds, if not thousands, of their employees. It was supposed to be a success story, a hopeful one for the masses, but it only reminded Olivia that not everyone had the privilege, support, and encouragement needed to overcome their demons.

After a few more questions, Landon nodded at Olivia and Allison, signaling the end of their interview with Shaun Grant. He stood up and shook the other man's hand with a practiced, confident pump. "Thank you for your time today, Mr. Grant," he said. "We'll be in touch."

"You're most welcome," Shaun responded politely while walking them to his office doors. "I truly hope this piece for The Seattle Tribune will encourage more companies to incorporate programs and workshops that deal with mental health and substance use. It's a start to have that here and to be spreading awareness, but it's far from enough. If there's anything else I can do, please give me a call. I want to help." He fished out some business cards from a case in his pocket and passed one to each of them.

Landon's tone was practiced and free of emotion when he spoke again. "Thanks for the offer. It's an important topic to us and we couldn't have done it without your insight. Again, thank you for your time, Mr. Grant. We'll be in touch."

He herded Allison and Olivia into the spacious elevator and jabbed at the button for the lobby. As the elevator doors began to close, Olivia's gaze fell on Shaun, who was now back at his desk and looking out the window as if searching for something. His shoulders drooped slightly, and even his expensive suit looked more rumpled and sad than when she first met him, but before she could look at him anymore, the elevator doors had closed and she was already heading back down with her coworkers.

She rushed to catch up with Allison, who was now walking a mile a minute across the lobby to reach their car in the parking lot, her blonde hair swinging as she balanced her large coffee and phone in one hand. "Well, *that* was interesting. I wouldn't have minded picking his brain some more," Allison said, her heels clicking on the linoleum.

"I don't think that's the only body part Allison is interested in," Landon whispered to Olivia.

She laughed.

"Shut up, Parker." Allison rolled her eyes.

The three of them reached their car and Landon slid into the driver's seat. "Well, everyone has their vices. For Allison, it's good-looking guys."

"Very funny," she said, flipping down the sun visor and smoothing down her hair, "but with Shaun, it's wasted potential, no pun intended. The guy is already married."

"Has that ever stopped you?" Landon laughed as Allison reached over to flick his arm, their banter comfortable and casual. "Anyway, we've got some time to kill before heading back to the office. As your supervisor for the day, I'm insisting that we swing by the gelato place on the way back."

He glanced at Olivia in the rear-view mirror, the two of them sharing a little smile before he turned the music up another notch. As Allison and Landon's conversation continued in the front, Olivia looked out the window at the trees and buildings passing by in a blur, her heart softening toward her father just a little more with every mile put between her and the law firm.

* * *

It was already mid-August by the time Olivia took her first day off that summer.

It was her birthday, and she and a couple of her closest friends were going to dinner together before ending the night with some drinks at the beach. Turning twenty-two felt like a big deal. She was going to graduate in the spring and planned on taking a solo trip to Asia, either to Taiwan or Japan. She was growing more confident in her ability to write, she had plans to pitch her articles to a few more places, and she was spending more time with her mom. It was funny, but the older Olivia got, the more she seemed to understand her mom's point of view. It was nice to go to dim sum and the movies together, to bond over new things instead of what they lost so long ago.

The year ahead felt like a fresh start in many ways, and her birthday was just a reminder of how much life had changed in 365 days.

Jamie had sent her a big bouquet that morning—it was the biggest one she had ever received—and even though it made her smile, a small part of her wondered if it was a way to make up for being so far apart. No amount of expensive flowers or video calls would ever do, but they would have to suffice for now.

Olivia studied herself in her room mirror—the vintage one with the gold edges she had saved up to buy years ago—and leaned in a little closer. The silver airplane necklace that Jamie had gifted her dangled from her neck, sparkling in the light, and she touched it gently, wishing more than anything that she could spend the day with him.

She took a photo of herself and sent it to Jamie instead. Letting out a breath, Olivia turned back to her reflection. Her dark hair was thankfully cooperating and staying in the loose waves she had put them in earlier, and she had to admit that her sun-kissed skin was positively glowing in the lavender dress she had picked out for the evening. It had been on clearance at Macy's and it was what she gravitated to right away. She was going to be even more frugal than usual and save more of the money she made at The Seattle Tribune and the restaurant so that she could use it to see Jamie as soon as possible—whenever that would be.

With one last look, she turned her back on her reflection and left the house.

The whole way down to the restaurant, she fantasized about Jamie being

CHAPTER 8

in Seattle to surprise her on her birthday, knowing full well that he was out with his friends that night, thousands of miles away.

Dinner passed by in a blur, with laughter and cake and candles.

Her friends had surprised her by getting the restaurant decorated on their side, with the typical Mylar balloons and tissue paper flowers hanging from their table. The cake she had picked out was delicious—chocolate cherry ganache with candied orange—and it was so good she had two and a half slices in between conversations. All of her friends were so curious about Jamie, asking questions about his job and family and when they were going to see each other next, all of them one after the next.

It had been a while since she was last in a relationship.

Most of them started so sweetly and innocently but ended with a bitter taste in her mouth, their history defaced by their worst moments and most heated arguments. Dating was one of those things that Olivia had a pretty fatalistic outlook on, once upon a time. Things either worked out, or they didn't. People would end up together for a lifetime, or they would break up and get a nasty divorce. It seemed a little odd—even to herself—that she was so hopeful about Jamie without any guarantee, but she didn't want to question it and ruin a good thing.

Sometimes, good things just *happened*.

And instead of questioning it and analyzing it from top to bottom, she was going to enjoy it for what it was—a love that she didn't expect.

As she and her friends trekked down to the beach that night, most of them a little tipsy from the cocktails at dinner, Olivia tilted her head up and looked at all the stars that had been poured across the summer sky. Jamie once taught her how to find constellations when she visited him in Texas. It was harder to make them out now without his help, but she still found a few.

"Look." She nudged her friend, Hannah, and pointed at the sky. "There's the Little Dipper."

"Oh, I see it." Hannah squinted. "Think your man can see it from New York?"

Olivia shook her head. "I doubt it. I think he's asleep by now. He's three hours ahead."

Hannah shrugged and took a seat on the sand. Olivia joined her, digging her toes into the warm sand, enjoying the smell of the salt-stained air and the predictable sounds of the rolling waves. "How long are you willing to wait for him?" Hannah suddenly asked, oblivious to the fact that the rest of the group was listening just a few feet away. "I mean, you guys live on opposite sides of the country and you'll see each other a few times a year *if* you're lucky. What's got you so committed to him?"

"Yeah, what's so great about the guy?" Another one of their friends sat down next to them, linking arms with Olivia and Hannah in an affectionate manner, her dark curls falling into her eyes. "I want to know."

"I'll wait as long as I can. I mean, distance aside, I'm really happy in our relationship. And at the end of the day, it's not the time together or apart that matters, right? It's the happiness." Olivia tucked her hair behind her ears and looked down at her feet buried beneath the dark brown sand. "Some people spend their whole lives just trying to get to a place in their relationship where they're happy with each other, but Jamie and I already have that. So, our goal is to hold on to that for as long as we can. I know there's plenty of fish in the sea, but I already found my favorite."

"Okay, but metaphorically speaking, you won't ever be able to catch that fish."

A small smile appeared on Olivia's lips. "Well, maybe I don't have to."

Hannah's eyes grew wide. "Don't tell me he's *moving* here."

"Everything's still too early in the game to be set in stone, but he's thinking about it. With the distance, either *that* ends or the relationship will." She shrugged, trying to act nonchalant. "There's no third option." It seemed like a rather fatalistic mindset to have about something filled with possibility, so Olivia changed the subject. "Anyway, I thought we were here to celebrate *me*. Enough about Jamie, right? Jamie *who*?"

Her friends laughed and agreed, and they talked about many more things that night. More stars poured across the sky and the waves continued rolling in, all of it predictable and the same. Far in the distance, one star shone particularly brightly, glimmering in space as Olivia stared at it from below, an old saying running through her mind as she did so. It was about the fact that no matter how far apart in space and time two people were, they would always be sharing the same moon, sun, and stars. She wasn't even sure who first said it, but she found herself being comforted by the fact that whoever said it was right. She closed her eyes and tilted her face toward the sky, keeping that thought in mind.

It was her birthday, so maybe she'd get a little extra luck that night. She blocked out the sound of her friends and their chatter and the ocean waves, allowing all the noise to fade into the background. She knew the chances of a long-distance relationship working out were slim, but the probability of having something as special as what she had with Jamie was even slimmer.

Keeping her eyes closed, she wished that she would someday get to be in the same place as him, that they would make it to one another in the end. Maybe it was too much to ask, but there had to be a reason they were in each other's lives—even if it was only to learn some hard lessons.

* * *

Summer came and went, but Seattle was consoled with an uncharacteristically warm and bright September that year. The autumn leaves on the sidewalk below Olivia's office building boasted a variety of vibrant oranges, reds, and yellows. Most people had just returned from their travels, looking fresh-faced and relaxed as they went around the office, chatting up a storm and sipping coffees at their leisure since their minds were still stuck in vacation mode. Besides a weekend trip to Whidbey Island with three of her close friends, there wasn't much traveling Olivia did that summer, especially since money would be tight with flights and paying off her student loans in the spring.

Things with Jamie had been harder the past few weeks. He had been working longer hours at the hospital and outpatient care clinic, and seemed a lot more distracted and distant with Olivia, often zoning out during their conversations and sharing less about his day. It was one thing to argue and have time apart when she was dating someone in the same city, but the silence that came from Jamie some nights would keep her up, just because she couldn't read his emotions or see exactly what was going on for him with the thousands of miles between them.

One night, he called her and simply said, "I miss you."

It made Olivia feel both relief and anger. He put her through sleepless nights just to tell her that he *missed* her? He was making things harder in an already difficult relationship and the thought of him trying to placate her with three words really pissed her off.

Jamie had apologized and agreed that he hadn't been as attentive, but that the distance had been especially hard on him because he was spending more and more time adjusting to his old life in New York, with his friends and family and work taking up most of his time. He said that he'd do better, and would see her again soon when things settled down.

When Olivia asked for a tentative date, he had no answer, but he said that moving to Seattle was still very much on his mind and promised that it was what he was working toward every single day.

She had told him that she hated when people made promises they couldn't keep and to just let her know if the distance was getting to him, that she would rather lose him than spend her time and energy on someone who only kept her hopes up because it was comfortable and easier to do than to let her down.

Olivia hung up and cried herself to sleep that night.

One apology, two phone calls, and three days later, she forgave him.

"I'm sorry I put you through that," he said when they spoke on the phone again, sounding genuinely apologetic and embarrassed. "I got caught up in my own life and didn't prioritize us when it mattered most. I want to do better and stop letting you down. Just give me some time, okay?"

She said she would.

* * *

It had been a while since Olivia last saw Landon at The Seattle Tribune's office.

CHAPTER 8

They had each been so caught up in their assignments and been in and out of the office at different times, making it hard to properly catch up. Olivia enjoyed working with him—he taught her new things all the time, and they'd grab coffee together and joke around during work hours. It made adjusting to her position ten times easier with him around during the last few months.

Olivia glanced over at him sitting a few feet away at his desk, sipping coffee from a mug shaped like a duck-banana hybrid as he worked. It had been an inside joke of theirs when they saw them on sale at a store for sixty percent off and decided to get a bunch for the office during their lunch break. The fact that nobody wanted to use the mugs except the two of them made it even funnier.

Landon looked up and flashed her a smile over his laptop, one that crinkled up his eyes when he did so. His skin had darkened from all the sun he got to enjoy while in Bora Bora for his brother's bachelor party, and the fact that his cheeks were a little sunburned somehow made him look endearing.

A moment later, he texted her. *Want to grab some food? I've been craving the fish tacos at Blue's since I came back. We can catch up.*

She grabbed her tote bag. *You read my mind. Let's go.*

On the way to Blue's, he seemed even more energized and talkative than usual.

Blue's was a restaurant about three blocks from their office that Landon frequented, often waxing poetic about their spacious patio and fish tacos, but it was the first time they had gone alone together without the rest of their team.

Sunlight poured across the patio like melted butter, warm and soft, and the autumn leaves carpeted the ground in a blur of browns and oranges. Olivia took a seat across from Landon, savoring the unusually warm October afternoon as the two of them perused the happy hour menu.

"I read your article about the new restaurant opening downtown," Landon said. "I'm actually going there with a couple of my buddies this weekend. You should come out with us sometime."

"Make sure you try their strawberry and hazelnut crêpes," she said, taking a sip of her lemonade and dodging the last part of his sentence. "It's their best one."

Their food came and she watched Landon dig into his favorite fish tacos, grinning as he chewed. "Damn, these are so good that I don't know if I'd ever be able to leave Seattle and leave 'em behind."

Olivia smiled, tucking her hair behind her ears. "Not even for Bora Bora?"

"Okay, now you're just pushing it." Landon smiled luxuriously, his skin glowing in the afternoon light. He took another bite of his taco. "How are things with your guy?"

"To be honest, that saying about being out of sight and out of mind is garbage. He's out of sight, but he's always on my mind." She stirred her drink with the straw. "Maybe a little too often."

Landon leaned forward, close enough that she could make out the familiar blend of spice, leather, and citrus in his cologne. "Are you happy?"

"I am."

"You don't look it."

She looked away into the distance, then back at Landon. "Yeah, well, looks can be deceiving."

"Okay," he said, putting his hands up in the air. "I'm sorry I brought it up. I know long-distance relationships aren't easy, so I just hope you feel comfortable enough to fire off about it if you ever need an ear. We might work together, but I've still got your back outside of it. I mean, I want you to be happy, but it's not my business unless you want it to be." He looked at her with kind and patient eyes, his beloved fish tacos half-eaten on his plate.

"I'm fine, I promise," she lied. "My love life isn't half as interesting as what I'm about to tell you."

"And what's that?" Landon took a sip of his lager.

"Remember Shaun Grant from Forster & Warren?" Olivia pulled out her work phone and scrolled to an email. "He reached out while you were gone and said that they're hosting a fundraiser this winter, with the funds going to the Seattle Addictions Association. He extended an invite to us for press coverage."

Shaun's motivation was to extend the generosity he had given to his

CHAPTER 8

employees to others who couldn't afford treatment or counseling services. There were plenty of treatment centers and support groups that could use the funds, and by having media coverage and different sponsors for the event, the holiday fundraiser would draw in more people than if they went at it alone.

It was a shrewd move, and at least it was for a good cause.

Landon nudged her phone back toward her, taking a long drink of his lager. He wrapped his slender fingers around the cold glass, the effervescent liquid sparkling in the fading autumn light as he contemplated the idea. "Honestly, it's mostly a business move at the heart of it because it's still great publicity for the law firm, but I don't see a reason why we can't do it."

Olivia grinned. "I'm glad you're down with the idea because I was going to do it anyway."

"You're really something, you know that?" he laughed, showing off his perfect teeth as he did so. "I never told you this, but I'm really happy you joined us. You've got everything I could ask for as a partner, so cheers to us." He raised his glass and clinked it against Olivia's. "We make a great team."

There was something about the way he said the last part that felt more intimate than professional. Olivia took a sip of her drink, discreetly studying Landon over the rim of her glass. He had broken up with his partner just a few months back and seemed happier than ever. He was confident, charismatic, and successful, and it was becoming clearer to both herself and their colleagues that he had taken a liking to her over the past few months since she started working there. It would make things so much easier if she just took the simple route and picked someone like Landon Parker, available both geographically and emotionally.

But he wasn't Jamie—the most important factor—so she sat back in her seat, closing herself off from the idea of anything more. "Yeah, we do make a great team, especially when it comes to devouring an insane amount of tacos," she quipped, nodding at their plates.

Landon laughed, then signaled for the bill. "No kidding. We'll have to try the place down the street some other time. Anyway, let's head out. I'll give you a ride home."

As the two of them leisurely made their way back, Olivia checked her phone for messages from Jamie, but there was nothing. He told her how very busy it had been with work and that he needed some time to adjust to being back in New York again, so she tried to be understanding of his silence and distance. Still, she wished he'd just say something. *Anything.*

Vibrant colors began to tinge the corners of the sky to mark the arrival of evening. It was usually her favorite time of year, but as she walked past a loving couple walking arm in arm on the sidewalk, laughing and talking intimately, Olivia felt loneliness creep into her heart like an unwelcome ghost. She wondered if her absence was haunting Jamie as well—because if it was, it sure didn't feel like it.

Chapter 9

When Olivia was fifteen, she had her first appointment with a therapist. That was when life at home had soured, with her parents announcing that things just weren't working out between them as a family. Her dad left for New York and didn't look back. She told her mom that she was feeling depressed, and it was enough to warrant some phone calls and appointments. A few weeks later, Olivia found herself sitting in a room that smelled strongly of potpourri and staring at a kindly lady with a penchant for old cardigans that looked like they had been in a thrift shop for about a hundred years. No one—not even Olivia—expected it to be as helpful as it ended up being.

For forty-five minutes every week, Olivia sat there and regurgitated everything that had been stewing inside of her, hoping that the lady sitting across from her would say or do or offer *something* that would make her feel better, make her feel whole again. The therapist simply listened patiently and asked questions here and there to clarify her thoughts. After six weeks of sessions, they reached a conclusion together—Olivia and her dad could rebuild their relationship in time. They could pick up the scraps and crumbs from their old relationship, dust them off, and piece them together into something new if that was what Olivia wanted. In time, she would come to accept her father and mourn the loss of the one she wanted.

Seven years later, she realized that the therapist had been right about all of it. Rebuilding their relationship and starting over seemed like the right decision at one point in time, but Olivia knew in her heart of hearts that moving on was the best option—for everyone. It had been almost a year since she and her dad last spoke, and she was okay with it. All she wanted was for him to be happy and healthy, wherever he was. The fact that he probably had a completely different life or family didn't even bother her anymore. Their time together had already run out and there was no amount of bargaining with the universe that would change that.

Her father's silence was all the closure she needed in the end.

Besides, it was supposed to be the most wonderful time of the year. There was too much going on for her to occupy her mind with the past anymore. Outside her window, the homes in her neighborhood looked like little gingerbread houses with their colorful lights all strung up and warm fires flickering through glass windows. Christmas was in two weeks, and Jamie had surprised her with an impromptu visit to Seattle earlier that month. He had been able to take some time off work to spend five days with her, claiming that was the reason he had been so preoccupied with his overtime shifts. On top of that, he had gifted her with an early Christmas present—a visit to New York in February so she could spend some time with his friends and family, to be a part of his life back home. When Olivia saw him at the airport in Seattle, she cried.

"Remember how we met?" he had asked, pointing to a row of seats occupied by strangers. "We were sitting just over there, a year ago. And now we're back."

The holidays were meant to be spent with loved ones, and Olivia never expected him to just show up out of the blue so they could spend a precious handful of days together, but they didn't let a minute go to waste. They exchanged their Christmas gifts early in her living room, walked around the neighborhood at night to admire all the festive decorations that had been put up, had dinner at their favorite restaurant together, and visited Olivia's favorite museum in Seattle—Chihuly Garden and Glass—where they wandered through halls full of colorful and unique creations and an outdoor garden made up of gorgeous glass sculptures. They got to hold hands and sit in coffee shops while snow swirled outside, and they went to sleep at night knowing the other person was right there beside them. It was the best present that either of them could've asked for.

CHAPTER 9

Before he left, Jamie had kissed Olivia for what felt like forever at the entrance to the airport. There was always another flight and another goodbye waiting just around the corner for them. Their time together was so short, but their fleeting moments always seemed to stay for so much longer in her mind.

He had seemed so happy with her in Seattle. He raved about everything there and was like a little kid, his energy and optimism at an all-time high as they spent every minute of every day together. He didn't bring up moving there—not even once—and it was beginning to feel like it was a fantasy he committed to too quickly. Just when Olivia felt like it was a good moment to talk about their plans for the future, he'd launch into another distraction tactic. She loved him dearly, there was no denying it, but her patience was beginning to run thin.

She had watched him leave that day at the airport while bundled up in her favorite red scarf and coat, waving until he disappeared into the crowd. Their hard-earned time together meant the world to her and their relationship still felt like magic in many ways, but all she had to show for it was a promise still waiting to be kept and a little paper airplane necklace hanging around her neck.

* * *

There were only a few days left until Christmas. New York City was as cold as ever, with snow sweeping mercilessly through the streets of Brooklyn as people bundled up in their warmest coats and gloves.

Even with the cold, Jamie was happier than ever to be back home. It had been a few months since he moved back, and it felt like he was finally getting back into the swing of things and back where he belonged. His mother was back to working most days and doing hot yoga on the weekends, while Jamie's father happily tested out new recipes for his catering business, including alcohol-spiked cake pops and white truffle ravioli. Work at the hospital and clinic was back in full swing for Jamie, and there was hardly ever a moment to slow down. He was back to working out at the gym before shifts, catching up with some of his old friends from his university days, and jogging around Central Park in the mornings—the frigid air always invigorated him and it gave him some much-needed alone time.

To say the least, everything was back to normal—almost.

His parents invited over a crowd of family and friends for that evening to celebrate their first Christmas back in New York. They had decorated the house with enough ornaments and lights to be mistaken for the Macy's department store light show that year. Jamie didn't care much for the excessive holiday displays, but the gorgeous fir tree downstairs in their living room *did* brighten up the place. He knew the parties that his parents threw were renowned—when they put their money and ingenuity together, an over-the-top party was often the festive and welcome result.

The party was still in full swing hours later, but after countless conversations and gingerbread cookies devoured, Jamie retreated to his room. He took off the customary ugly holiday sweater his mom had gifted him earlier and changed into a cream sweater and black jeans. He couldn't tell if the music or the laughter was louder, but he was glad to have some privacy for a few minutes.

Olivia had been talking about a fundraiser hosted by some big law firm for the past few days, but he barely had time to slow down and respond, even though he was so proud of her and all the work that she had been doing at The Seattle Tribune. He sat down at his desk and carefully placed his mug of apple cider down, pulling out his phone at last. It was his fault that things between them had been rocky even if it wasn't his intention. He scrolled to her number and was just about to call when a figure appeared at his bedroom door.

"You admiring the wallpaper in here by yourself or what?" Lynn entered the room, smelling of wine and cigarettes with a slice of chocolate bundt cake in her hand. She was his best friend, the only one who knew him like the back of her hand, and had called countless times to see how he was doing when he was in Texas with his grandfather. "Thought you'd be down there getting drunk with your dad, at the very least."

"Very funny, Lynnie. Did you come bearing gifts?"

CHAPTER 9

"I *am* the gift, but if you're referring to the cake, I'm feeling generous tonight, so I'll share." Lynn walked over to where he was and took a seat on the carpet with her back against his bed. She crossed her long legs and patted the spot beside her. "Join me."

Jamie pocketed his phone and took a seat, figuring he'd call Olivia later since she was probably busy anyway. The two of them ate the cake together, chewing in comfortable silence for a few minutes until Lynn spoke again. "I have to admit," she said, swallowing a bite, "it's really good to have you back, J. Shit hasn't been the same without you here."

"I know, but I had to go. I couldn't just leave my grandpa there without saying goodbye. And with my mom being the way she is, she never would've forgiven me if I didn't go with her." He sighed, running a hand over his face. "You know how she is. She even gave me a hard time about Olivia's dad."

"Mama didn't approve? Look, I love the lady, but I swear your mom has beef with everyone." Lynn took out a pack of cigarettes from her bag and carefully dug one out, expertly lighting it up with a flick of her wrist and a match, sticking the cigarette between her lips and inhaling deeply.

Jamie gave her a look, but she only shrugged and moved to crack open his bedroom window a couple of inches. "Cigarettes again?" he groaned. "Lynnie, come on."

"Well, guess I found *one* thing I didn't miss," she said, puffing out a little wisp of smoke. "You being my mom."

Jamie rolled his eyes and smiled. "You love me."

"I do. Even though you're as annoying as the dog-sized rats I see on the subway floors at Times Square."

"Poetic. And weirdly specific." He raised his eyebrows. "You could be the next Sylvia Plath."

"I'm probably Sylvia Plath reincarnated. Did you know that she was severely depressed and stuck her head in the oven?"

"That's bleak. I didn't."

"Of course you didn't," Lynn snorted. "You were all the way out in the middle of nowhere in freaking Texas when you could've been learning morbid facts from yours truly, right here in New York."

"You know, I sense some emotion from you. Are you sure you didn't get more sentimental while I was away?"

"Maybe a little bit," Lynn admitted, her face softening for a fraction of a second. After a few minutes passed, she broke the silence again. "So, how are things with your woman? It's been a hot minute since I heard you talk about her. Are you guys over already?"

"No, but I've been acting like a coward," he groaned, leaning his head back against the mattress.

"Shit." Lynn raised her eyebrows in mock surprise, her slender fingers twirling the cigarette. "What happened?"

"I told her I'd move to Seattle eventually."

The cigarette in Lynn's mouth turned acrid. The last thing she expected was for her best friend to drop everything and leave New York again for someone who lived clear across the country. There was nothing romantic about her relationship with Jamie and she wasn't planning on meeting him at the altar in bridal gear one day, but she still loved him as a friend—and losing him again for an indefinite amount of time made her feel sick.

New York was where he belonged, where he was happiest, and where he was meant to be.

"But before you get upset with me," he continued, "the reason I'm saying that I've been a coward is because I haven't done anything about it yet."

"Why not?"

Jamie chewed on the inside of his cheek, lost in thought. "Think I feel stuck. Half of my heart is wherever she is, and the other is right here in New York. It's scary because I never thought I'd leave this place, but then I realized that I'm willing to do it for the people I love, like my grandpa and Olivia. But if I go to Seattle, it's forever." He looked over at Lynn, his eyes big and wide with innocence. "How do I know I'm making the right choice?"

"You don't. But why doesn't she move to New York instead if you're on the fence?"

"I already promised her I'd be there, and I meant it. It's not like I said it just to be romantic or to string her along. I know she wants to build her life in Seattle and stay close to where her mom is, so it makes sense that Olivia

CHAPTER 9

wants to stay. She never asked me to leave everything behind or to sacrifice anything for her, but I *wanted* to do it."

"And now?"

"Now I'm just overwhelmed. Being back here the past few months just made me realize how attached I am to this place."

"So, why don't you tell her the truth?" Lynn waved her hand in the air. "The whole truth, I mean. I hate to say it, but if you're making promises with no intention of keeping them, then you're stringing her along and romanticizing everything. This stuff isn't a fantasy."

"I know." Jamie stared out the window, the music and chatter from the party downstairs floating up. "I'm flying her here in February, by the way. It's about time my two favorite people met each other."

"How lucky for me," Lynn replied dryly. She tossed her stubbed-out cigarette through his window and watched it sail into the dark.

"Come on. Don't be like that." He nudged her with his shoulder. "You'll get along."

"Yeah, yeah, whatever you say." She moved closer and rested her head on his shoulder as the party continued downstairs without them.

Jamie had to admit it was nice to see that his friendship with Lynn never changed, despite everything else being so completely different.

* * *

It was Olivia's last week of work before the holiday break and she found herself in the passenger seat of Landon's black Porsche one evening, the two of them laughing and talking about nothing in particular as he sped down the snowy city streets.

They were practically matching that evening—he wore a custom suit in an elegant shade of mulberry while she had on a dark red dress that was the color of rich wine.

"It's too bad Allison is out of commission tonight with the flu," Landon sighed, pulling into a parking spot. "Hope you're okay being stuck with me for tonight's fundraiser."

"As long as you're okay leaving before midnight. I barely had enough energy to scrape myself together to look presentable tonight," she laughed. "Finals wrecked me this semester."

They entered the venue together and pretended not to notice the glances that people gave them, admiring what looked like a put-together power couple. The entire place was decked out with soft lights, lush fabrics, and holiday blooms, lending the whole space a cozy and sophisticated feel. Shaun Grant had put so much effort into all of the little details, and it was clear that the event was going to be a big success.

Olivia and Landon moved to their table and took a seat. Landon took a sip of wine, drumming his fingers against the tablecloth as they waited for the opening speech. His gaze trailed over to Olivia, who was waiting patiently and observing the rest of the room with a soft expression, a few tendrils of hair falling gently against her cheekbones. From where he sat, he could see how the candlelight caressed her skin in liquid gold while her eyes reflected most of the light.

Something in Landon shifted and he opened his mouth, ready to confess. "Olivia, there's something I've been wanting to tell you. I'm—"

"Oh, there's Shaun Grant," she interrupted, pointing to the front.

The room erupted into applause as Shaun took his place in front of a podium and introduced himself. He ended the speech three minutes later, saying, "Every one of us can make a difference, and I'm so thankful to all of you tonight for making it possible. The proceeds from our holiday fundraiser will benefit the Seattle Addictions Association to fund their programs and assist with affordable treatment. I encourage us all as a community to continue educating ourselves around this topic and doing what we can to reduce stigma and to encourage healing and hope."

Everyone clapped and cheered, eager to enjoy the rest of the festivities for the evening.

Landon left their table and returned moments later with two glasses of sparkling Dom Pérignon, stating, "I know you don't normally drink, but you can't turn down good champagne."

She politely accepted the drink and took a cautious sip, surprisingly

CHAPTER 9

enjoying the way it bubbled luxuriously on her tongue before turning cool and sweet. She had alcohol maybe only once before—some cheap tequila—but this tasted expensive and foreign, and she found that she liked it immensely. "Ooh, that's good," she murmured, closing her eyes. "Thanks, Landon."

The absence of Jamie still hit her like a runaway train most times, but as she sat next to Landon casually twirling the stem of his champagne glass between his thumb and forefinger without a care in the world, something in her snapped.

"You know, you've asked about my relationship about a dozen times by now, but I never really opened up about it." She stared into her glass. "It's been really hard lately and I feel like my head isn't where it's meant to be tonight."

Landon's eyebrows scrunched together in concern for a moment, then melted into a lighthearted one that erased whatever trace of empathy was there. He opened his mouth, closed it, then opened it again, debating on what to say.

"Look," he finally said, his voice velvety, "we'll take a couple of pictures and get some quotes from Shaun first. Then, we're going to have some good food, dance, and drink some more of that champagne. And if you still want to talk about it by the end of all that, then we can talk." He stood up, extending his hand to her. "What do you say? Make the night one to remember with me?"

She hadn't danced in a long time, but she danced that night. She ate roast beef and crème brûlée and introduced herself to some new people. For hours, she forgot all about Jamie and New York and the distance that sat between them like a gaping hole. She had ways to find him anywhere, but that habit had to go.

At last, the night drew to a close with everyone satisfied and a few guests drunk off flirtation as much as liquor. There was always something intimate about that little window of time after a party had run its course—when the night still held possibility and there was secrecy laced in every hushed conversation between party guests.

"Ready to go?" Landon came up behind Olivia with her coat, flattening his hand against the small of her back. The warmth of his skin seeped right through the silky fabric of her dress.

"I'm good if you are," she replied, moving discreetly away from his hand and the light cloud of expensive cologne that always surrounded him. "Let's go home."

It was one of the coldest December nights that year, but there was nothing but warmth and laughter in Landon's car as they drove back.

Olivia's lipstick had worn off from sipping champagne and laughing and talking all night, her hair had come undone, and her feet ached from all the dancing she hadn't done in a long time. The night had turned out wonderfully and she was absolutely drunk with happiness. Olivia swept her fingertips against the material of her dress, smiling at the lazy ripples it made. She rolled down the window, the snowflakes kissing her cheeks as if they were long-lost lovers. Maybe it was from all the champagne she had and all the dancing she had done, but for the first time in a long time, she felt free.

"You were right," she said, raising her voice to be heard above the music. The wind flying past the car whipped her hair into a state of dark disarray as she glanced over at him.

"About what?" Landon turned the music down a notch, smiling at her.

"About us making a great team. You dragged me out of my shell even when you didn't have to." She shrugged. "Thanks for tonight."

"Is the idea of us together so hard to imagine then?"

Something shifted once the words were out of his mouth, and even though the change was as slight as the wind changing direction, both of them felt it. Landon glanced over at her while stopped at a red light, but she looked out the window and pretended not to hear him.

"Sorry, that came out differently than I intended," he said. "What I mean is that we have a lot more in common than you think, and I've been in your corner since you started here. It's frustrating sometimes that you don't see the potential." The light turned green and he stepped on the gas with more force than necessary. "Everyone at work sees us as the dream team, and we've been busting ass together for months."

CHAPTER 9

"Look, I appreciate everything that you've done for me, I really do. I *know* that there's chemistry and we work well as a team, but—"

"But what?" Landon gripped the steering wheel, his elegant features warped with frustration.

"I'm with Jamie. You know that."

"But are you even happy? It sure as hell doesn't seem like it. Because *I'm* the one who's driving you home right now, *I'm* the one making you laugh at parties, and *I'm* the one making sure you're taken care of at work. Does he do any of those things for you?" Landon paused. "Maybe the better question is whether he *can* do any of those things."

There was no way to respond with dignity, so Olivia kept quiet.

He pulled up to her house at last and killed the engine, the winter moonlight spilling over the dashboard. "Well? Talk to me."

"There's nothing to talk about," she said, looking away. Any other sane person would have cut their losses at this point, but not Landon Parker. She moved to open the door. "Anyway, thanks for the ride. I'll see you at work."

"Wait!" Landon reached over and grabbed her wrist. "I'm sorry. I—I didn't mean to make you uncomfortable." He raked a hand through his hair, looking flustered for the first time since she met him. He loosened his grip on her wrist and took her hand instead, the gesture so intimate and unfamiliar that Olivia immediately wanted to recoil from him. "Don't tell me that you don't crave having someone around to take care of you and to give you attention. Everybody does."

"I don't."

With his other hand, Landon's fingers quickly moved to her thigh, with only the thin fabric of her dress separating them. His lips brushed her hair as he spoke, his breath hot in her ear. "Olivia, don't be like that," he whispered. "We're both missing something we could be getting right now."

His hand slipped underneath the hem of her dress and she felt him squeeze her bare thigh right as his hot, wet lips pressed against her neck in a kiss.

It all happened so quickly that she didn't have time to think.

There was a stinging sensation in her hand, and when she looked at him holding his throbbing cheek and cursing, Olivia realized she had slapped him on instinct. The disgust that she felt strongly overruled the need to apologize for what she had done—he deserved it.

Olivia threw open the passenger door and flung herself out, her high heels sinking into the snow. Her stomach churned and her vision was blurry, but she forced down the humiliation, anger, and shame, and hurried across the street to her home.

"Olivia!" Landon honked at her from across the street.

Her legs felt like they would give out at any moment and blood was rushing past her ears in a roar, but Olivia unlocked the door with clumsy hands and hurried inside. She undressed, washed her face, and brushed through her curls in silence, unable to look at herself in the mirror. She climbed into bed, took out her phone, and scrolled to Jamie's name, her thumb hovering over it.

He had hosted a little holiday party at his place with friends and family that same night, but she never got to ask how it went and he didn't call either.

He was already asleep since it was almost three in the morning in New York, so Olivia shut her phone off and threw it into her bedside drawer.

She turned off the lights and went to bed, the loneliness crushing her heart in a way she never knew possible until then.

Chapter 10

In the light of the new year, Landon Parker didn't seem nearly as shiny or impressive. Olivia saw him again at the office again when everyone was back after the holiday break. She kept her head down and worked, mostly keeping to herself. She didn't tell anybody what happened after the fundraiser, and by the look on Landon's face when he saw her show up day after day, it was obvious he hadn't expected her to stick around. The last thing she wanted was for someone like Landon Parker to deny everything and turn it into a sideshow act. He didn't deserve to have the satisfaction of screwing things up for her a second time.

He walked up to her desk one morning with a smirk on his face that she wanted to slap right off, speaking to her for the first time since the night of the fundraiser. "Marcia wants to see you for your final review. She sent me to grab you," he said, hooking a thumb over his shoulder in the direction of his aunt's office. "I'd wish you luck, but I don't wanna get a report from HR for inappropriate behavior."

Ignoring him, Olivia left her desk and headed to Marcia's office on the other side of the room. Olivia's entire outfit was black from head to toe that day. She was aware that it looked like funeral garb compared to everyone's holiday-inspired outfits, but she didn't really care—she didn't care about much lately, honestly.

The dull January skies outside did little to brighten her mood, but the very colorful and very overpriced flowers on Marcia's desk certainly did. Olivia liked Marcia a lot—they got along well, she was a thoughtful and caring mentor, and also a straight shooter who championed the people around her. It didn't matter whether it was the delivery driver or the vice president she was working with—she treated everyone with kindness, respect, and compassion, which was more than Olivia could say for the Landon Parkers of the world.

Marcia took off her glasses and set them on her desk, her lips pulling up in a genuine smile as she studied Olivia. "You're likely well aware that your internship with us is drawing to a close very soon. It's hard to believe how quickly the months have gone by, isn't it? I've heard nothing but wonderful things about your work here, and I hope you know that your passion for writing did not go unnoticed. With that being said, I'm curious to know what your plans are after this."

"I'm graduating in May with my journalism degree," Olivia began slowly, almost surprised at how quickly time had passed. "It's been a really busy year with finishing school and juggling two jobs, but it's helped me prioritize what I love. I'm not one hundred percent sure what I'll be doing after this, but I know it'll have something to do with writing. I love it so much, and I can't imagine being happy working at a job that doesn't value it the way I do."

She was an architect with words, bringing anything and everything to life with them. It was that sense of freedom that she loved, the idea of carving out whole worlds and bringing characters and emotions to life that she couldn't live without.

"I can see that. Your articles on our site have been viewed more times than any other intern over the past few years." Marcia leaned forward. "To be transparent with you, we can really use you here. I know eight months isn't a long time, but it's enough time for me to see that you really love what you do and that you do it well."

"Is this an offer?" Olivia stared at the older woman, her expression melting into a mix between happiness and disbelief.

"I don't see why not. We have several positions here that seem like a good starting point for you." Marcia clicked her tongue as she remembered something. "Oh, I almost forgot. I know you've been working closely with Landon, Allison, and Mike on their team, but if you should choose to stay

CHAPTER 10

with us at The Seattle Tribune, you'll be working under new supervision. I know you've gotten quite close with your team here, so I hope it's not too much of a deterrent."

"I won't be working with Landon anymore?"

"You may still work on the same projects from time to time, but you'll likely be in different departments since your work focuses mostly on the writing aspect while he shines in media production." Marcia gave her a sad smile, unaware that Olivia's sigh was one of relief and not disappointment. "I know it's a bit of a transition in that way, but I always encourage my staff to apply for the positions that best reflect their passion and skills. Your work can speak for itself."

"I'm honestly a little speechless right now. I just didn't think this would happen."

Marcia laughed. "We always like to say that news hits hardest on an unsuspecting Wednesday afternoon, right? Well, Olivia? What do you think?"

"I can't imagine *not* working for The Seattle Tribune." Olivia finally let the offer sink in as a mixture of emotions flooded through her body. "Thank you so much, Marcia."

The older woman stood up and extended a hand to her across the table. "Happy to have you. Welcome to the team, Olivia." She chuckled. "Not that you weren't already a part of it from the very beginning."

***

"You're back to being a world traveler, I see."

Olivia smiled at her mother sitting next to her in the car while they were parked at the airport. "I'm hardly traveling the world by going to New York. It's just the life of someone in a long-distance relationship."

A month had already passed by in the blink of an eye. Outside the passenger window, the February chill was taking its toll on jacket-clad passengers as they rushed to the entrance of the airport. In just a few minutes, she'd be joining them, too.

"You know, I went to New York for the first time when I was about your age. It was with your dad." Her mother paused, a faraway look in her eyes. "But that was a long time ago. To be honest, I barely remember anything about that trip, but I just remember being so excited to even be there. I hope that Jamie shows you all there is to see and do. Don't forget to send me photos."

"Thanks, Mom. And thanks for driving me. I know you had to leave work early for this."

"It's okay. You can take me out for lunch when you're back. We can go to that new Hong Kong-style café that opened up near Broadway and Commercial."

"I'd do that even if you didn't drive me, but it's a deal." Olivia reached over the console with outstretched arms and hugged her mom, feeling homesick even though she hadn't even left yet. "Ugh, I'm going to miss you. I know I'm not gone for long, but still."

It had been a long time coming, but it felt like that was the year when they finally reached an unspoken understanding about everything their family had been through. They had been at odds ever since her father left, and there was no equation, no linear path, and no cheat sheet when it came to what grief and healing would look like. They hurt in different ways and over time, they would also heal together, albeit a little differently. They both did the best they could with what they knew at the time, moving on and moving forward with the big question mark that her dad left. If anything, time just revealed the truth of the situation—sit showed how much her mother had sacrificed to support the two of them, to never let Olivia feel less than anything but loved.

"What can I say?" Her mother finally pulled back from the hug, looking her daughter over. "You're growing up! You're graduating in May, you're going to be working full-time, and …" She paused. "Well, I don't know what else to say. I'm proud of you, that's all."

"Whoa, that's a first. My Asian mom finally saying that she's proud of me. I've waited for this moment for twenty-two years."

"Alright, enough. Let's get you into the airport before you miss your flight."

CHAPTER 10

Her mother laughed and got out of the car, pulling Olivia's luggage from the trunk. "Have a safe trip, and don't forget to send pictures." She waved one last time before getting back into her Honda Civic and driving home. It wasn't too long ago when they disagreed about Olivia's long-distance relationship, but after more than a year of it, her mother had softened a little toward the idea that love made people do crazy things sometimes, and even she hadn't been immune to its effects.

Olivia watched her go, then turned and headed toward the airport doors. It had been almost two months since she last saw Jamie over the holidays, but things between them had been slowly and steadily improving. He seemed more talkative and relaxed, more like the guy she fell in love with all those months ago. She reached for the little plane resting against her ribbed turtleneck—the necklace calmed her, a little reminder that things were going to turn out just fine.

All the way to New York, she thought about him and what he was going to do when he finally had to choose to face that fork in the road. She had a choice to make as well—she could choose to wait for him to make up his mind or to walk away.

She imagined what it would be like to have a normal life with him, one where they wouldn't have to fly thousands of miles and miss out on birthdays and holidays and even mundane days.

What would it be like to wake up in the morning with him still next to her, dreaming while sunlight crept into their room?

Would they get to have their own routine of spending Thursday nights with Chinese takeout by candlelight, talking about their day while sitting cross-legged on some couch they picked together?

What would it feel like to experience all 365 days of the year together, to experience all those little moments that most couples took for granted?

Olivia closed her eyes and rested her head against the airplane window, wondering about their future and getting more questions than answers.

* * *

Jamie blew into his cupped hands, grateful for the indoor heating as he entered the airport with Lynn.

He brushed some stray snowflakes from his wool jacket and hair, craning his neck to see past the hordes of travelers. A frazzled older woman narrowly missed colliding with him as she rushed past to make her flight on time. It was chaotic at JFK that morning, but it didn't bother him—he was much too excited to let anything get to him.

"Come on, let's go." He ushered Lynn to the arrivals area, spotting Olivia almost immediately. He cupped a hand around his mouth and shouted at her, waving his other hand in the air. "Liv, over here!"

A moment later, she was in his arms, pressing her cheek against his coat collar as she nestled against him. It was the kind of embrace that was full of unspoken words. When they finally pulled apart, she was breathless and happy and her cheeks flushed a shade of pink so pleasing that he couldn't help but press his lips against them.

Olivia's gaze flicked over to the slightly-familiar woman standing just behind Jamie, who was watching their reunion with a reserved expression. She had toffee-colored hair styled in a wavy bob, her eyes were much greener in person, and her unblemished skin was almost doll-like when paired with her small and delicate facial features. Everything from her understated and elegant style to her poised expression matched Jamie's descriptions. It had to be Lynn—Jamie's oldest friend from New York.

"Hi, I'm Lynn," she said, sticking her hand out and shaking Olivia's, confirming her identity. "I've heard so much about you."

"Good things, I hope." Olivia grinned as Jamie took her hand and the three of them headed out to the airport parking lot together.

"Are you hungry? Let's go to Milk & Moka," Lynn suggested, answering her own question and throwing a smile over her shoulder at Olivia. "J and I go there all the time." They reached Jamie's car and Lynn faced him with her hand outstretched. "Can I drive?"

Jamie sighed, hesitantly pulling his car keys out of his pocket and dropping them into her open palm. "Be careful. Olivia's not replaceable like your last car."

CHAPTER 10

"If the traffic here in New York doesn't scare her, then nothing will. Not even you."

"Keep talking like that and I won't buy you lunch," he retorted, buckling up in the passenger seat. "Oh, and take a left on Victoria Drive instead. Traffic's pretty backed up on Cornelia Street right now."

"Right-o." Lynn backed out of the parking spot and swerved onto the road without checking her mirrors.

"We're not going to live to see next year if you keep driving like that."

As the two of them bantered in the front, Olivia relaxed in the backseat as the car whizzed by department stores and Chanel billboards and heaps of New Yorkers crowded at crosswalks. Being back in New York filled her with a mixture of emotions and memories, but there was just one question that she couldn't seem to get out of her mind, one that she often wondered about back home.

What was going to happen to her and Jamie?

At Milk & Moka—a spacious brunch spot with lots of ivory, green, and cream tones with an airiness that rivaled a country club patio—Lynn kept her eyes on Jamie and his new love interest.

"You should try their biscuits and gravy," Jamie said to Olivia, pointing at an item on the menu. "It comes with poached eggs and honey butter and it's one of the best items on the menu by far. My dad and I are huge fans of it." He scanned the options on the last page. "Oh, they added a new item here. A cheddar scramble that comes with a side of hash browns and fruit."

"What are you going to get, Lynn?" Olivia glanced across the table at her, looking innocent with her big doe eyes and dark hair falling against her pink cheeks. No wonder Jamie considered leaving New York for her, Lynn thought. "Do you have a usual?"

"Ah, not really. Everything here is good."

"Lynn's a vegetarian, so she gets full from kale and photosynthesis," Jamie joked. "And she'll remind you every single time you eat with her."

"Well, I gotta do *something* to make up for all the smoking I do. My lungs are looking like a head of charred broccoli right now, but at least I'm avoiding synthetic hormones in meat, right?"

"Remember telling Ryan you didn't eat meat during his family's Thanksgiving dinner junior year?" Jamie laughed, his eyes crinkling up at the memory. "I thought he was going to start funneling meat down your throat or something."

"Good times." Lynn nodded.

"Ryan's an old friend of ours who was crazy about Lynn way back," Jamie explained. "He was a beefy, strong-headed guy who wasn't going to give up Kobe beef or chicken tacos for *anyone*." He shrugged. "Well, anyone but Lynn. She's the glue that holds our friend group together. I can't wait for you to meet the rest of them."

It was true—there was some sort of magic about Lynn, some gravitational pull that held everyone and everything in her orbit. But no one—not even her old flames who faded in and out of the fabric of her life for years on end hoping she'd someday change her mind about them—remained as special to her as Jamie. They were friends for life, for better or worse, and the thought of him leaving New York forever to be with Olivia made her stomach turn.

But she loved him and his happiness was hers, so she would just have to be an adult about it.

Lynn ordered her usual latte with almond milk and brioche toast, and both Jamie and Olivia opted for the malted pancakes with hazelnut maple praline and brown butter. As they ate, Jamie and Lynn talked comfortably and traded stories about work, and though Olivia tried to pipe in with questions or comments, Lynn would only shoot her a polite smile each time to subtly say that she was interrupting. It was frustrating, but Olivia tried not to dwell on it—maybe she just needed more time to warm up.

Underneath the table, Jamie reached over and clutched Olivia's hand in his and gave it a reassuring squeeze, a subtle reminder that he was right there with her. That one touch gave Olivia the push she needed to get out of her head. It didn't matter if Lynn was being distant and aloof or not, because she wasn't there to impress anyone. She had already done that same song and dance with Jamie's parents and it had turned out horribly when they found out she was anything less than perfect, so it didn't matter what

CHAPTER 10

people thought of her anymore. What mattered was making the most of every second she had left in New York with Jamie, and finally getting some answers to the questions that he had been avoiding all year.

She wasn't going to leave without them this time.

* * *

After lunch, they all went back to Jamie's parents' house—a suburban dream nestled just on the outskirts of the city.

Olivia shielded her eyes from the winter sun and looked out the passenger window. It wasn't exactly what she was picturing in her mind as his childhood home when he brought it up. It was a gorgeous three-story stucco house with a manicured front yard that she couldn't imagine little Jamie kicking a soccer ball around on without getting reprimanded. Spacious windows flanked the front and sides of the house, letting sunlight grace the spacious foyer and bedrooms inside. The lush backyard had a covered stone porch with wicker armchairs for friends and family to sit for a chat on weekend mornings, and a fire pit sat in the middle to curl in front during chilly autumn evenings.

"There it is. Home sweet home." He winked at Olivia, then moved around to the back of the car to grab her luggage.

"Home sweet home *indeed*," Lynn echoed with sarcasm. "This place is big enough to host an entire wedding reception for hundreds."

"Maybe yours and Ryan's if he's still alive from all the bird food you force him to eat," he retorted. "Come on, let's go inside."

The three of them went in and were greeted by his parents, their faces lighting up immediately upon seeing Lynn and hugging her. There was a comfortable and familiar air around the way they interacted with her, another reminder that Olivia was still an outsider and didn't know him and his life back home the way everyone else around him seemed to.

His mother had dyed her hair a reddish shade that was fitting for her fiery personality. "Love the hair," Lynn commented, leaning against the counter and nodding at the older woman.

"Thank you, hon." His mother's gaze landed on Olivia standing just behind her son. "Oh! Olivia, so nice to see you again." She stalked over in her heels and hugged her as well. "Mind if I steal you for a minute?"

"Not at all." Olivia flashed Jamie a knowing look, then followed his mother into the den.

Lynn, Jamie, and his father went to the kitchen to prepare a batch of hot chocolate while the two women spoke in hushed tones in the next room over.

When Olivia came back fifteen minutes later, her shoulders had relaxed and there was a lightness in the way she maneuvered her body as she walked toward them standing at the kitchen counter.

"Good talk?" Jamie whispered, nudging a mug of hot chocolate toward her.

"Believe it or not, your mom apologized. For what she said in Texas." Olivia took a small sip of the liquid, keeping her voice down. "When I overheard you two arguing about my dad? She said she was sorry that she overstepped and didn't mean to make me feel inadequate or unwelcome, but she was just in her head after your grandpa passed away. I told her that I already forgot about it, but the apology was still really nice of her to do."

"That's Mama Reyes for you. Act first, apologize later," Lynn chimed in, overhearing their conversation. She moved to grab some ingredients from the cupboards with the familiarity of someone moving around their own home. "By the way, how do you two feel about some skillet brownies? I want to try out a new recipe that Ryan taught me." She glanced at Olivia. "My boyfriend's a pastry chef, by the way. You'll meet him later this week, I'm sure."

"Do you eat eggs as a vegetarian?" she asked.

"You can help me beat the eggs, sugar, coffee powder, and vanilla in a bowl. I heard you like to bake." Lynn smiled and pushed a bowl toward her before collecting the rest of the ingredients. "And to answer your question, it depends who you ask. Going meatless kind of exists on a spectrum for me."

"You eat eggs if they're in baked goods," Jamie said. "Dessert overrides

CHAPTER 10

your values."

Lynn shrugged, tucking her short hair behind her ears, her gold earrings glinting underneath the kitchen lights. "Isn't it a cardinal rule that everything should be in moderation, including vegetarianism?"

The three of them laughed for the first time together.

When the skillet brownies were done, they brought them outside to Jamie's undercover patio along with the hot chocolate, the three of them settling comfortably into their seats with some faux fur blankets. Olivia curled up and took a bite of the brownie with fresh nectarine ice cream on top. She knew for a fact that Lynn actually hated baking—Jamie told her so a while back, but maybe it was Lynn's way of extending an olive branch, a sign that she wanted the two of them to get the chance to do something together and get along better.

As the three of them sat and talked about one thing or another, Olivia realized that Lynn was incredibly intelligent, self-aware, and witty. There was a softness beneath her tough exterior, and she recognized it almost right away because she was the same way to some extent—it was a defense mechanism. Whatever Jamie had done to earn her trust and keep their friendship strong, it had to have been something worthwhile. Even if Olivia could never earn her trust and friendship the way she wanted to, she knew that Lynn was only looking out for her friend, and that was something Olivia would never blame her for.

"Are you going to the rooftop bar with us on Friday?"

The question caught her off guard and Olivia looked up at Lynn with her eyes wide. "Sorry?"

"The rooftop bar. A few of our friends are back in town this long weekend and we're going to meet up tomorrow night. Didn't Jamie tell you?"

"No, I—"

"Well, consider this your official invitation." Lynn wagged her fork at her. "You're coming with us."

Jamie and Olivia exchanged a look, both surprised at how suddenly Lynn had warmed up to her. "Well, I *did* say that it'd be nice for you to meet the rest of the group, so tomorrow night it is," he said, his eyebrows raised.

"Great. It's settled then." Lynn wrapped her dainty hands around the ceramic mug and shot them a smile that seemed to suggest that Olivia's time in New York was suddenly going to get a whole lot more interesting.

* * *

An hour later, Olivia found herself sitting solo on a park bench, staring at the Brooklyn Bridge from the top of a hill, alone for the first time since landing in New York.

She wrapped her coat tighter around herself to block out the chill of the February air and squinted against the winter sun at the looming structure before her. The last time she was in New York was over a year ago and she had been on that very same bridge with her dad, feeling optimistic and ready to start over.

Looking at it then, there was nothing but emptiness.

But it wasn't the kind of emptiness that made her feel sad or lonely, it was the kind of emptiness that left space for other things and people—better things.

"Someone looks deep in thought." Jamie appeared behind her from where she sat on the bench, his hands shoved deep inside his navy-blue coat pockets. He had made a quick detour to the post office twenty minutes ago and Olivia said she'd explore the area for a little bit on her own, only to end up entranced by the limestone-and-granite bridge. "What did you get up to while I was gone?"

She patted the spot on the bench next to her and scooted over to make room for him. "I was just thinking about my dad," she admitted. After Jamie took a seat, she gestured to the bridge. "When I came to visit my dad last year, I remember we walked across it together. It was one of the first places he took me. It was before everything went down."

She felt Jamie's gaze land on her, studying her with those warm brown eyes that she loved and knew so well. His hand rested over hers on the bench between them for a minute, then he gently asked, "Do you want to go somewhere else?"

CHAPTER 10

Above the water, two birds played a perpetual game of tag, one always bridging the distance between them whenever the other wandered slightly off course. Olivia watched them in silence and breathed in the salt-stained air as she thought about his question.

"No," she said at last, "I'm fine. I'd be lying if I said that I never think about him or wonder if I'll run into him here, but I'm fine." She pulled her shoulders up to her ears in a shrug, letting out a little breath. "Honestly, it wasn't just the drinking or his outbursts or his absence. It's not even about all the damage he's caused over the years or how he wouldn't listen or let me explain before losing his temper when I visited him."

"Then what is it?"

"It's how I lost myself so completely. I let it seep into everything and I was tying my entire existence to him. I kept trying to figure out why he left or why I wasn't good enough, and I reinvented myself so many times after he was gone, just trying to mold myself into a daughter that he would be proud of or at least miss. I wanted him to feel sorry for what he had done."

"Do you think he is?"

Olivia laughed. "No, I don't think so, but I'm fine with things the way they are now. I was punishing myself more than he ever did by letting him affect me so much. But I realize that I'm actually a lot stronger and resilient than I give myself credit for."

"There's going to be versions of that our whole life. We're always going to face some loss, some disappointment, some sudden change in our plans that screws everything up." Jamie squeezed her hand. "But we're resilient. If there's anything I've learned from working in palliative care, it's that people are resilient." He paused. "More resilient than we give them credit for."

"True, we never know if things will pan out the way we expect," she agreed. A moment later, she turned to face him. "And speaking of plans, I know we haven't been able to talk much about our plan for you to move to Seattle in the past few months, but it hasn't fallen off my radar. It would mean a lot if we could just talk about it some more. I feel like we're getting nowhere."

"There's not much to say, Liv. You just have to trust me when I say that I'm doing everything I can to get to you. You just need to give me some more time."

"But how much time?"

Jamie scrubbed a hand through his hair and sighed, his brows furrowed as he tried and failed to hide his frustration. "I don't know. I've been trying to figure things out here so I can be in a good spot to go to Seattle, but it's not that simple. You're not the one leaving everything behind. I asked you once before if you'd ever come to New York and it was a hard pass for you, so I don't have any other option but to relocate to Seattle."

"I never asked you to do that for me." There was an awkward silence, one that stretched on for what felt like forever. Irritation pricked at Olivia when she realized that he was silent because he wasn't going to deny it. He *couldn't*—because it was true. "I never asked you to leave everything behind or to sacrifice your whole life here for me. And if you were to follow me across the country and end up in a place that you have no business being in, you'll eventually resent me for it. And the thought of you ever resenting me honestly breaks my heart."

"I would never resent you—"

"You don't know that." Olivia leaned her head wearily against his shoulder, not wanting him to see the disappointment written all over her face. "And please, just this once, don't say things you can't guarantee."

For months, he had avoided answering her questions about where he was at mentally and emotionally when it came to bridging the distance. There was always some excuse he spouted about being swamped at work and needing more time to think about it, or that he needed to save up some more money before making any concrete decisions—without ever letting her in on the timeline or progress.

Olivia didn't want to call him out on the fact that he had plenty of free time on his days off to think and had no trouble buying expensive gadgets or splashing out on flights whenever he felt like it. Everything that he said just felt like an excuse meant to keep her around without ever giving her what she needed. For someone who preached about appreciating life and resiliency so much, Jamie sure didn't seem to notice how much appreciation and resiliency existed in her as she patiently waited without any definite

CHAPTER 10

answers.

He used to tell her that at the end of the day, New York was just a place, one that he was willing to give up to be with her even though he loved it very much. It had been a grand declaration of sacrifice, hard work, and commitment—but there was nothing to show for it.

She looked over at Jamie now, studying him in the afternoon light. His hand was warm against hers and his breath came out in little clouds in the cold. He was right there, oblivious to the fact that she wasn't disappointed because of anything he did—it was what he *didn't* do.

It was one thing to be let down by her dad, but to be let down by the person she had chosen to fall in love with felt worse in some odd way. Jamie was so good at making her feel understood and validated and hopeful, but also somehow terrible at giving her the answers and reassurance that she sorely needed.

* * *

After dinner—a rather quiet one—at one of Jamie's favorite restaurants in Brooklyn, Olivia found herself at Rockefeller Center while staring out at an enormous rink of ivory.

Towering buildings flanked the rink on both sides against an onyx sky and golden lights wrapped effortlessly around trees that lined the perimeter. Prometheus was in the middle of it all, a beautiful cast bronze sculpture that would forever be falling from the heavens, watching as skaters stumbled their way around the ice rink—it was like a scene straight from the movies.

"So, *this* is the world-renowned Rockefeller Center," she said, awestruck by the gorgeous setting as they walked with their ice skates dangling from their gloved hands. "Mighty impressive." She squeezed in beside him on a bench as they laced up. "And crowded."

"No trip to New York in the winter is complete without a lap around here." Jamie took her hand as he stepped carefully onto the ice, trying to find his balance. "I remember how much you love to skate." He took a tentative step forward, then smiled at her over his shoulder.

He wore a black bomber jacket with a white sweater, grey scarf, and matching toque, and for some reason, Olivia was suddenly overcome with nostalgia, thinking about the way he looked when they first met at the airport over a year ago, both of them bundled up because of the snow. Everything between them had been so new and full of possibility, and they had been free to fall for one another without ever looking down.

The two of them went around the rink, faster and faster each time as their skates scraped expertly against the ice, propelling them forward through the crowd. After a few more rounds, Jamie gestured to the benches on the side, looking a little weary. "I'm going to sit this lap out and join you on the next one!" he called out to Olivia, giving her a little wave. "Just going to rest my feet for a few."

"Sure thing, grandpa," she responded, smiling as she skated off on her own.

The crowd became a blur of coats and legs as she looped around the rink, that familiar feeling of freedom and exhilaration rushing back to her almost immediately as soon as she was alone. She moved her legs rhythmically, whisking across the ice as adrenaline coursed through her veins.

Ice skating had always been something she loved, even when she was little. It was a time to have space in her head, a time for her to push out all the worries and thoughts that weighed her down and to simply move in a way that felt natural to her. When Olivia was ten, her mother dropped her off at the local ice rink every weekend for months. She had begged her mom to save up for group lessons because she had been so adamant about doing and having the same things that her friends did. Eventually, one by one, they all moved on to other interests and dropped out of skating lessons, but Olivia stayed—it became something she looked forward to every single weekend, having that one hour of focusing on nothing else but her body gliding across the ice on two thin blades.

A few feet ahead of her, Jamie stepped back onto the ice and immediately swerved to one side, narrowly avoiding a collision with a small child clad in a puffer coat. "You're fast on your feet, I see." She glided effortlessly up behind him. "When did you first learn to skate?"

"My first time was right here at Rockefeller Center." Jamie reached for her

CHAPTER 10

hand and the two of them started going around the rink together, slower this time. "My parents took me and a couple of my friends during Christmas break one year when we were kids. They had that enormous tree set up at the front with all the lights and everything. I said I wouldn't get off the ice until I could make it across the rink all by myself."

"Did you do it?" she asked. "Make it all the way across the rink, I mean."

"Took forever, but I did." He squeezed her hand, looking relaxed and happy as the two of them continued on an endless loop around the rink like two figurines in a music box.

Olivia stole a glance at him, the cold wind rushing against her face. She hadn't seen him this way before—not in Texas, and definitely not in Seattle.

"You know, I don't think you'll admit it, but New York seems like where you're happiest," she remarked.

"What makes you say that?"

She shrugged. "It's easy to see. It's written all over your face. Besides, your career's really taking off, your family and friends all live here, and you know this place like the back of your hand. You just belong here."

Jamie pulled back and stopped in the middle of the rink, oblivious to the fact that multiple people were giving him dirty looks for blocking the way. "Why do you keep thinking I won't be happy anywhere else?"

"I'm just making an observation," she mumbled, feeling suddenly defensive. "Sometimes I feel like *I* should be the one making the move and closing the distance since we've been talking in circles for months and have gotten nowhere."

"I don't want you to rush into anything that isn't right for you, Liv." Jamie pressed his lips together, considering his next words carefully. "At the end of the day, I just want you to be happy. I want you to do something because you want to, not because you have to. And we have time to think about all of this, right?"

"Do we?" Olivia asked. She was still holding his hand, but it felt cold and lifeless in hers and she had half a mind to let go. "We're in our twenties right now without any idea about what's coming next, but time is a finite resource. I'm not saying we need to lock everything down right this second, but I need to know what you're thinking and what the timeline is. Closing the distance isn't a fantasy. We have to put in the work and make some hard decisions together."

"We've had this discussion a hundred times, Liv."

"Because we never resolve it!" She pulled her hand away in frustration, searching his face for a hint of understanding. "You think I *want* to be pushy or to feel like I'm asking for too much? Frankly, I don't think I'm asking for much at all. All I want is for you to be honest with me, even when it's hard or uncomfortable." Olivia sighed, looking away and softening her voice a touch. "I'm starting to think that you just love the idea of me. It's like you just expect me to be patient and supportive forever."

"What are you even talking about?"

"You expect me to just play my role without ever asking for anything or holding you accountable when it comes to keeping your promises. And when I break that image, you get upset with me for calling you out, for being brutally honest when no one else is. I'd be much happier if you would just tell me the truth and say that you don't actually want to leave New York, that it was a stupid idea you were never planning on really going through with. Because if you meant it, you would've done something by now."

"I think you're just expecting everything to happen right away. You want things to be perfect and to go your way all the time so you can feel secure."

"That's bullshit." The heat started to build in Olivia's cheeks and her mouth felt dry. "I don't need you to feel secure."

"Then what do you need?"

"I need you to decide." She met his eyes. "Decide if you want to stay in New York or not. Decide if you want to move to Seattle or not. Decide if you want to be with me or not. And once you've made those decisions, stick with them and do what you need to do so we can both move on and live our lives. I don't want to be stuck in limbo waiting for you to make up your mind for the rest of my life. It's selfish."

"You're one to talk. You don't even want to give New York a chance!"

Figuring they weren't going to solve their issues right then and there, Olivia moved to the side of the rink to let others pass by. There was a lump

CHAPTER 10

in her throat and her legs were starting to feel wobbly. "Let's take a break," she said, looking away. "I'm tired."

The two of them made their way to an empty bench and sat down to unlace their skates, but her fingers were so stiff and clumsy from the cold that she struggled to pick the knots apart from the lacing hooks.

"Let me get that for you." Jamie knelt in front of her and bent forward, unhooking her laces with ease and practiced swiftness, his gaze never wandering to meet her eyes.

"Jamie?"

"Hmm?"

She reached down to stop him from fussing with her ice skates and waited until he looked at her. "I love New York and I love you, I really do," she said. "And I'm sorry if what I said came off as harsh. I never meant for it to hurt you."

Jamie simply nodded and went back to untying Olivia's skates, carefully unhooking each lace before finally sliding her feet out of them. "It's okay. I know you didn't mean it."

She blinked, wondering how many days she had left in New York. On one hand, she could argue that it was not enough time to try and fix a crumbling relationship with the person she loved, but on the other hand, it was a very long time to be stuck with someone whose heart wasn't in the relationship anymore.

The two of them left Rockefeller Center together hand in hand, but there was a loneliness between them that felt even colder than the chill drifting through the air.

Chapter 11

"I've never seen the guy so happy." One of Jamie's oldest friends sidled up next to Olivia, leaning against the railing of the rooftop bar to join her. He had been kind enough to strike up a conversation when he first saw her by herself and even introduced her to a few of their other friends.

The venue granted them a breathtaking view of Times Square glittering beneath them while towering buildings stretched far into the distance against a darkening sky. Far below them, little yellow taxis crawled along the city grid, honking and inching forward with their restless passengers.

Olivia glanced over at Danny, Jamie's friend, and gave him a polite smile, their faces lit up by the glow coming from the string lights and the outdoor fire pit's dancing flames.

"Everyone keeps telling me that," she said, her voice chipper even though she didn't feel it. "I'm glad he's having a great time."

She had on a little black dress with delicate mesh sleeves and she rubbed them absentmindedly now, thinking back to how Jamie had been his old self again on the way to the rooftop bar, their argument at Rockefeller Center all but forgotten or forgiven.

A part of her almost preferred the arguing instead of them walking on eggshells and acting like it never happened.

Jamie sat a few feet away from them, laughing with the group over something Olivia couldn't quite hear from where she stood. He was unfairly handsome that night, more social and vibrant than usual, and looked like he was having a grand time.

It was hard not to notice him and want to join in, but things weren't quite

CHAPTER 11

so simple anymore. The last thing Olivia wanted was to ruin the night for him by making a scene or asking for him to be her social crutch—their problem was theirs alone and she was more than capable of acting jovial for one night to keep everything in harmony. It was probably for the best that he was spending some time with his friends and letting off steam after their heated discussion at Rockefeller.

"How long are you staying in New York for?" Danny tilted his head to study her, a sliver of the tattoo on the side of his neck peeking over his collar.

"Just until the weekend is over. I go back to Seattle on Monday morning."

"Ah, that's coming up soon," Danny noted. He was close enough that she caught a whiff of cigarette smoke clinging to his sweater. "What do you do there?"

"Well, I graduate in three months and after that, I'll see what life throws at me. I'm working in journalism right now, so expecting the unexpected is literally my job."

Danny laughed, his blue eyes sparkling like precious stones from behind thick glasses that lent him a bookish appearance. "Any articles you're especially proud of?"

"Why, are you going to read them?"

"I might." Danny took another swig of his drink and grinned. "I love a good exposé."

"I hate to disappoint you, but I don't have anything gripping in the works." She paused. "Well, unless you consider a manuscript gripping news."

"You're writing a book? No way."

"It's just a manuscript right now, but I'll pitch it eventually." Olivia took in a breath and stared at the city below them, her arms resting on the railing. "It's always been a goal of mine to pitch it here. I mean, New York is well-known for its abundance of authors and publishing houses."

"Funny you should say that. My brother works as an agent at a publishing company. Granted, it's not a big one, but I'm sure he's got a few connections if you just want some feedback. Why don't you give me a shout when you finish that manuscript?"

"You're kidding."

"I kid around a lot, but not about this. Give me your phone." He typed in his contact information and passed it back. "Seriously, reach out if you ever need some guidance or more information after you're done with the writing. I promise it's not a scam or pyramid scheme or anything."

"Hey, if that's what it takes to get published," she quipped, shrugging her shoulders. "Thanks a million."

Ethereal dark blues and inky black filled the sky as night came upon them, and Danny held up his empty glass. "I'm going to get another drink and rejoin the group in a sec, but I just gotta tell you something about Jamie," he said, lowering his voice to a confidential whisper. "I've known the guy for a long time, and this is the happiest I've seen him. You didn't look like you believed me the first time, so I had to say it again."

"Alright, alright, I got the message this time." Olivia gave Danny a smile and moved away from the railing. "Why don't you join them first? I'm going to grab a round of drinks for the table."

Danny raised his glass and saluted her, walking backwards to their table. "You're my hero."

She came back a few minutes later with a round of overpriced tequila-inspired cocktails, much to the delight of Jamie's friends as they welcomed her back with a boisterous round of cheers. They were great people—friendly and ambitious with a lot to talk about. As she sipped her drink and watched Jamie interact with them, laughing and reminiscing about moments she wasn't there for, she knew that he wasn't just hers alone.

He made her feel things she never knew were possible and convinced her that the unpredictable nature of their relationship was beautiful and unique. She was willing to wait for him, but no matter how much she loved and wanted him, if he wasn't ready to leave New York and the life he had there, she wasn't going to force him to do anything. People promised things all the time without thinking them through, and as Olivia sat beside Jamie at the rooftop bar that Friday night, she knew she'd have to make a decision for herself, even if he was willing to put it off for the rest of their lives.

"Are you having a good time?" Jamie leaned closer and wrapped an arm protectively around her shoulders. "You've been quiet."

CHAPTER 11

"Just thinking," she said, shooting him a placating smile. "I'm fine."

"You're sure?" he asked. "Because we can always head home if you're tired or if you just want to talk. You know you can talk to me about anything."

"I know, but—" Before Olivia could finish, she saw Lynn coming toward them with an expression on her face that she could only describe as bewildered.

"Jamie, you're not going to believe this," Lynn said, reaching their table, her gaze darting back and forth between them as if debating whether to tell the truth. "Emma's back."

* * *

Jamie's ex, Emma. The name that held so much history for Jamie and so much curiosity for Olivia.

Emma sat across from them at the table, all smiles and laughter as she recounted stories about her life in the U.K. to all their friends. She already knew everybody at the table, each of them more than happy to welcome her back, ready to reminisce and drink the night away, to listen to her go on about how much she missed New York-style pizza and her old life there. A part of Olivia wondered if maybe she was missing a particular *someone* from her old life more than she missed the other things.

Noticing the white dress that a stranger was wearing a few feet away, Emma looked right at Jamie and, in a voice loud enough for everyone at their table to hear, exclaimed, "Look at that dress, Jamie! Remember when we went to Boston for our anniversary and you took me to that Spanish tapas restaurant? I was wearing something just like it, wasn't I?"

When one of their friends expressed interest in hearing the rest of the story, Emma just laughed and went on to share an anecdote about how her dress had blown up when the two of them stepped over a subway grate after leaving the restaurant, resulting in a very Marilyn Monroe-esque moment. The whole time, Emma didn't acknowledge Olivia. Instead, she chose to share yet another anecdote about a time when she was dating the person sitting right next to her instead.

Emma had tiny, delicate features and a little button of a nose that was spattered with auburn freckles on a face that was otherwise quite plain—but not in an unappealing way. She wore stacked gold rings on all her fingers and had an oversize, plaid coat draped around her bony shoulders. Her lips were colored by a Yves Saint Laurent lipstick shade that matched the strawberry daiquiri she was sipping, and she openly laughed at the dirty jokes being passed back and forth across the table.

It was hard not to notice Emma—she seemed to melt into the foreground without even trying, and as she sat there with Jamie and their friends, it was hard for Olivia not to feel like she was the outsider who just came back from London instead.

With her eyes fixed on the ice in her drink while squeezed between two of Jamie's friends, Olivia pretended not to notice every flirty laugh coming from Emma's lips as she caught up with Jamie and how she'd rest her hand on his arm mid-sentence as if the thought of not touching him for one second would decimate her. Emma's arrival only seemed to underline the fact that there were plenty of people still within Jamie's orbit, and anyone looking their way that night would've made the incorrect assumption that they were still together just based on the way they looked at each other.

"It's been so long since we've all been together like this," Emma was saying now, seeming quite at home in the spotlight with Jamie beside her. Her voice was an airy meringue, all cloying sweetness. "I'm so glad I took the earliest flight out of London. I've missed all of you."

She gave each of her friends a warm smile, ignoring Olivia sitting right in front of her. It was probably for the best, because there were very few nice things Olivia could think of to say to her anyway. Moments later, the familiar and jubilant notes of "Dancing in the Dark" piped loudly through the speakers of the rooftop bar, replacing the ambient jazz from the hours before, and a handful of people got up from their seats and started dancing in a little circle right by the bar on the far side.

Springsteen was a shared favorite between Jamie and Olivia, but as soon as he reached for her hand across the table to ask her to dance, Emma's eyes lit up in dramatic ecstasy and she looped her arms with Jamie and Lynn. "We

CHAPTER 11

have to dance at least once while I'm here," she declared, impatiently pulling them toward the group of people dancing. "I haven't heard this song in ages."

Jamie looked over his shoulder with an apologetic expression as he got whisked away, but Olivia just smiled and shrugged with pretend nonchalance. When she had a moment, she would talk to him.

"She's not always like that," Danny said from beside her as if reading her mind. "She's changed a bit since moving away a couple of years back, but she's not a bad person."

"Don't worry, it's not like I'm going to go up there and rip the hair straight from her head."

Danny laughed. "I hope not. I know she's been sticking to Jamie all night like a bad rash, but I think it's bizarre for her to come home and find everything different, like her ex being happy and moving on with someone new."

"It's just throwing me for a loop that she's back in New York all of a sudden. Jamie never told me she'd be here."

"None of us knew until today." He paused. "Well, except Lynn. I guess one thing that hasn't changed about Emma is the fact that she likes to make an entrance."

The two of them watched as their group of friends continued to dance and sing on the other side of the bar, even after the music switched from Springsteen to a slower song.

Danny leaned back in his seat and rested an ankle over his opposite knee, taking a pensive sip of his drink. "They started dating during their senior year of high school and went to the same university. They had all these big plans of graduating and working in healthcare together, and even getting engaged."

"What happened?" Olivia tried to keep her tone neutral, even though every part of her was aching with curiosity as much as hesitation. "I know they dated for four years and she moved to London, but he never told me why."

"They grew up and grew apart like any other couple that didn't make it, I guess. Emma had some family back in the U.K. that she'd visit once in a while, and all I know is that she and Jamie fought a lot over their future plans, so she ended up finishing her last year of university in London and ended up staying there instead of coming back. All of their future plans probably freaked her out a little, but she's doing well for herself now," Danny explained, an earnest expression on his face. "She's making over six figures working in public policy and just finished graduate school this year. She's happy. He's happy. They just weren't happy *together*."

"They look pretty chummy right now, if you ask me."

"Yeah, but that's after lots of distance and time apart. Sometimes, things work better between two people when they're not in a relationship." Danny shrugged, his gaze roaming across the bar. "Besides, she decided what was best for her. I don't think Jamie could ever blame her for that. She made a decision about what she wanted, even if that decision didn't include him."

"When you put it that way, it makes sense. It was probably a hard decision for her to make."

For the first time that night, she felt a little bit of empathy for the other woman and she couldn't argue with Danny's logic, but it was hard not to think about Jamie and Emma's past in that city. They probably ordered Thai food as a ritual every Friday night from their favorite place and checked out university campuses together during summer road trips. She imagined them going on double dates to Broadway shows, celebrating the holidays with their families, and drawing up plans for a whole life together that Olivia knew nothing about. A part of her regretted asking Danny because it didn't really matter what Jamie had said or done before he met her. Everyone had history, including herself. His story with Emma was just like any other love that had dissolved with time, their problems starting out as little rips and tears in the fabric of their relationship until they turned into gaping holes big enough to swallow them whole.

Olivia took a deep breath, shaking the image of Emma and Jamie out of her mind.

She was determined to have a great night since it was one of her last in New York, even if she wasn't spending much of it with the person she came to see. They had a hotel suite booked for her last day in New York and that was probably a good time to sit and really talk with Jamie, but she didn't

CHAPTER 11

want to spend the rest of the night overthinking anymore.

Olivia brushed off her black dress and got up, pasting a smile on her face and committing herself to a good time. "I'm going to go dance. Wanna come?"

"Dancing at a *bar?*" Danny downed the rest of his drink and stood up. "Crazy idea, but why not?"

An hour later, people had gathered in small, intimate groups to chat and wind down for the rest of the night before heading home. At the bar, Lynn was talking to the bartender with a thinly concealed grimace, barely listening to a word he was saying as he mixed her grapefruit mimosa. She was recognizable to Olivia almost immediately, dressed in a grey duster jacket with a white sweater and velvet cigarette pants that shone whenever she moved in the low light, her svelte figure and understated style discernible even in the crowd of people.

As Olivia got closer, Lynn locked eyes with her, a glimpse of relief in them.

The bartender slid Lynn's drink across the counter toward her, lingering there for a moment to show off the muscles on his forearms with his white sleeves rolled to his elbows. "You should stop by again when I'm done with my shift," he was saying. "I'm off in an hour."

"We'll see, bud." She grabbed her drink and joined Olivia as they slid onto some bar stools several feet away. "I'm glad you came by when you did," she confessed. "Because if I have to spend another second being hit on by that bartender, I'm going to lose my mind. The only highlight is that he didn't charge me for this twenty-five-dollar drink." She slid it toward Olivia with a smirk. "Shit is criminally overpriced here. Anyway, try some."

After having equally-overpriced non-alcoholic drinks all night, Olivia figured it wouldn't hurt to take a sip. The drink was sweet and a little tart and the freshness of the mint felt refreshing on her tongue as she swallowed.

"Told you it's good." Lynn lit a cigarette and held it between her slender fingers and crossed her long legs, looking like a movie star against the luxurious backdrop of a million stars and city lights. "You mind if I smoke?"

Olivia shook her head.

Lynn blew out ribbons of smoke that obscured her face, her gaze still on the horizon. "Had enough of Jamie for one night?"

"Jamie who?"

This made Lynn laugh, the sound rich and warm.

The two of them sat in comfortable silence while Lynn smoked and drank, the hustle of the city beneath them somehow calming as background noise. There was something almost intimate about being alone together on a crowded rooftop bar. They could share secrets and drinks and dances, and all of it would be forgotten the next day or recounted in blurry detail at most.

There was also a sense of hidden wisdom attached to Lynn, as if she knew and understood things that other people didn't, and it was this sense of awareness that drew Olivia to her. She watched as Lynn blew out a plume of smoke that swirled into its own galaxy until finally disappearing above their heads.

"I might be overstepping here, but why are you sitting with me when Jamie is over there?" she asked, gesturing with her cigarette.

"It's hard to explain."

Lynn cocked her head, her copper-colored eyelids glimmering in the low light. "Try me."

What was there to say when even Jamie's friends noticed that there was something off between the two of them that night? Olivia's gaze drifted to her hands in her lap, a wave of sadness crashing over her. "No, I mean it," she said, finally bringing her gaze back to Lynn's face. "It's *really* not easy to explain. I don't even know where to start."

"Does anyone?" Lynn studied the other woman carefully through the wisps of cigarette smoke. "Again, just try me."

A few seconds passed where they just looked at each other, a few seconds where Olivia contemplated the consequences of being honest. Closing her eyes and deciding to just go for it, she blurted, "I don't think that things are going to work out between me and Jamie."

"What?"

"I never expected things to be easy for us, and we always knew that distance was going to be hard. But I have a feeling that he's not ready to say goodbye

CHAPTER 11

to everyone and everything here, and I don't know if that's because he needs more time or if it's because I'm not the one for him."

"Have you talked to him about it?"

"I've tried, but we keep going in circles and he keeps avoiding the topic." Olivia rolled her eyes up to the sky and sighed as if the stars might rearrange themselves and spell the solution out for her somehow. "I just don't know if I can keep doing this forever."

"Oh boy, isn't this déjà vu?" Lynn muttered to herself, the remnants of smoke from her cigarette making ghostly shapes in the air as she stubbed it out. "Look, this isn't my first rodeo when it comes to grievances about our boy here, but if you're talking to me because you want advice on breaking up, I think you're talking to the wrong person."

"No, wait." Olivia's hand shot across the table and rested firmly over Lynn's, asking her to stay. "I'm sorry, I know you'd never do anything to hurt him. I don't want to hurt him either."

"I know J can be indecisive and do too much, too soon," she said, "but this is between you and Jamie."

"Has he ever talked to you about this? About us, I mean."

Lynn drew her hand away and sighed, almost as if regretting her next words for being so truthful. "He has. He really loves you, and I know his actions and words aren't matching up right now, but I think he meant it when he said that he wanted to make it to you. But maybe his head hasn't caught up with his heart yet."

"What do you mean?"

"I'm going to hate myself for saying this to you, but as much as I love J, you need to do yourself a favor and take a long, hard look at your future with him. He's a great person and he's my best friend, but he's not perfect. If you're putting your whole life on hold for someone who doesn't even know what he wants, then that's on you."

There was no malicious intent in her words; all Olivia could hear was Lynn's genuine concern for her.

Holding back tears, she thanked Lynn and got up from the bar stool, their conversation quite over. Her dress felt too tight and the rooftop bar felt too loud and everything just felt *wrong*. Walking quickly, she kept her head down and moved through the crowd to the exit, ignoring the drunken laughter and conversation following her. Jamie was also nowhere to be found—he had probably sneaked off with Emma somewhere, but Olivia couldn't find it in herself to care right then.

She hurried into the elevator and left the building a few minutes later, the rooftop bar's glowing lights and faded music still calling out to her from behind. She walked, lost in her thoughts, for many blocks. The sad howl of the February wind was oddly satisfying to her, and the solitude and sound of her footsteps comforted her as she rewound the tape in her head from the past week.

She thought about all the different facets of Jamie that had made her fall in love in the first place and all the ones that made her hurt and confused now. Their relationship felt like a train derailing from the tracks and it was so much harder to get it back to the way it was.

Snow began to fall in little flakes around her, swirling in arcs and loops across the sky before settling on the sidewalk. Olivia peered up at the sky, closing her eyes and letting the snow settle gently on her eyelids and cheeks until she heard someone calling her name from behind.

She spun around and squinted, shielding her eyes from the snow to see who had called out to her. Jamie appeared, his coat flapping open as he jogged toward her, his hair coated in fresh snowflakes.

"Hey," he breathed, slowing down when he reached her at last. "What are you doing out here? I thought you were back at the bar with everybody."

"I could say the same to you." Olivia took a step closer so that the two of them were standing and facing each other underneath the glow of the street lights. "Are you sure you won't be missed by Emma if you're out here for a few minutes?" she teased.

Jamie chuckled. "Oh, is that what it is? She might be a bit *much* at times, but she's a good person. I'm sorry we haven't been able to spend much time together tonight. Everything's been kind of ... unexpected."

"Yeah, it has. How did you know I was out here?"

"I asked Lynn where you had gone and she said she saw you heading out.

CHAPTER 11

I figured you couldn't have gone far." Jamie shook some snowflakes from his hair and took her hands in his, his expression quickly changing to one of concern. "Jesus, your hands are about to fall off from the cold, Liv."

"I'm fine." She blew on her hands and then stuffed them into her coat pockets. "Want to take a walk before heading back?"

Jamie smiled softly at her, smoothing her hair from her face and planting a kiss on her forehead. "Sure, why not?" He offered her an arm in such an exaggerated gentlemanly manner that it made her laugh.

They walked side by side in silence down the city block, watching as the bright and colorful lights from shops and billboards colored the falling snow above them. Olivia moved closer to him, breathing in the familiar scent of his skin mixed with soap and cologne, imprinting that moment in time. It was a little stolen moment in an avalanche of hundreds, but it was those moments of solitude and love and comfort that meant the most to Olivia.

What made her sad was the thought that it might be one of their last.

Chapter 12

It was late afternoon when Jamie and Olivia stepped foot into the hotel suite during her last day in New York. With the sunlight pouring in through the hotel curtains into the warm and spacious room, it was a welcome change after a long week. It had been a sweet surprise that Jamie had planned for her—a day and night for just the two of them.

Jamie kicked off his shoes and fell backward onto the bed, looking like a happy camper as he sighed contentedly, ready for a night of room service and quality time. Olivia set down her bag and took a look around. The hotel bathroom housed a gorgeous vanity carved from maple with essential oils on the counter and the claw foot tub draped with warm towels was just begging to be soaked in.

It was going to be one relaxing night for the two of them.
"Look, they left us presents." She pointed to a little tray sitting on their bedside table with a bottle of champagne in an ice bucket and a plate of chocolate truffles. "What did you book us? The honeymoon suite or something?" she laughed.

"I might have mentioned that we're celebrating something tonight, even if that's just being in the same place for once."

Olivia turned away from the windows and joined Jamie on the bed, resting her head on his chest. She was going to leave and go back to Seattle the next morning, but right then, they were curled up together on the bed in some fancy hotel in New York City with nothing to do and nowhere to go. Still, one thing kept running through Olivia's mind in an endless loop, never letting her get very far without thinking about it. They were at an impasse,

CHAPTER 12

a fork in the road.

Deep down, she had a feeling that they were going to break up, but it seemed like neither one of them wanted to do the brave thing and just address it. They weren't happy together anymore for different reasons, and if they weren't going to be happy together in the present, then there was no point in even thinking about the future. They could continue letting their relationship crack down the middle and rot away, or they could do the mature thing and walk away with some of their optimism and pride still intact.

Before Jamie, she had only ever loved one other person—a beautiful blonde boy with eyes so blue that they reminded Olivia of robins' eggs. They went to the same elementary and high school but never really talked until they both happened to be at the same festival one summer and ended up completely forgetting about the people they had come with.

They were inseparable, but after a year of holding hands and kissing in secret, they broke up. She had been too afraid of what people would say about them, what other people thought, and spent too much time wondering if he was the right person for her.

It didn't end up mattering in the end, because he told her he didn't want to wait forever for her to decide that he was good enough, and that was that. He kissed her one last time outside of her house one evening and then they never spoke again. She was seventeen at the time, and although she had cried for days afterward, it didn't hurt the way it hurt with Jamie.

Looking back at it now, Olivia wasn't even sure if it was love because it definitely didn't hurt the way she was hurting now. The kind of pain she felt from what was happening between her and Jamie felt like an entire kingdom crumbling down, crushing her beneath its weight. Whatever love she had before felt like the tip of the iceberg.

"You know what? I would actually *love* a drink right now," she stated, extricating herself from Jamie's arms and wandering over to where the champagne was waiting patiently in its silver bucket. "Want one?"

"We don't have to drink it. There's plenty of tea and coffee available for room service." Jamie sat up, resting on his elbows as he watched her pour two glasses of fizzy champagne. He knew she didn't drink alcohol because of her father, so her sudden thirst for a drink made little sense to him. He picked up the hotel phone. "Want me to call them?"

"Don't worry so much," Olivia laughed. She handed him a glass. "It's a special occasion, right? Might as well celebrate and not let it go to waste."

"If you say so."

She took a seat on the bed, sitting cross-legged as she took her first sip, the bubbles frothy and sweet on her tongue. She found that she liked it immensely, just like the first time she had tried it with Landon at the fundraiser a few months back. She had already buried Landon's existence deep in her mind's graveyard, but the intrusive thought of him popped up anyway, turning the champagne sour in her mouth as she swallowed it with difficulty.

Olivia never ended up telling Jamie about what happened that night with Landon being a snake. They had both been so busy with work and he was adjusting back to life in New York—it never seemed like the right time to bring it up.

Ironically, that seemed to be the theme of their relationship: It was never the right time or the right place.

As thoughts swirled through her mind, she took mouthful after mouthful, each fizzy gulp filling her with lightness as her head began to swim with pleasant airiness. The hotel room was their very overpriced happy place for the evening, and Olivia suddenly decided that she wanted to be very, very drunk for the first time in her life. She kind of hated herself at that moment and hated how badly she was avoiding what needed to be done.

After putting on some boring movie that neither of them was going to watch and finishing most of the champagne, she leaned across Jamie on the bed and reached for the hotel phone, feeling gloriously warm and energetic.

"I'm going to order room service," she announced to no one in particular, the numbers and letters on the menu swimming before her eyes. It took two good tries before she placed the order correctly and hung up. "A bottle of merlot and a plate of chocolate lava cake are comin' right up."

"Living recklessly, I see."

CHAPTER 12

"For once." She kicked off her cognac-colored ankle boots and sat cross-legged on the bed. "We're going to make it a night to remember."

There came an interruption in the form of three polite knocks at their hotel room door fifteen minutes later. Jamie returned with the chocolate lava cake and bottle of red wine, looking slightly more relaxed than he had a moment ago. "This is a great idea—wine and dessert. You're really tugging on my heartstrings here, Liv."

He joined her on the bed and she smiled at him, digging a little silver fork into the middle of the chocolate cake and pulling it apart, letting a stream of rich chocolate spill out of its center, cracked right open like a broken heart.

After a few contented bites, she gestured to the bottle of red wine in his hand with her fork. "Can you pour me a glass of that?" she asked sweetly.

She was well aware that their time together was slowly running out and she had done nothing but eat cake and get drunk. The thought of it was delightfully amusing to her for some reason, and she bit back a laugh as Jamie handed her another glass.

"Liv, maybe we should slow down on the wine and have some actual dinner. Are you hungry? We can go to the restaurant across the street," Jamie said, trying to sound lighthearted. "They do a great flatbread pizza and I've been—"

"Let's talk about dinner later. I've got other things on my mind right now."

She finished her glass of wine and pulled him close with one hand, placing luxurious kisses along his jawline as she did so. His skin was warm and soft and she finally brought his mouth to hers, tasting the remnants of the sweet champagne on his lips.

There was a buzz vibrating throughout her body, everything in the entire room seemed extra bright and loud, and her confidence was through the roof as she ignored all the alarm bells in her head. There was absolutely nothing she wanted more at that moment than to be with Jamie, to give them something they would both never forget.

She reached down and pulled Jamie's shirt over his head, admiring every inch of exposed skin before tossing it to the side. He looked gorgeous beneath her in the dim light, his brown eyes filled with desire and surprise as he stared up at her, his hands firmly gripping her waist.

She unbuttoned his jeans and slid them off, feeling the heat from his body mix with hers in an intoxicating rush as he pulled her down at last to join him.

An hour later, she was alone in the hotel bathtub.

Jamie had gone out to grab some takeout from the Italian place he mentioned earlier and she asked to stay behind, claiming that she wanted to take a hot bath and have some time to herself to clean up before dinner. But she mostly wanted to be alone so she could fall apart.

She sat in the tub in the dark, the hot water enveloping her in its comforting heat as she stared straight ahead. It was quiet in the room without Jamie, but she preferred it right then.

A headache was gnawing at her skull and she felt gross and empty and clumsy and just terribly sad. She drew her knees up to her chest and rested her arms on them, propping her chin there as she let out a heavy sigh. She was terrified of losing him, but she was afraid of losing herself more. And with every month that passed by without any answers or reassurance from him, a little piece of herself floated away alongside the big hopes she had for them.

The faucet dripped every few seconds, interrupting the welcome silence. She stared at the ripples each droplet created, thinking about what to do when he returned.

Drip. Drip. Drip.

Olivia leaned back in the tub and stared at the ceiling, feeling tears well in her eyes. Jamie would be back any minute, but she couldn't bring herself to leave the bathtub, let alone the bathroom.

She knew that time was running out, and it killed her to think about all the times when it was magic, back when she knew Jamie like the back of her hand and felt comfortable sharing anything and everything with him. Now, she just missed that person deeply, and if she were to be honest, she also missed the person *she* used to be. This new version of herself that was skeptical and lonely and jealous wasn't who she wanted to be at all.

CHAPTER 12

Olivia cried, her tears falling into the tub of water one by one as they rolled off her cheeks.

She gingerly washed her hair and face before getting out of the tub at last, wrapping one of the hotel terrycloth robes tightly around her body, her morose reflection almost unrecognizable in the foggy mirror as she left the bathroom.

Moments later, Jamie entered the hotel room again with both hands full of takeout and some ibuprofen for her head.

"I'm back," he singsonged, raising both arms to show her the goods as he kicked off his shoes. "Ready to eat takeout on the bed like the classy couple we are?" When she didn't reply, he moved closer, studying Olivia's blotchy face and puffy eyes. His shoulders sagged with worry and he dropped his arms back down to his sides. "Liv, are you alright?"

"No," she said, meeting his eyes. "I'm not. I think we should talk."

* * *

The silence was almost unbearable.

Olivia sat on the bed, the white hotel robe still wrapped around her slim body as the last rays of the sun filtered in through the curtains, washing her in a soft blend of yellow and gold. The takeout had gone cold in their respective containers, but neither of them touched it. Truthfully, neither of them felt hungry anymore.

The reckless and detached feelings that she felt when she was intoxicated finally faded away and only sadness lingered there now, a deep-seated sadness that she couldn't ignore or escape from as long as she sat there across from him.

After what seemed like ages, Jamie went over and held her chin gently between his thumb and forefinger, tilting her face up so he could look into her red-rimmed eyes.

"I'm worried about you," he said, breaking the silence at last. "I just don't know where this is coming from."

She wanted to speak, but no words came.

"I know it's tough to be apart, but what other option do we have right now?" His eyes rolled up to the ceiling with the decorative tiles as if searching for an answer there that would satisfy them both. "We've got responsibilities, Liv. There are bills to pay, jobs we have to show up for, and places we have to be. What other option do we have but to wait and see?"

"We have the option of breaking up." Her voice was soft.

Jamie looked at her as if he had just been punched, the hurt plain in his eyes. It was permanent damage inflicted, but Olivia realized the bravest thing she had ever done wasn't about choosing to fall in love with someone living on the opposite side of the country, it was choosing to leave them.

Jamie moved away from her and walked to the other side of the room, leaning against the wall with his arms crossed defensively over his chest. "So you want to give up."

"I don't want to. I never wanted any of this, but I love you and I want us to make decisions based on what we want, not what we're afraid of."

Jamie threw his hands up in frustration. "What are you talking about?"

"You're always asking for me to give you more time, to keep waiting and holding on. But you're only saying that because you're afraid to lose me. You're afraid to admit the truth."

"And what's the truth?"

"That you were never really going to keep your word about moving to Seattle in the first place. You want to believe it so badly, you want to convince us both that it's going to happen." She took in a deep breath. "I'm not giving up on us and I wish I didn't have to have this conversation with you right now, but I mean it. I'm not going to let you keep breaking my heart."

She loved him—all the messy and radiant parts of him that made him who he was—but it hardly seemed to matter when the relationship they had built together was crumbling before their eyes.

After more than a year of distance, their story had come to a dead end.

Olivia watched as Jamie moved to the bed and sat on a corner of the mattress in disbelief, slouching over with his elbows resting on his knees and his chin propped on knotted-up fists.

For several minutes, neither of them spoke.

CHAPTER 12

Jamie looked at her clothes lying in careless piles on the hotel floor from their earlier bout of passion and their empty wine glasses sitting next to the bed, wondering how their last night together had gone so terribly wrong.

All at once, the hotel room felt both suffocating and somehow too big for him.

Avoiding Olivia's gaze, he grabbed his phone and the hotel key and opened the door to their suite, his voice tired as he said, "I need some time alone to think. I'll be back."

And then he was gone.

* * *

It was past midnight when he came back, a thin triangle of light crawling across the carpeted floor as he cracked open the hotel room door.

Olivia had spent the last few hours flipping through television channels without really watching anything, glancing at her phone every few minutes to see if he had texted or called, wondering if he was out there somewhere feeling every bit as empty as she did. After washing her face and climbing into bed, she just lay there and stared at the empty spot next to her, wondering if she had made the wrong decision and whether she'd change her mind when she saw him again.

Now, she lay quietly in bed with her back to him as Jamie slipped underneath the sheets to join her in the dark. The scent of her clean skin and rose-scented face cream was so familiar that it almost hurt to breathe.

He couldn't see Olivia's face in the navy shadows, but the hotel sheets were pulled all the way up past her shoulders and scrunched beneath her neck—the way she liked to sleep whenever she was troubled by something—as her body rose and fell with each dejected breath she took.

Jamie wished she would say something, but the minutes crawled by with nothing.

"I know you're awake," he said, reaching over and touching her back.

There was no response, so he started to rub her back in little comforting circles instead, her warmth beneath his palm a reminder that she was only human and likely hurting just as much as he was. It was hard to tell where they stood now, halfway between strangers and lovers, and even though a part of him wanted to pull her close, it felt too intimate, so he just watched her.

After what felt like a lifetime, Olivia turned over in the dark, her brown eyes settling on his with a softness and vulnerability that made him want to cry, inching forward little by little until they were finally resting on the same pillow, their faces but an inch apart.

The necklace he had given her shone in the dark as it fell against her throat. Jamie reached over to touch it, the tiny silver plane smooth and warm between his fingers, the irony of his gift not lost on him. They were just two paper planes crossing paths, fragile and destructible, never meant to get very far together. He knew the reasons why they were breaking up like the back of his hand, but none of them seemed good enough to him. None of them could justify why they had to end it.

"I can't sleep." Her voice was soft.

"I know," Jamie responded. Pushing away the hesitation in his mind, he kissed her forehead gently. "I'm sorry. I'm sorry that I left you here by yourself when I should have been trying to figure things out and fix them. I should've known better than to do that to you." He shook his head. "To *us*. I'm just really sorry about everything, Liv. I never meant to hurt you."

Olivia didn't respond, just touched his hands wrapped around her face, her eyes never leaving his.

"I don't want us to end," he said, his voice tinged with so much pain that it was almost a plea. "I fucked up. I'm sorry, Liv, I fucked up." He tipped his head down and, to her surprise, started crying, his breath coming out in heaving sobs. She had never seen him like this before, not even when his grandfather passed away the year prior.

She didn't resist when he leaned in to kiss her, each one more desperate and final than the last. There was so much love and hope that had existed between them at one point in time, but they weren't inseparable if they were constantly being separated, constantly being given reasons to be apart. She was done holding onto careless people and promises.

CHAPTER 12

As she held him, forcing herself to be strong, she hoped that he would forgive her one day for breaking up with him. Letting him go was going to be one of the hardest things to do and though it was killing her to see him fall apart in front of her, there was a sense of clarity and relief, too.

When they finally pulled apart, Jamie was no longer crying, but he refused to look at her.

"It's really over, isn't it?" he asked.

"Yeah." She blinked at him, exhausted and brokenhearted. There was no glossing over it or lying to themselves anymore. "It's over."

Jamie nodded, closing his eyes in defeat as Olivia let him hold her one last time, their final moments together already slipping away into the past.

* * *

At the crack of dawn, Olivia went to the airport in a taxi.

She had insisted to go by herself, even though Jamie said he could drive her to JFK and it wasn't an issue, but it *was* an issue.

It was morning by then and they were broken up.

Done. Separate. Single.

The thought of being stuck in a car with her newly-minted ex for thirty-five minutes while sitting in New York traffic felt like asking for a miserable time, so she dragged her suitcase into a taxi, hugged Jamie goodbye, and left. She tried not to look into his eyes or to linger too long because she had a feeling that a part of her would change her mind if he so much as touched her the way he used to.

All the way to the airport, she had her earbuds in and listened to music, exhausted and in no mood for friendly chatter with the driver.

The plane was mostly full when she boarded, but the seats beside her were miraculously empty. Situated between the clouds, thousands of miles up in the air, Olivia had all the time and space in the world to rest or think, but she did neither of those things. The package of complimentary pretzels lay unopened on her tray even though she hadn't eaten anything for hours, and the idea of sleep felt impossible even though she was the most tired she had been all week.

Sighing, she opened up her laptop and stared at the screen, the cursor blinking at her, then back down at her lap where her notebook was. She hadn't slept a wink all night and still had a five-hour flight looming before her, but something was pulsing in her veins that was all too familiar. It was the same feeling she got when she first met Jamie in the beginning, when things were new and fresh and full of hope.

Everything that she had written over the past year during her visits with Jamie was in that notebook and everything was suddenly clicking into place, all the cogs in her brain turning together with a jumble of dialogue and settings and characters and plots. It was inspiration and artistry, but the kind that only came once in a blue moon. It was clear then what she wanted her book to be about. Writing was something she worked at every day since she was aware that pure talent only got people so far without hard work, but as she sat in seat E8 that morning, Olivia found that she didn't need to use an ounce of effort to write at all—she simply couldn't *stop* writing.

As her fingers flew across the silver keys, she realized that broken hearts had a lot to say and hers was no exception.

All that time, she had been stupid to think that there was some place where she and Jamie could just exist together, some fair compromise in which neither of them had to sacrifice so much in order to be together. But that was a fantasy—that place didn't exist.

As her pain poured out in the form of dialogue and plot lines, she finally let herself break, her eyes welling with tears and blurring the words in front of her, but she didn't stop writing. It felt like the only thing that would give her closure and peace at that moment, knowing they were really over. If she was going to think about Jamie and have a rerun of everything playing nonstop in her head anyway, a film of their greatest hits, it was justified to write about it for processing, for catharsis, for closure. If she wrote about their relationship from the hopeful beginning all the way to the bitter end, it would somehow be okay.

It was with this flawed logic that Olivia even made it all the way home to Seattle.

Chapter 13

Time moved differently for the brokenhearted. The first week following their breakup was the easiest to manage. There was only a feeling of numbness and overwhelming silence, her phone quiet without the usual texts wishing her a good morning or calls to hear about her day when she got home from work. It was still painful to be alone without that old familiar voice on the line, but there was the feeling that maybe it was temporary, maybe it was just a bad fight and they'd smooth it over in a few days.

But then those days turned into weeks, and those weeks turned into months. Denial passed and memories came back to fill its place instead, with his heartbeat joining her underneath the sheets at night and his face haunting all her what-if scenarios. Every time she heard Springsteen, Sinatra, or Billy Joel on the radio or even just saw a package at her door that wasn't from New York, she'd get inexplicably sad even though it made little sense.

Whenever time she saw white cars on the road, she thought about Jamie driving them around in his, his hand holding hers across the console, the two of them laughing over all the noise of the traffic about things she couldn't remember now. Olivia still saw his face in the places they used to go and on passing strangers in the streets—everything in Seattle reminded her of what they used to have and the echoes of their old selves haunted Olivia everywhere she went.

It seemed like everything in her world had become black and white; all the colors that had once blossomed so brightly for her back when they were in love seemed to fade away until there was nothing left. Gone were the dates circled in red in her agenda planner to mark their hard-earned visits, and new events and lunch dates with friends and appointments filled the space instead.

As the days crawled by, one after the other, she found that there were little pockets of time where she felt okay. She wasn't one hundred percent, but she was okay, and she lived for those moments in time when she would almost forget.

All those feelings and memories with Jamie—both the good and bad—started to fade as time wore on, little by little, like a Polaroid developing in reverse. It left a gaping hole where their memories and feelings once took place. Every day, Olivia prayed that her old self would fill its space instead, but that version of her was nowhere to be found.

* * *

Two months later, she and Ingrid sat in one of the local coffee shops together, the comforting scent of fresh blueberry muffins and steaming cappuccinos wafting through the air as they caught up.

"I feel like I'm going crazy," she lamented. "I can't stop thinking about him. It's been over two months and I still can't stop replaying everything. Tell me I'm going crazy." Olivia slumped in her chair, plucking at a loose thread on the hem of her brown corduroy skirt. The sadness was finally settling in now, and she honestly preferred the numbness—the absolute nothingness—because at least it didn't hurt. "Tell me I'm going crazy."

"You're *not* crazy." Ingrid studied her over the rim of her coffee mug. "You haven't missed a day of work, you're still going about your life, and you've remained civil about all of it. In fact, I'm a little surprised you're not having a bigger reaction to it. I know the guy was really something to you."

"Maybe it's my coping mechanism." Olivia lifted the corners of her mouth in a small smile. "Act like everything is in order and going perfectly and no one will be wise to the fact that you're depressed." She sighed and leaned forward, resting her forehead over her folded arms on the wooden table. A small groan escaped her lips. "I don't even know why I do it anymore."

CHAPTER 13

"Because it's all you know."

"I know I'm not going to erase Jamie overnight, but even if I could, I don't know if I want to."

Ingrid blinked, her eyes shiny and inquisitive against the April sunlight streaming through the windows. "Have you gone out with anyone new yet?"

"No, I haven't even thought about it." Olivia sat up again and shrugged. "It just feels wrong to me. I don't think I'm ready. Sometimes it feels like I'll never be ready again." She was being dramatic, but she couldn't help it.

"Is Jamie seeing anyone?"

Olivia sputtered out a laugh and draped her arms around her body as if to protect herself from the possibility that he had already moved on. "How would *I* know?"

The unfortunate truth was that she *did* know.

She knew he had already moved on and found someone new in just a matter of weeks. It was near impossible for Olivia to remain civil and nonchalant watching Jamie share about his new relationship at every possible turn. It was almost sickening seeing all the photos and not-so-subtle declarations of love being posted publicly for everyone to see. It was a cruel way to broadcast to everyone around them just how little Olivia meant to him, how easy it was for him to find the sunlight and beauty in someone else, and how easy it was to replace the woman he once swore made him the happiest man alive.

It was a different kind of betrayal learning who the new woman was—a blonde girl that Jamie swore was only a friend back when he and Olivia were together. He always said there was nothing going on between them, but it felt way too convenient that just fourteen days after breaking up, he was already in a committed relationship and spewing all kinds of mush about her. She was three years younger than Olivia and sported pink, dip-dyed ends, worked as a receptionist, had an apparent obsession with the *Twilight* franchise, and liked to call Jamie saccharine nicknames inspired by the characters.

As much as Olivia wanted to pick her apart over some flaw or fault, she couldn't. The new girl hadn't done anything wrong except fall for someone inconsistent and unreliable, someone who probably didn't even know what he was doing.

In some ways, Olivia even felt bad for her. She was falling for the same lies Olivia once fell for, and there would be other problems Jamie's inconsistencies and unreliable nature would bring out in time.

But the new girl looked beautiful and kind, and she was exactly what Jamie needed to distract himself from what had happened between them.

None of it really mattered anyway, because he wasn't her problem anymore. If he wanted to make a spectacle of himself in front of everyone and Olivia, that was completely up to him.

Seeing Jamie move on in a matter of weeks was a different kind of pain and betrayal. It was like their entire relationship never mattered—like *she* never mattered.

All of it was confusing and pointless and painful, and she was never going to heal if she let him take up space in her head that way.

She told him not to reach out to her again because she needed her own space and time to heal, and Jamie's apathetic and passive-aggressive response and attitude toward her after that confirmed what Olivia already suspected—he was always going to act like a child when he didn't get his way.

The combination of indifference and blatant disrespect for what they once had felt like rubbing salt in a wound. As if flaunting Olivia's shiny, new replacement in her face wasn't enough, he said it didn't matter if they spoke or not, or if they even remained friends.

In every way he possibly could, he made sure to let her know that their relationship mattered less to him than it did to her, that she had just been a commodity to him, ready to be loved and shown off when she was shiny and new and then discarded and replaced when he got bored of running her empty.

Soon after that, Olivia bagged up all his clothes that he had left behind and donated them to Goodwill and threw the paper airplane necklace he had given her straight into Elliott Bay.

It felt like bad karma to keep anything of his around.

Bringing herself back to the present where she was sitting across from

CHAPTER 13

Ingrid in a coffee shop, Olivia let out a small breath and sat up a little straighter.

"Even if he's moved on, it doesn't matter anymore. He could be in Antarctica for all I care," she said. "The only thing that really hurt was how he promised something so big and then acted like it was nothing. A part of me feels really cheated and betrayed. It's as if he set everything up for us only to take it away when I wanted it most and trusted him. What's even worse is the fact that it hurt me more than it'll ever hurt him. He's perfectly fine in New York doing whatever he's doing because he's not the one who had to wait for someone to make up their mind, to follow through on what they said they would do." Olivia shrugged, but sadness weighed down her shoulders. "And that's the part I can't get over. I'm pissed that none of it even mattered to him, that I'm the one who's still hurting when it should be him."

"People put on a front all the time." Ingrid's voice was gentle and she put down her ceramic mug, her mauve lipstick coloring the rim in a little half-moon shape. "I wouldn't be surprised if he was still hurting in his own way. Whatever he says and does is not a reflection of how much he loved you or how worthy you are as a person. I know you want him to hurt because you're hurting, but all that's going to do is take up more of your precious time and headspace. He's already hurt you and wasted your time, so why let him take even more?" She smiled reassuringly at Olivia. "Act first and the healing will come later. You don't need to be at a hundred percent in order to take a step forward."

"I guess."

"And I know it's cliché, but if you two aren't together anymore, it's probably for a very good reason. Maybe Jamie just isn't the one for you."

"But what if he is?"

"Let me ask you a question then." Ingrid leaned forward. "Do you feel like it was the right decision to end your relationship with him?"

"Sometimes. It feels like a relief, but there are all these other emotions too, like anger, disappointment, shame, sadness." Olivia paused. "Honestly, it's everything all at once. It's hard to know where one emotion begins and the other ends."

"Can I be frank?"

"You can be Bob, too."

Ingrid laughed. "Glad to see you haven't lost your wit. But if I had to pick a word to describe you right now, I'd say that you're afraid."

"Of what?"

"Lots of things. Being hurt again, moving forward, remembering him, or even forgetting him. But most times, I think we're most afraid of losing ourselves in the process. You feel like you'll never get back to being the person you were before them."

"I think you hit the nail on the head with that one."

"Okay, but is it really that bad?" Ingrid's eyes sparkled as she spoke. "You won't be the same person you were before Jamie, but maybe that's a good thing. I know it sounds like I'm pulling things out of my geriatric arse right now to make you feel better, but I've had my fair share of heartbreaks and lessons learned when I was in my twenties too. Believe me when I say that the best part of a broken heart is getting to decide which pieces you want to keep and which pieces you want to fill with something new. You get to decide, you're in control, and there's nothing more empowering than that."

"Thanks, Ing. I needed that." Olivia smiled at her friend, reaching across the wooden table with both arms to hug the older woman. She put a few bills on the table and got up, shrugging on her wool cardigan. "My treat."

As they took off down the block to where Ingrid's car was parked, Ingrid looked over at Olivia and affectionately wrapped an arm around her shoulders. "I know that it'll take some time to move on, but you'll get there. I know you must really miss him, even if you don't want to admit it."

It was true. She didn't know how she could ever love someone else. The past year with him felt like some dream that had turned into a nightmare, and everything that she had hoped for and planned for the two of them was now water under the bridge, something meant for another lifetime or another couple. But those hopes and lost plans kept washing up to shore day in and day out, reminding her over and over again that she wouldn't ever get to find out what it would have been like if things worked out the way she wanted them to.

CHAPTER 13

It was true that she did miss him in her own way, even if she never saw him again or said it straight to his face.

"If you ask me, it's the poor bastard's loss." Ingrid playfully nudged Olivia with her shoulder, the two of them reaching her car at last. "Before you know it, you'll be happy again and he'll still be making the same mistakes over and over again with different people. But what's important is you being happy and being back on your feet again, not what he's doing or who he's seeing. I know you're going to be just fine."

Olivia got in the car and buckled up, letting out the breath she didn't know she had been holding. "I hope you're right."

* * *

Graduation day fell on a perfect spring morning in May.

The air was fresh and crisp and the sound of twittering birds was a welcome change after the city's long and icy slumber. The campus buzzed with activity as her fellow graduates got their maroon gowns fitted and their caps pinned for their parade across the stage. There was enough nervous energy going around to fuel the entirety of Seattle, but it was also mixed with excitement, relief, and gratification.

Olivia waited patiently behind the other students in line, waiting to follow the bagpipes and valedictorian out to where friends and family waited with smiles and smartphones to commemorate the end of their journey as university students. She adjusted the red hood pinned to her gown, well aware that her maroon gown was just a little too loose on her and looking a little frumpy. She had unintentionally lost quite a bit of weight over the past few months, with her poor appetite and busy schedule to blame.

Taking a deep breath and trying her best to fill out the graduation gown she had tried on months ago with the rest of her fellow graduates, Olivia silently made a promise to herself that she would start working with a nutritionist and get back on track with her health that week. Her family doctor had suspected that she was severely depressed and had referred her to a therapist as well as a nutritionist to make sure she was getting the help she needed.

It would all get better over time with that support, but right then, Olivia wanted to be happy and proud of herself and focus on the present. The late nights of studying and writing papers were long gone, and so were the lazy afternoons by the campus pond with her friends and cheap takeout sushi. She remembered how excited she had been to go to her first dorm party where everyone drank too much and remembered too little after playing beer pong, and how proud her mom had been when they got the news about Olivia's scholarship. She was even going to miss the little koi fish ponds by the side of the campus buildings where she spent so many hours eating lunch and studying over the past few years.

As she followed the other graduates into the open space where their loved ones gathered patiently for the beginning of the ceremony, she glanced at the crowd. Her eyes roamed across the hundreds of faces, and the thought of Jamie being in the crowd edged its way into her thoughts. He was the last person she wanted to think about that day, but before they broke up, he had promised to go to her graduation at all costs.

A small part of Olivia wondered if he'd show up anyway or find some way to reach out to her, but she pushed those thoughts out of her mind.

She made it through the valedictorian's moving speech and clapped for the dozens of other graduates who had been called up before her to accept their hard-earned diplomas and congratulations. When her name was called, she carefully made her way up the carpeted stairs in her heels, aware that her proud mother was somewhere out there in the sea of people beaming up at her—it was just as much her mother's achievement as it was hers.

Olivia shook the chancellor's hand and posed for a quick photo with her diploma before making her way off the stage as a new graduate. When she took her seat again, her phone vibrated with a text from an unknown number. *So proud of you! Congratulations, my dearest daughter,* it read.

As everyone clapped and cheered from their seats for the last few people crossing the stage, Olivia just sat there, her thumbs hovering hesitantly over the screen.

But for some reason, she couldn't find the words and pocketed her phone instead, forcing her eyes back to the stage. Little did Olivia know that it

CHAPTER 13

would be the last time he'd be in touch for many years, though the reason she didn't reply wasn't out of spite—it was out of self-preservation.

For that one day, she was going to make it all about herself and not let anything or anyone from her past take precedence over that.

She smiled, clapping for the others crossing the stage now as a sense of relief washed over her.

It felt like she was finally choosing herself first, and that made her prouder than any piece of paper with her name and degree on it.

Over steak and ginger beer later that night with her friends, there came an epiphany.

"You know, I think you should give dating a try again." She was sitting next to Evan, one of her closest friends, and the confident statement came out of left field. "It's been almost half a year since you and Jamie split up, right?"

"It's been three months," she corrected him, her voice flat. "I know for a fact that I'm not a hundred percent over him yet, so there's no point in dating someone new. I'm just going to hurt them or get hurt myself."

Olivia loved her friends, but they were dead wrong about moving on. She wasn't ready and it made zero sense to bring it up during the celebratory dinner she was having. She met Evan during their first year of university together and quickly bonded after going to a very chaotic fraternity party one night with some mutual friends that resulted in a bloody toe and a complimentary piggyback ride back to their friend's dorm room. They ended the night with cheese pizza at 2 a.m. and some bandages scavenged from a questionable-looking first aid kit in the lobby.

She loved him to death, but there was no way she was venturing back out into the swampy depths of dating anytime soon. Evan took a bite of his food, chewing thoughtfully. "True, it's only been a hot minute," he said, "and I'm sorry if that came off as blunt. I know it can feel like scouring the bottom of the barrel for leftovers right now, but maybe something frivolous with zero expectations is just the antidote you need. Just get out there and have some fun, Liv."

"And why is my love life suddenly so interesting to you, hm?" Olivia gave him a goofy grin. "Am I *that* pitiful and sad right now?"

"Maybe a little," he quipped, laughing as she elbowed him in the ribs, "but it can't hurt to go on just one date." Evan hugged her from the side with one arm, leaning against her. "But seriously, I love you and you deserve to be happy. Mr. Perfect from New York isn't even all that."

"Just *one* date? Is that all it'll take to get you off my case?"

"It really is."

Olivia scrunched her face, skeptical. "I doubt that, but I guess it wouldn't hurt to go on just one little date. Maybe you're right."

"You know I'm right." A little smirk played on Evan's lips. "You know, when things didn't work out with Michael a year ago, I thought it was the end of the world, but look at me now." He leaned back and opened his arms wide. "I'm as happy as ever. I didn't know what else was out there."

"You didn't know *Chris* was out there, to be clear."

The two of them stole a glance at Evan's boyfriend, Chris, sitting across the table, laughing about something with the others, his contagious smile and sparkling eyes enough to get everyone's attention in the room. "Right," Evan responded, a shy smile blooming on his lips. "I didn't know Chris was out there."

Olivia shook her head with resignation, but she was smiling. "I hate the fact that I'm listening to you right now."

"Look, all I'm saying is that love doesn't only come once in a lifetime and it's rom-com bullshit to only have *one* person on the planet that we're meant to be with."

The idea of falling in love with somebody else felt pretty far-fetched to Olivia, but being open to the idea of what else was out there seemed slightly more feasible. It would be hard to find anything or anyone that matched the intensity of the feelings and love that she felt for Jamie, which came in a burning red, and the thought of never having someone stack up to what she once had with him was scary—but it wasn't insurmountable.

She could give it a try and go on a date or two, make small talk with a stranger in a restaurant, and maybe even feel more like herself than she had in weeks. With the gears already turning in her head, Olivia took another

CHAPTER 13

bite of her food and stared straight ahead, the noise from the restaurant fading away into the background. She knew that comparison was going to kill her, but the thought of Jamie living it up in New York doing all the things they used to do with his new girl and having the time of his life while she sat in a Seattle restaurant still tending to her broken heart seemed sad.

She didn't want to feel sorry for herself anymore, but there was another emotion buried in her heart—anger.

She had left their relationship with as much dignity, respect, and love as she could muster at the time, and all Jamie ever did was mess things up. If he was going to let her go so easily and make sure the entire world knew about it, then he didn't deserve a second more of her time. Olivia was well aware that she had already given him more hours of her life than he ever deserved.

She took a sip of her ice water, indignation and irritation burning in her throat.

She was mad, but that was good. It meant that she would no longer have to waste any more time being heartbroken over someone who didn't think enough of her when they were together and thought even less of her now that they were apart.

The stages of grief felt way too real.

On the way home, Olivia hesitantly downloaded the dating app Evan had suggested and made a profile for herself, feeling slightly awkward as she uploaded some photos and details like her favorite coffee shop and movie series and whether she was an outdoors person.

There was a photo she uploaded of her standing in front of the glistening blue, bronze, and rose-colored stainless steel and aluminum tiles of the Museum of Pop Culture. She was mid-laugh and looking as happy as ever in a candid moment captured by Jamie. She had been wearing her favorite lavender wool coat with the gold heart-shaped buttons in the photo, the one he never ended up mailing back to her when she left it in New York. They had found it together at a vintage shop in Manhattan and she fell in love with it, buying it on the spot that afternoon. After wearing it nonstop for a few days, she accidentally left it in the trunk of Jamie's car before their breakup and her flight.

It seemed like a minor consolation that at least she had a great photo for her dating profile now.

***

It took seven days and a hundred matches for her to take a shot and pick someone to go on a date with.

Joshua was a well-read engineer who liked cold brews, had surprisingly good taste in music, volunteered at an animal sanctuary, and had eyes so green they looked almost otherworldly.

He picked her up one Friday evening after a few days of flirtatious back-and-forth about where to get the best flame-seared sushi in Seattle. Everything at the restaurant he had chosen was made fresh in front of them and cost four times more than the place with the kitschy paper lanterns and little wooden booths with cloth pillows just a couple blocks from them. Olivia actually liked that place a lot, but she wasn't going to burst Joshua's bubble on their two-hundred-dollar first date.

She learned that she had much to learn when it came to dating again.

Joshua was so foreign to her, and even though she told herself it was exciting to be seeing someone new after so long, she couldn't help but to look into his eyes only to see that he wasn't Jamie. But Joshua had soulful eyes and a personality that made her feel safe, so she tried harder to focus as he said, "I spent a couple of years in Japan—three in Tokyo and one in Nagoya. My mom was an expat and so we moved frequently, but I enjoyed Japan so much when I got there and just fell in love with the culture and the food and the pace." He took a polite bite of tempura, the coating breaking neatly between his teeth. "I ended up staying there on my own and finished up my degree while being in a different country. That's how I learned to speak Japanese, but coming back to Seattle has definitely turned me back into somewhat of an amateur."

The two of them laughed amiably. "An engineer *and* a man of culture. I'm into that."

CHAPTER 13

"I was hoping you'd be." He smiled, forgetting about the sushi on his plate as he studied her. Olivia crossed her legs and leaned back in her seat, well aware that his eyes followed her every move. It felt good to be wanted and it felt even better knowing that she wasn't somehow exposing herself on the outside—no one had to know that she had been so broken, not if she didn't tell them. She could be confident and charismatic and it was an addictive feeling to be someone who had it all together, even if only on the surface.

They held eye contact, the tension palpable as it hung in the air between the two of them, sparkling with potential until they finally looked away.

During their date, he showed her a little magic trick by making his chopsticks disappear and reappear from behind his hand, which was both silly and endearing. They debated a little over social justice issues and unsolved mysteries and ended up changing each other's minds about some topics. He showed her photos of his dogs back in Japan and she told him a story about the time she met a famous actor at the restaurant where she waited tables with Ingrid.

An hour later, the two of them left the restaurant together, interrupting each other and sputtering out laughs in between telling stories. She liked the way Joshua would lean close whenever he told a joke just to make sure she didn't miss the punchline, and the way his eyes would light up with interest over her words, whether they were witty or plain nonsense.

They took a few tentative steps forward, the warm breeze comfortable as they made their way down the block. Olivia moved a little closer to Joshua, surprised that she didn't mind it when his fingers brushed hers for a brief moment before slipping into her hand as they crossed the street.

"You know, I had a really fun time this evening. To be honest, I haven't done this in a long time." Joshua glanced over at her, looking a little embarrassed all of a sudden. "Go on dates, I mean. Things ended pretty poorly with the last person I was with and I just didn't feel ready to meet anyone new for a really long time." He laughed. "This probably makes me sound like a loser, but I realized I was only sabotaging myself by hiding away. It was like I didn't want to let myself be happy as a way to punish myself." When Olivia didn't say anything, he apologized. "Sorry," he mumbled, "I'm already putting too much out there."

"You're a human being," she said. "There's nothing to be sorry about."

"Damn, I was hoping you'd think I was an android or something for being so perfect."

"You showed your true colors too soon. Should've waited until your clones took over the planet or something."

He chuckled and shoved his hands into his coat pockets as if to stuff his earlier confession away.

"If it makes you feel any better, this is my first date in a long time," she said.

Joshua stopped walking and looked at her, a sweet smile gracing his lips. "You could have fooled me."

"I'd much rather be honest with you."

"The honesty is attractive."

Before she could process what was happening, they were kissing.

His hands pressed warmly against her back, pulling her to him as they leaned into one another. A mix of emotions crossed Olivia, but she didn't stop kissing him back.

A moment later, he pulled away, her face still in his hands. Everything about him was new and unfamiliar, but it wasn't necessarily a bad thing.

Joshua smiled shyly, his hair ruffled by the breeze. "Can I see you again?"

It was a question that was unplanned and unexpected, just something that came naturally after a good first date. It was the start of something new, something different.

Instead of answering, she closed the space between them on the sidewalk and pulled his lips down to meet hers again.

***

For three weeks, there were matinees and happy hour tapas, coffee dates and window shopping, kisses in his car, and long drives out to the beach with the windows down.

She even had her first—and last—cigarette with him one night, the two of them smoking underneath a bar awning while rain poured from the

CHAPTER 13

dark skies. The smoke singed her lungs and tasted like a mixture of burnt newspaper and tar and Olivia wondered for a moment if all of it was just a distraction, just another way to dissociate from whatever she had experienced with Jamie. She would have to sit and face the feelings eventually, the ones she had worked so hard to try to avoid in the beginning, but the thought of it wasn't so scary anymore.

Little by little, she was going to move on and be okay in the end.

One Saturday morning in late June, she woke up feeling unusually cold and frustrated, aware that her night terrors had returned with a vengeance. She was supposed to see Joshua that day and go down to Pike Place Market for some lunch, but as her alarm increased in urgency and volume, a part of her longed to just stay in bed and become a pile of dusty bones.

Sighing, Olivia kicked off her sheets, washed up, and changed into a fresh outfit in record time, slipping into her sandals right as Joshua texted her to say that he was at her door.

She stepped out and saw him waiting patiently for her, leaning against the side of the house with a maroon windbreaker thrown over a soft grey tee and jeans, his hands shoved in his pockets as his green eyes landed on her with something she could only identify as desire.

"Hey, you," he said, pulling her into a hug. "You look great. Ready to go?"

Olivia nodded and hooked her arm through his as they walked to his car.

On their first date, he opened up to her about being in the middle of getting over somebody. That nugget of information seemed to bond them in some sad and strange way. There were no expectations they had of one another, no requirement to be logical and reasonably functioning adults when they were still cleaning up the mess that somebody else had left behind, the fragments of their hearts still being pieced back together.

It felt strangely good to want *nothing.*

It was a gorgeous day and everyone was out and about enjoying the salty ocean air by the market, perusing the open stalls, and chattering happily.

A little bit of color had finally returned to Olivia's world and she was desperate to keep it. Even if it would never again be the bright kaleidoscope of color that she saw with Jamie, at least some of it was returning.

She ate fresh lobster rolls and sat by the pier with Joshua, their legs hanging out over the edge while they talked about work and family and travel, and later that afternoon, they walked by the stalls boasting fresh fruit, marzipan, sweets, and handmade jewelry and crafts. There were boats out in the diamond-dusted waters and the sun caressed their skin with its warmth, and as they walked by the familiar vendors together, Joshua reached over and interlaced his fingers with hers.

"Have you ever been to Mount Rainier at sunset?" Olivia looked over at him, shielding her eyes from the sun. It was a random question, but she didn't much care.

"If I say I haven't, is it over between us?" Joshua asked, squeezing her hand. The gesture was so familiar that it made her heart squeeze, but she blocked it out and forced herself to focus on the present.

"No, I'd just say that you're missing out. We should go."

"Right now?"

"Right now."

"It's two hours away," Joshua said, glancing hesitantly at his watch. "It's almost two in the afternoon, so we'll get there around four."

"Well, it's not like either of us has anything to do tonight or tomorrow morning, so why not?" Olivia spoke with the carefree attitude of someone spontaneous, someone that wasn't her.

Joshua's expression was hard to read—it was stuck between being impressed and hesitant.

Finally, he nodded, a spark passing through his eyes. "You know, that's what I like about you so much. You live in the present and you don't worry about the future."

"Well, why worry about things we can't control, right?"

"Exactly."

The glimmer of mischief in Joshua's eyes was so tempting that it didn't seem too much of a stretch that she *could* be a carefree and spontaneous person if she wanted to be.

"I can drive us," she said, grinning with newfound confidence as Joshua handed her his keys.

CHAPTER 13

"If you drive, it's only fair that I buy us iced coffees on the way then."

"You've got yourself a deal. But I have to warn you, I prefer to listen to music in the car instead of talking, so I hope you're okay with that."

Joshua opened his mouth and then closed it, only nodding. "Yeah, yeah. That's cool with me."

As Olivia turned up the volume of the music and merged into the I-5 traffic to leave Seattle, she surprised herself by actually feeling better. It wasn't because Joshua was there, but because it had been a minute since she last felt so free. She was in the driver's seat with the open road ahead of her, and as the wind whipped through the windows, Olivia couldn't help but smile again.

It had been four months since she last saw Jamie. Four months since they last kissed or saw each other in person, four months since they were together and facing the world and the distance as a duo. At one point in time, it felt like they could do anything as long as they were together, but she now realized that she had so much left to learn. She loved him, but she had to love herself more.

As Olivia drove with Joshua next to her, she felt some of the tension and heartache that she had been holding onto for months begin to slowly melt away.

Two hours later, she threw the white Subaru in park before flinging open the door to greet the last golden rays of sunlight that were now dipping below the trees and casting her skin in a bronze glow.

It was gorgeous up there, with sloping hills and a variety of wildflowers and wildlife that stretched for as far as she could see. It was like something out of The Sound of Music when Julie Andrews' character, Maria, sang about how entranced she was by the beauty of the hills that stretched out endlessly before her. Up there on Mount Rainier, Olivia felt the same as Maria, surrounded only by trees that whispered in the wind and the rest of civilization somewhere far beneath her. There was something magical about all of it.

Jamie had always wanted to go, she remembered. He told her one time in the middle of the night after they had stayed up too late watching a documentary about places to travel to within the states. He said that less than half of the hundreds of thousands of people who tried to reach the peak of Mount Rainier ended up succeeding, but that wasn't the reason he wanted to go.

"It's like a whole world just by itself. It has so much contrast," he had said. "It's an active volcano with 25 glaciers and there's so much wildlife there. Even if I don't make it to the top, I'd love to see it someday and just take photos, especially at sunset."

"Well, it's only a two-hour drive from Seattle," Olivia said at the time. "Maybe we can go next time you visit me."

"You'd better put it in your calendar because we're going to make it a day trip. Our first one together. A day trip, a road trip, an eat-everything-we-find-along-the-way trip."

"Our first everything together."

He had leaned over and kissed her, slow and sweet. "Yeah, our first everything. After we go to Mount Rainier, I'm going to take you to one of my favorite little getaways in New York next time you come, okay?"

That never ended up happening, but here she was now at Mount Rainier with Joshua.

"You were right," Joshua said now, breaking her out of her thoughts as he moved closer behind Olivia and placed a kiss on her mouth. He tasted like the iced coffee they had on the drive over, his mouth cool and sweet. "I don't think I've ever seen Mount Rainier like this. What made you want to come?"

"No reason." She let him slide his arms around her from behind, pressing her back against his chest. The two of them stared out at the sherbet sunset in silence, aware that the most beautiful time of the day lasted only mere minutes.

* * *

Back at Joshua's apartment a few hours later, she waited patiently as he made his way over with some hot lemon tea, smiling as he joined her on the couch

CHAPTER 13

in his living room.

"Thank you." She took the mug and smiled, noticing that he was sitting close enough for his leg to be brushing hers. "This really hits the spot after all that walking."

Olivia rested the mug in her lap and looked around the room. Joshua's apartment was small, but relatively neat and tastefully decorated. There were a few pieces of modern art hanging on the walls from artists that she didn't recognize, a collection of old board games tucked underneath the mahogany coffee table, and biographies from big shots in the tech industry lined his bookcases while a record player sat on top. She got up off the couch and moved to the record player, riffling through the vinyls. "The Beatles, Arctic Monkeys, Nirvana, The 1975, Oasis, Bon Iver …" She turned to look at him over her shoulder. "You really have a thing for bands, don't you?"

Joshua's gaze followed her as she moved around the room, the tension between them growing steadily. Noticing an acoustic guitar sitting abandoned in one corner of the room, Olivia moved toward it and ran one finger down the strings. "Do you still play?"

"Here and there, but it's honestly been some time since I've picked it up. I used to play along to records to learn some of the more classic stuff, but it's been a hot minute since I tried."

"I'll bet you leave the guitar lying around because you're just *dying* for somebody to ask you to play something."

"Guess you caught me." Joshua winked at her, then walked over to where Olivia stood, lifting the guitar out of its hiding place in the corner. "Any requests, madam?"

She crossed her arms over her chest and leaned against the wall, blanking out. "Not that I can think of."

"Well, how about a classic then?" Joshua gestured for her to take a seat beside him on the couch again, and Olivia watched as he strummed a few notes and adjusted the capo. "I'm sure you'll know this one. It's by Sinatra."

As the first few notes of "Fly Me to the Moon" sweetly filled the air, Olivia thought back to how she and Jamie had talked about Sinatra when they first met at the airport, and she was immediately reminded of Seattle snowstorms and postcards and airport coffees and hotel lobbies. But as easy as it would have been to spiral down into the past again, Olivia forced herself to notice the way Joshua's fingers expertly moved and the color of his eyes, appreciating that moment between them in time. It was bound to happen over and over again. There would be thousands of things that would remind her of Jamie over the course of her lifetime, and she was just going to have to rewrite those memories and make space for the new ones.

To her surprise, Joshua started singing halfway through. He had a great voice, she found, and as he coaxed each chord from the instrument with ease, she found herself softening toward him as well. Olivia broke out in applause as the last of the music faded away into the recesses of the apartment, and Joshua tipped his head down in a little bow.

"Want to learn a few notes?" he asked, offering the guitar. "I can teach you."

"I've never even held one before."

"All good. If you've got patience, you can learn. It's the same as learning any other instrument." He placed the guitar gently in her lap and she cradled it awkwardly, watching as he moved three of her fingers to rest over the strings. "This is the C chord. Draw your thumb gently down the strings, from top to bottom."

Carefully, she did as he instructed and a clear note filled the air.

"Look at you, you're a natural," he commented, his emerald eyes gleaming in the dim light.

Joshua was patient and cracked jokes the whole way through, and before long, the guitar lesson had turned into kissing on his couch. It didn't have to be love to feel good, she knew, but there was a small part of her that felt like it was a little rushed. It was like the gentlemanly version of Joshua had morphed into an insatiable one, his lips against her neck and his hands in her hair coming off as hungry more than romantic.

The two of them moved backward into his bedroom, still kissing, and Joshua stripped his shirt off, tossing it to the side before moving forward to meet Olivia's lips again.

As she tried to take a step forward, she accidentally knocked something

CHAPTER 13

off his dresser.

"Sorry," she said. Olivia bent down and reached for the picture frame that had landed harmlessly on the carpet, but her smile faltered a little as she saw who was in the photo. There was Joshua, looking dapper in a dress shirt and black pants as he smiled happily at the camera with another woman who had her hand resting lovingly on his chest, her eyes sparkling with joy as she looked up at him.

Sitting on her left hand was a glittering, pavé diamond ring.

"Is that—"

"Yeah. That's my ex," Joshua said, stepping forward as if to protect Olivia from what she had already seen.

"You were *engaged?*"

Olivia knew he still had some ghosts from his past, but she never thought she'd be seeing someone who was getting over a fiancée.

"Yeah, we had been together for five years before I finally got the nerve to propose to her. I didn't have the guts to do it before." Joshua laughed, but the sound of it was bitter. He took a small step closer, his eyes still trained on the woman in the photo. "I thought she was too good for me. I mean, her family always made sure to remind me. Then I found out that she had been sleeping with someone she worked with. I broke it off because I didn't have it in me to forgive her. I just couldn't get past the betrayal. It killed me. I gave her a ring and my word, and I kept it. But she didn't."

"Do you still think about her sometimes?"

For a moment, Joshua's gaze softened and he looked as if he might admit it, but then his eyes hardened and whatever ounce of wistfulness was there before was gone. "No, I don't," he replied. "At least, I try not to. Last time I checked, she's happy and healthy and the guy is a big hit with her parents, so I guess everyone got what they wanted in the end."

Olivia didn't know what to say, so she just nodded.

"It doesn't matter anymore." Joshua reached over and took the frame from her hands, putting it inside a drawer and shutting it. "It's out of my hands and it is what it is. To be honest, I'd rather focus on you and me right now. So, can you please forget you ever saw that?"

He looked at her, and for the first time, she realized how much hurt was actually behind those green eyes she was so captivated by.

"Okay."

"Come to bed."

He extended an open palm toward her in the dark. In some screwed-up way, it felt like a relief to know that he wasn't perfect. He was probably grieving even more than she was. They were just two people who were trying their best, but it wasn't going to fix what had happened in their past. There was nothing left to do but strip off their masks and stand naked and vulnerable in front of each other with the truth—they were both hurting.

For a fraction of a moment, Olivia wanted to leave because sleeping together wasn't going to solve anything. But then again, playing by the rules and trying their best to be a good person and a good partner hadn't been enough anyway.

With this thought in mind, she slipped under Joshua's sheets without another word, shutting out the noise in her head as his hands reached for her body once again.

* * *

It was about to be morning.

The first rays of dawn filtered through the curtains like a humble guest, polite and shy as light snaked through. She had barely slept, but she wasn't tired.

Her gaze flicked over to the silhouette of Joshua lying on the pillow next to her, sleeping soundly while facing away from her. He had fallen asleep before her last night, and he was now wrapped in the duvet with one bare leg hanging off the edge of the mattress on the opposite side of the bed. He murmured something under his breath and shifted slightly, shedding part of the duvet and revealing the single tattoo on the side of his torso.

It was an intricate-looking compass with sharp points and jarring lines, all ink and precision and sharpness. Just a handful of hours ago, she had been running her fingertips gently over where it lived permanently on his skin,

CHAPTER 13

watching as the tattoo shifted and danced with her touch. She didn't say it to Joshua at the time, but she thought it was ironic how something as simple and inanimate as black ink could stay with someone forever, when people—even with all their memories and complexities and intricacies—could easily be dismissed and erased like yesterday's headlines.

The sex wasn't bad with Joshua, but she couldn't remember much of it. It felt like she had been floating around the ceiling the whole time, as if she wasn't even in her own body. She couldn't remember feeling him or what they had done or when it stopped.

Olivia sat up quietly in bed and pulled on her shirt, trying her best not to wake him. There was no disgust or remorse or shame with what she had done because she didn't really feel much of anything. It was strange because she never thought she'd be the kind of person to be okay after something like that.

She left Joshua's apartment after stealing one last look at him sleeping soundly in the bath of warm light coming in through his windows. She hoped that he would heal and she hoped that he wouldn't take it personally if she never spoke to him or saw him again.

When she got home, she crawled into bed but didn't sleep. Instead, Olivia opened up her notebook and picked up a pen, writing one last letter to Jamie that she would never send.

Dear Jamie,

I know we're not talking, but I still have so much to say to you. If you're wondering how I am, the truth is that I'm not really sure anymore. Just when I think I'm moving on, the decisions and mistakes that we made still find a way to follow me around. It honestly surprises me how long it's taking for me to get used to your absence even though we were apart for most of our relationship. I guess life is ironic that way.

We both know that our relationship ending was for the best because we weren't happy and things were clearly not working out for us anymore. Deep down, what hurts the most is feeling like all the love and time we shared didn't really mean anything to you, that what we had didn't matter enough to pull us through in the end. I know we weren't perfect, but I can't even begin to tell you how much the past year meant to me. I still see your face and hear your voice all the time, and all the places that we used to go to are now haunted. Everything that we had planned for the years ahead was just gone in the blink of an eye, and now we'll never get to know what more in life we could have experienced together.

Our parallel lives will continue to move on and we'll go about the years without each other. I know that I'll never get the answer, but I wonder if you hurt the way I do or if you even think about me from time to time. People always say the best way to get over someone is to practice gratitude, but I'm having a hard time with that. I hope I'll be able to find gratitude for all of this in time and that it won't hurt so much when your name comes up in casual conversation or when I hear that you got everything you wanted in life.

The one thing I can't seem to wrap my head around is how easy it was for you to give me your word without keeping it in the end. When it mattered and when I needed you, you were a coward and let me down and that's what hurts the most. I've never felt this way about anyone, and I don't know if I ever will again. Maybe it hurts more when you really loved someone—when you really tried.

I guess our relationship wasn't enough for you in the end. But with that being said, I know that in time, I won't feel hurt, disappointed, or even angry at you anymore, and that's when I'll know it's really over. But even as I write this now, I don't regret having loved you. I don't regret it because I know that I gave you my best and tried hard to make our relationship as strong as possible. It felt like I had the world back when I had you, but we still live in the real world where things don't work out, people don't always get what they want, and being a good person isn't the winning card we throw on the table. I never imagined that I would fall in love with you, just some guy stranded at an airport with me on New Year's Eve, but I always figured that we met for a very good reason. Maybe it was meant to teach us the lesson that some things aren't meant to last forever, no matter how

CHAPTER 13

extraordinary or important.

I know it's over, and it's not the day we met or the day it all fell apart that left the biggest mark on me. It was everything in between—all those little moments that didn't seem very important or memorable while they were happening, the ones I didn't realize were actually the most meaningful until it was all over. Now that I'm nearing the end of this letter, I finally know what to be grateful for. I'm grateful that we don't have to struggle with the distance anymore. I'm grateful that I don't have to wait on you to make up your mind or make me feel important. I'm grateful that all these words I had saved in my heart for so many months are now free. But most of all, I'm grateful that I get to love myself now the way that I loved you—with all my heart.

Olivia

Chapter 14

Two years passed before Olivia once again found herself in New York. It took some time and at least a dozen rejections, but with some pointers from Jamie's friend, Danny—who she met at a rooftop bar almost two years ago—she managed to get her manuscript into the hands of the right people and had it turned into a novel. It was the novel that brought her back to New York for the first time in years. She was there for some book signings and author events and would be flying back to Seattle soon after that to work on her next novel.

The trajectory of the past several hundred days both fascinated and unnerved her. Life moved at its own pace and the universe had plans for her that she had absolutely no idea about, but there was something really exciting about not knowing what was in store. Planning and preparing had been her comfort blanket for so long that just *existing* without expectation was scary, but it was the first time in her life that she really and truly felt free and in control. It was strange, but when she loosened her grip on things, they were free to bloom and fall into place better than she even thought possible.

She thought that being in New York would have her feeling some kind of way, but she was surprised to find that there was nothing there. There was no emotional attachment to the place anymore. It was just an empty shell, a ghost of the place where she was once in love. If she could have charted the ups and downs of their relationship, she'd have parabolas big enough to be considered mountains and valleys, but if not for those highs and lows, Olivia would have never known that she was capable of feeling such things.

Olivia stared out at the expansive city beneath her from her hotel window,

CHAPTER 14

her hair still damp from her morning shower. Her first book signing was that afternoon, and she planned on having a nice lunch, checking out a museum, and maybe doing some shopping at the vintage stores for her friends back home if she had the time. It was early summer and she knew the city would be alive with camaraderie and hidden gems and new adventures waiting around every street corner in the city that never slept.

She moved to the bathroom and ran a brush through her hair, smiling at herself as she stood barefoot in front of the bathroom mirror, still wrapped in the monogrammed hotel robe as the summer sun filtered in through the glass windows.

It was going to be a good day.

* * *

Olivia found herself still staring at a line of dozens an hour and a half later, her right hand cramping so bad that she wondered if she'd ever be able to write again.

The book signing had a bigger turnout than expected and there were now people staring at her from the second floor and friends crammed together on seats meant for one, patiently waiting as she signed copy after copy of her novel, answered questions, and took photos. She sat at a table draped with a red cloth with a box of Sharpies and her half-full iced latte sitting on top and she wore a blue satin blouse tucked into black pants with suede loafers—a very author-esque look—and wished she had worn something a little more eye-catching and bold for her first book signing, but it didn't really matter what she looked like. It was much more fulfilling knowing that her words had made an impact and made people *feel* things, made them think about their own lives, and relate to her story.

As Olivia signed another copy for a twenty-something redhead clad in a loose-fitting tee and jeans, her free hand drifted down to her thigh to pinch herself. It was hard to believe that it wasn't just a dream. Back when she wrote the first draft of her manuscript all those years ago, she never expected to pitch it or for it to sell more than a dozen copies even if it did get published, but as she looked out into the room full of people who loved her work and genuinely had an interest in what she had to say, her heart bloomed with gratitude.

"How much time do we have left?" Olivia whispered to her agent, Molly, who was standing just behind her in a stunning red suit with matching lips and nails. They had become good friends over the six months that it took to get everything in place for her novel to be published.

Molly glanced at her watch, then patted Olivia's shoulder fondly. "Just half an hour left. You're doing great. This is a really good turnout and you'll have two more signings over the next few days, so I've got my fingers crossed we'll see lots more people. You holding up okay?"

"All good." Olivia gently rolled her shoulders, tilting her head from side to side. She felt stiff from sitting but wasn't about to complain.

The next person in line set down a hardcover version of the novel, flipping open the cover to the title page. "I'd love an inscription if that's okay."

"I'm more than happy to do that." Olivia uncapped a pen and leaned over the page. "Who should I make it out to?"

When she didn't get an answer, Olivia looked up, her eyes widening as recognition set in.

"Lynn."

The two of them sat silently in Lynn's car a half hour later, parked just around the street corner from the bookstore with some coffee going cold in their laps.

"Why are we here?" Olivia glanced over at Lynn, the question coming out more abrasively than she intended. It wasn't that she had anything against Lynn, but sitting alone with Jamie's closest friend made her feel like she was repeating history and it was more than a little frightening.

"I saw the promotion for your book signing online and there were some fliers at the nearby coffee shop down Smith Street," Lynn explained. She seemed a little nervous, tapping her burgundy nails against the side of her coffee cup as she smiled uncomfortably. "Danny told me that you guys had been in touch about publishing a while back and that you'd be coming back

CHAPTER 14

to New York for a few days, so I thought I'd drop by."

"Okay, but I mean ... why are *we* here?"

It was a fair question.

They didn't keep in contact after Olivia's split with Jamie years ago, and out of all the millions of places to be in New York City on a Wednesday afternoon, sitting in Lynn's car outside of a small bookstore in Brooklyn was one of the last places she thought she'd be.

"I read your book," Lynn said. "I know it was inspired by what you and Jamie had."

"It's a work of fiction," Olivia said matter-of-factly, staring straight ahead. "I think you're giving me way too much credit here. And trust me, I'm here strictly for work purposes. I'm leaving in a few days after my book signings, so I don't know what the big fuss is about."

"I get it. I know he's been an asshole, but I also know J is the type of person to act like it didn't matter and that it didn't hurt him to lose you, but I *know* he was hurting. And I get that your time is valuable, but please give me five minutes to explain and then I'll leave you alone after I've said my piece, I promise."

Olivia looked into Lynn's eyes, gathering all the patience she had left inside of her. There was nothing to lose but five minutes of her time, so she nodded reluctantly. "Okay, I'm listening."

"I know this is going to sound absurd," Lynn said, subconsciously clutching her long-forgotten coffee cup, "but I think you should go see him before you leave."

"Why would I ever want to see him again?" The idea *was* absurd.

"Because it might change your point of view about what you had."

"I don't need to change my point of view. In fact, I'm glad things ended. I'm glad you had that conversation with me that night at the rooftop bar and I'm glad that things are over between us because I can't love someone like that. I wasn't even a second thought to him, and he made that *very* clear in the end." There was an awkward moment of silence—one that stretched on for a few seconds too long and made Olivia wonder if maybe she had been a little harsh—but then Lynn smiled, a compassionate one that felt surprising yet satisfactory. "Speaking of that night at the rooftop bar, I never got to thank you."

"For making you doubt Jamie?"

Olivia let out a laugh, one that was genuine. She relaxed into Lynn's passenger seat and took a sip of the cold coffee. "Well, *yeah*. You were the only person who was honest with me. You saw what was going on and told me the truth."

Lynn shifted in her seat, a faraway look in her eyes. "Truth hurts. And seriously, I'm sorry if I said too much that night. You and J broke up almost immediately afterward and I always had a feeling that it was because of what I said. I didn't know if I'd ever get a chance to see you again or to apologize in person. When I heard from Danny that you were coming here again, I just knew I had to tell you in person and say that it was never my intention to hurt you."

"I never blamed you. And it's for the best," Olivia reassured her. "I promise. If Jamie and I were supposed to work out, we would still be together today. And we aren't." She sucked in a breath. "But how are you and Ryan?"

"Not horrible." It was rare to see Lynn looking bashful, but there was no other way to describe her expression as she held her left hand out for Olivia to see. Sitting on her ring finger was a sparkling diamond in a modern marquise cut. "Our wedding is next May."

"I'm so happy for you! Congratulations to you and Ryan," Olivia gushed, pulling the other woman into a hug across the console. "With your taste and style and Ryan's cuisine expertise, it'll be a hell of a memorable wedding."

"Thank you so much. We're getting J's dad to do the catering. He always said he'd give us a good deal if we ever made it this far as a couple," she laughed, leaning back in her seat with a faraway look in her eyes. "I get to spend the rest of my life with that idiot and I'm so ridiculously happy about it." She glanced at Olivia. "I know it's not my place to say this, but I really think you should go talk to Jamie. So much has changed since you last saw him."

"You think that we'll get back together or something?"

"I don't think anything." Lynn shrugged, tapping her fingernails against the

CHAPTER 14

steering wheel. "Maybe I'm just reaching here, but it feels like you wrote that book as a way to tell him everything you didn't get to say. But you're literally in the same city now and maybe your life circumstances have changed enough to make things work this time around."

"Sure, maybe every writer is inspired by someone or something, but I wrote every word and created every character and set every scene. I did it for myself, to give myself closure and hope. Jamie inspired it, but I finished it."

"Good." A little smile danced across Lynn's pink lips. "Anyway, I've held you hostage for long enough. I keep my promises, so I'm gonna let you go now." She popped open the car door and stepped out, regarding Olivia in the afternoon light with new understanding and respect. "Give me a shout if you're ever in my neck of the woods again, okay?"

"Will do."

"Oh, and in case you change your mind, take this." Lynn gave Olivia a small piece of notebook paper, folded in half with something scrawled inside.

"Thanks." She didn't have to ask what it was—she already knew.

As she walked down the block to her car, Olivia closed her fist around the piece of paper, crushing it.

* * *

It was two in the morning.

Olivia rolled over in her hotel bed. There was the comforting hum of the air conditioner as she snuggled underneath her sheets, breathing in that distinct smell that hotels always seemed to have—something clean and warm and woody—but she still couldn't sleep.

She had ordered room service for one earlier, wearing the same hotel robe she wore getting ready that morning. She was set to grab dinner with her agent, Molly, at the end of their trip, and a small part of Olivia wanted to call and vent, but Molly slept through anything—even a fire alarm—so there was no point.

She threw the covers over her shoulders and squeezed her eyes shut, trying hard to push back against the memories that were starting to surface, the ones that had been locked away.

Another hour passed, but sleep didn't come.

Frustrated, Olivia slipped out of bed and flicked on the bedside lamp, pulling her hair back in a ponytail. She went into the bathroom, splashed some cold water on her face, and stared at herself in the mirror, studying the flecks of brown in her eyes as if looking into the eyes of a stranger.

Her unexpected meeting with Lynn came back in echoes and snippets, their conversation replaying in Olivia's mind over and over.

She had little idea about who Jamie was anymore. She knew nothing about his life and the past two years remained a giant question mark for her.

Olivia curled back up in bed and pulled out her phone, slipping on her glasses as she went to her social media accounts. One by one, she unblocked Jamie from each one, her heart thumping.

It had been a long time since she last looked. She didn't want to be someone who scoured social media in a moment of weakness for any clue that he had moved on—or hadn't. Every picture of him with some girl she didn't recognize, every impromptu trip he took with friends that he promised they'd take together, every new post or comment that pushed their history down further—it would be a different kind of hell watching him forget her or even *pretend* to forget her.

Keeping his existence confined to the other side of the country helped her move on.

Little by little, day by day, that ache and memory finally began to fade. But now, for the first time in years, images and details of his life without her popped up one after the other and she was back in the belly of the beast, though she was prepared for it this time around.

Relationship status? Single.

Profile picture? Brand new.

New friends? Quite a few.

Olivia continued scrolling for a few minutes, surprised to find that their old photos were still left up after all that time, little fragments and snapshots of their past relationship suspended in time.

CHAPTER 14

There was one that made her pause. It had been taken a few years back at his parents' place, with the two of them laughing over something while curled up on the couch. She had one arm around Jamie's neck and the other over her mouth as she tried to cover up a big laugh. Jamie had been looking right at her, his eyes crinkled with joy as he joined in.

They had been so young and in love, but Lynn was wrong. It was too late to get back what they had and Olivia had come too far to fall back into those same patterns. In a city full of strangers and lovers, she and Jamie were somewhere in between—they were just two people who got to share a pocket of time together and made something special that only lasted for a fleeting moment.

A car honked in the distance and she could hear the hustle and bustle of the city below, even on the tenth floor. It was almost four in the morning by then, and it felt like a coincidence that she had insomnia in the city that never slept.

Groaning, she lifted herself out of bed again and trudged over to where her bag sat on the glass table. She was going to hate herself for it, but she did it anyway. Reaching in, she felt around the bottom of the bag until her fingertips brushed against some crumpled paper. She pulled it out, studying it in the dim light.

Olivia unfolded the paper carefully, smoothing out the edges and ironing out the wrinkles in the middle with her fingers, the letters and numbers of an address that Lynn had written down.

It was crazy how quickly the past came rushing back to her.

* * *

"Oat milk or almond?"

"What?" Olivia looked up from her phone. She was in line at a coffee shop she hadn't heard of before, just a block away from Jamie's new place. "Sorry, I didn't catch that."

The barista, a petite teenager with countless stacked rings and a ponytail extension, snapped her gum between her teeth in annoyance and repeated,

"Oat milk or almond?"

"Oh, almond. Thanks." Olivia pretended not to see the barista's eye roll and dropped a few dollars in the tip jar anyway.

She left the coffee shop with her almond milk latte and took a sip.

It was bitter and tasted like regular milk.

Resisting the urge to roll *her* eyes, Olivia adjusted the tote bag strap sitting on her shoulder and started walking down the block, keeping an eye out for one brownstone in particular. She kept it casual that day with faded blue jeans and a white tee and sneakers, barely a trace of makeup on her face. It wasn't like she was going to talk to him or see him. It was almost noon on a weekday and most people were already at work.

Olivia shielded her eyes from the sun, slowing to a stop in front of a brownstone apartment that looked just like all the other ones on the block. She couldn't see through the windows and there was nothing special on the outside. It was just a regular building, one of a million in New York to the everyday onlooker.

But inside, it was where Jamie slept every night, where he cooked Mexican dinner dishes and had friends over for board games on Saturday evenings, where he read his books and watched his shows and spent time with family when they visited. It was where he lived and breathed and existed.

It felt good to see that little place. It wasn't hers and Jamie would never know that she had stopped by, but it felt like closure in some way. He had moved on with his life and she had moved on with hers, and it was all good.

She smiled, taking another sip of her mediocre latte as she started to walk away. She wondered if his heart was still a little fractured or if it had healed completely, leaving an invisible scar that only Jamie could feel. She wondered if he still had love for her. Or more realistically, if he even just thought about her from time to time.

Either way, it was time to leave it all behind now because everything that she had saved in her heart was in that book. It was time to close the chapter with Jamie for good. She also no longer felt like a bystander the way she did all those years ago when she first visited New York—she was now part of the moving picture, part of the kaleidoscope of color and noise and brilliance.

CHAPTER 14

As she rounded the corner, she saw Jamie coming in her direction with his arms full of groceries. Even with her sunglasses on, Olivia was certain it was him.

"*Shit*," she hissed, scanning desperately for an emergency exit. Other than some skinny trees and a parked Volvo, the options for a good hiding spot were few and far between.

Clutching her latte so hard that the paper cup started to crumple, she kept her head down and turned around to head back in the direction she came, her cheeks burning red with embarrassment and anxiety.

"Olivia?" There were rapid footsteps behind her as Jamie jogged to catch up with her. "Is that you?"

With nowhere else to go and no other option but to face her consequences, Olivia turned around slowly, taking her sunglasses off so she could look right at the man she used to know.

There was a split second of surprise and unfamiliarity in his gaze, almost as if he didn't recognize her, but then his eyes softened a moment later.

"Hi," she said.

Jamie took a step forward, closing the distance between them. "Hi."

With his bags of groceries as a physical barricade, the two of them regarded each other carefully with curiosity and caution.

"Liv, it's been so long." Jamie finally spoke again. "Wow, I just—I don't know what to say. What are you doing here?"

He still looked the same in some ways, but mostly different. His hair had gotten longer and was now pulled back in a bun, and hard-earned muscles stuck out from behind a white tee and light chinos. There was a sprinkle of stubble across his jaw that made him look slightly older, and an air of newfound confidence that seemed to waft from him without effort. Judging by the amount of food he was buying from a grocery store known for its overpriced organic goods, Olivia made the assumption that he was living alone.

"Yeah, it has been some time, hasn't it? I'm actually here for work."

"What do you mean? You work here now?"

"Not exactly. It's for some book signings here since I published my first one about two months ago. My agent figured it'd be good marketing for a new author," Olivia explained, keeping her tone casual. She didn't want to go into detail about it. "I'm leaving soon, though. Then it's back to work on the next one."

Jamie set his bags on the sidewalk and opened his arms wide, pulling her into a hug that felt way too familiar and way too foreign all at once. "Congrats! That's amazing, Liv." He pulled back, looking slightly embarrassed as he shook his head. "Sorry, I got carried away. I'm just really happy for you. You deserve it."

"Thanks." Her eyes trailed to the yolky puddle slowly making its way from the bottom of Jamie's paper bags. "Um, I think your bags are leaking."

"What?" Jamie followed her gaze to the yellow slowly making its way toward his feet. "Oh, shit. I must have dropped those bags harder than I thought. Those eggs are goners."

"It's egg homicide," she chuckled. "Here, let me help you destroy the evidence."

"Thanks. My place is just around the corner from here, so we're in luck." Jamie picked up one of the paper bags, cradling the soggy bottom as he fished for the keys in his pocket. He shot a conspiratorial smile at her. "I always wanted a partner in crime."

The two of them brought the soggy bags over to the sink and found the soaked culprits at the bottom. Olivia salvaged a few unbroken eggs and tossed the gooey cardboard containers, rinsing her hands under the faucet as Jamie made a face at his yolk-covered hands.

"You could use some of the broken ones to make French toast so it's not a total loss," she said.

"You always have good ideas." He shot her a smile, then looked away. He pulled a hand through his disheveled hair, suddenly acutely aware of how he looked to her right then: unkempt, clumsy, unable to put two words together, and still wearing the same shirt he wore to sleep the night before to go on his morning grocery run. "Shoot, where are my manners?" he laughed. "Do you want to stay for a few minutes for coffee? I was just about to make some."

CHAPTER 14

"No, it's okay. I—" She glanced over at her lousy latte sitting on his counter, barely touched. "Actually, some tea or coffee would be great."

"Why don't you take a seat then?" he asked, clearing off an armchair littered with papers and a laptop. "Sorry, it's a little messy. I wasn't expecting guests, but welcome to my humble abode."

The living room was airy and light with cream-colored curtains and shiny bookshelves crammed with folders and books for his work, and little trinkets collected from various vacations. Colorful paper boats sat on top of a table next to a vintage camera and a succulent. Art prints were scattered around the room while snake plants peeked from corners.

From where Olivia stood, she could see his bedroom door slightly ajar just down the hall, teasing her with a glimpse of a life that she no longer knew anything about. It was hard to imagine that, once upon a time, they slept tangled together in bed with their noses touching and their breaths mingling, night after night. All those times they'd intertwine their legs and tell stories, laughing over something stupid and interrupting each other's sentences seemed so far away. "This is a really nice neighborhood and place, Jamie. When did you move in?" she asked.

Jamie paused, shoving his hands into his pockets. "About two years ago. I just felt like it was time to get a place of my own."

"Right."

"Anyway, I'm going to make the coffee. Make yourself comfortable." He quickly moved to the kitchen, wanting to kick himself for making it so obvious that he moved out immediately after their split at the time. Even worse, he had invited her in when they hadn't spoken in ages and had nothing to talk about. He never thought he'd see her again, but there she was appearing on his doorstep like in the movies, and a part of him wondered if maybe he was dreaming it all up.

Jamie picked up the two mugs and took them back to the living room where Olivia sat politely and stiffly on the couch, the sunlight lighting up her face through the window.

"Thanks." She accepted the mug he offered and took a tentative sip as Jamie took a seat across from her, the space and silence growing. "Are you working today?" she asked, attempting for casualness.

"Yeah, in a couple of hours. Still palliative care. It's not the happiest place on Earth, but I guess it's how you look at the situation too. The people there can teach you more about life in a single shift than some people learn in a lifetime."

"Got any good advice for me then?"

"Oh, plenty," Jamie said, grinning. "How much time ya got?"

She laughed, the sound of it so familiar that the dull ache from losing her all those years ago started to gnaw at him. He studied her discreetly over the rim of his coffee mug. Her hair was lighter and shorter than it used to be, and the way she carried herself had a new air of maturity and wisdom.

She looked nice. Healthy. Happy.

After catching up for a bit, Olivia set her mug on the coffee table and stood up, dusting off the seat of her pants. "Well, it was great seeing you. I'm glad you're doing well," she said, reaching for her tote bag. "And thanks for the coffee."

"Yeah, of course. Anytime."

He walked her to the door, realizing that it was nice to see her doing so well—that was all he ever really wanted for her anyway. He opened the door, close enough to Olivia that the sweet smell of the lemongrass soap she used that morning was evident, close enough that he questioned his resolve for a moment. "Hey, Liv?"

She turned around, halfway out the door, and looked at him with those big, brown eyes. "Yeah?"

"If you're free tomorrow night, do you want to have dinner together? I can cook and you can take care of dessert. That way, we'll get a chance to actually catch up before you leave." He paused, looking a little shy and uncertain all of a sudden. "I mean, if you want to, that is."

"Sure, why not?"

"Great!" Jamie grinned, watching as she made her way down the front steps, a summer breeze sweeping her hair back from her face. "I'll see you tomorrow at seven then."

"I'll be there." Olivia threw a wave over her left shoulder, keeping her eyes

CHAPTER 14

straight ahead as she made her way down the block, aware that Jamie was still watching her from his doorstep.

Chapter 15

It was a bad idea. The whole way from her hotel to Jamie's brownstone apartment the next evening, Olivia kept wondering if she was maybe making the biggest mistake of her life. Some things were better left behind and buried away, and now they were digging up the grave together.

But it was also likely that she was blowing things out of proportion and things were not as stressful as they seemed. It had been years since they last spoke and she was sure that two adults were more than capable of having a civil dinner together and talking about things other than who they had slept with or what their parents *really* thought about them together back then.

Raking in a deep breath to calm her racing heart, she made her way up to Jamie's front door and knocked. She wore a floral wrap dress with a pair of espadrille wedges and a little bit of makeup. It was nice that even though they didn't end on good terms, time and distance gave them enough space to process everything and to maybe have a friendship instead.

She heard Jamie's footsteps, then she was greeted by his welcoming smile and the scent of something delicious wafting from inside. "Hey, glad you made it," he said, hugging her with one arm, an oven mitt still on his hand. "You're just in time. Give me a few more minutes to finish up, but make yourself comfortable."

Olivia handed him a blue bakery box. "It's a chocolate-raspberry torte. Hope you're a fan."

"I'm always a fan of Malcolm's Bakery. It's one of the best ones here. How'd you know?"

"As someone who enjoys dessert more than actual meals, I'd say it comes

CHAPTER 15

from experience," she replied, moving past him in the doorway. "Wow, the place looks amazing. Look at you with your fancy, grown-up napkins and matching plates and all."

"Bit of a change from my usual takeout box, but let's keep that a secret between us." Jamie smiled warmly at her, walking backward toward the kitchen. "You look really nice, by the way."

"Thanks. You don't look too shabby yourself," she replied, noticing his fresh button-up tucked neatly into some dark pants and fading summer sunlight made his skin glow after a fresh shave. His hair was still slightly damp from a shower and the smell of his eucalyptus body wash trailed after him as he moved around the apartment. "What's on the menu tonight?"

"Take a seat at the table and you'll find out in a sec."

She did a little drum roll on the edge of the table with her hands. "I'm ready!" she called back.

Jamie emerged from the kitchen wearing a chef's hat that looked incredibly stupid and lopsided, making her laugh. "Tonight," he said, "we have fresh rolls, potato salad, Tuscan shrimp and garlic pasta, and pear punch. To finish it off, we have a chocolate-raspberry torte, courtesy of our bestselling author here."

"Ha. Funny." She raised her brow, smirking. "In all seriousness, you've outdone yourself with dinner. Everything looks great."

Jamie took a seat across from her and poured them both some punch, wondering if he had made the right decision by getting something non-alcoholic. It had been years since he last had a meal with her, but he didn't want to make assumptions. "I'm glad you approve. I don't usually cook this much because it's just myself here. Shifts are long and exhausting sometimes and I just want to grab some takeout, watch some crappy reality show, and then scrub the day away. When you live alone, you get to do anything you want and it's great, but then the caveat is that you become this lazy slob sometimes. So, thank you for making me put on a fresh shirt today."

"I'm going to be leaving for Seattle in a few days after my book signings are done, but I have something for those days when you just want to be a hermit crab at home." Olivia reached into her bag and took something out. She passed him a rectangular package wrapped in blue paper. "I'm going to ruin the surprise and tell you that it's exactly what you think it is."

Jamie unwrapped it with care, his eyes widening as he uncovered the hardcover edition of her novel, the front cover glistening underneath the lights.

"I promised I'd save you a copy a long time ago," she said, shooting him a smile that verged on the side of flirtatious. "Lucky for you, you don't need to go to my book signing tomorrow in order to get a signed copy."

Jamie laughed. "Liv, this is incredible," he exclaimed, flipping to the title page to find that she had signed it and written a little note just for him. "I'm so happy for you."

"Thanks."

He reached across the table to rest his hand over hers. "This calls for a toast." Jamie picked up his glass and held it high. "To dreams coming true."

Olivia followed suit and raised hers too, her hand still tingling from where Jamie's fingertips had been resting just a moment ago. "To dreams coming true," she echoed.

It was like nothing had changed that summer evening.

They ate and talked and laughed, enjoying fresh rolls and bites of pasta in between old jokes and new stories. When Jamie got up to clear the table, Olivia helped him gather the plates and bowls for the dishwasher, grateful for something to do with her hands. The two of them working together in silence while side by side made her miss something she never got to have with him.

It could've been a simple life together doing mundane tasks like cleaning up the kitchen, going grocery shopping on the weekends, coming home to each other after a long day at work, and falling asleep knowing they'd have another day together tomorrow.

Jamie tapped on her shoulder, snapping her out of her thoughts. "Want to have dessert outside?" he asked. "There's a place I want to show you."

She followed him as he grabbed two forks and the torte, leading her up

CHAPTER 15

several floors to the rooftop deck. It gave them a generous view of the skyscrapers and buildings beyond as the sun dipped lower in the summer sky, the atmosphere burning in orange and yellow hues.

To their surprise and delight, there was not a single soul up on that deck with them that evening.

"Here." Jamie took a seat on an empty wooden bench in front of a rectangular planter bursting with flowers. "Let's claim these seats before some of my neighbors get a chance to."

Olivia sat beside him, looking up at the sky and watching as two birds flew in dizzying circles above them, the faint sounds of the city dancing through the wind like music notes. "Surprisingly peaceful here. I didn't think you'd get much peace and quiet living in New York."

"Maybe it just depends on where you look." Jamie set the torte between them on the bench and passed her a fork. "It's like my little getaway here. I know it's hard to get some space in this city, let alone peace and quiet. So, when I see one of my neighbors up here, I just go right back down to my apartment to give them some time to breathe and do what they need to do. They do the same thing for me when they see me up here. It's like our unspoken rule, and we don't mess with it."

Olivia laughed, accepting the fork and cutting into the torte with the tines. "It's a good rule. I like it. But I don't think I'll need to be that stingy in Seattle. Lucky for me, I have plenty of places to go when I need to just be alone." She took a bite of the cake.

"Speaking of Seattle, how are things at home? How's your mom doing?"

"She's doing great. We've been traveling a lot more recently. We just went to Taiwan and Japan, actually."

Jamie grinned. "I remember you telling me she always wanted to go."

"Well, now that we both have a little more time and money on our hands, why not?" She took another bite of cake. "What about your parents? I heard your dad is still in the catering business."

"Yeah, they're doing great. My dad's going to be catering for Lynn's wedding. She and Ryan are getting married next year, if you can believe it." Jamie paused, keeping his gaze ahead. "How did you know my dad was still doing catering?"

"A little bird told me so."

"I'm willing to bet a million dollars that little bird is Lynn."

"Congrats, you just became a millionaire," Olivia cheekily replied, taking another bite. "I ran into her the other day at my book signing."

"Was it fate or meddling?"

"The latter," she laughed.

Jamie rolled his eyes, smiling. "Figures. Us meddling New Yorkers are the worst."

They ate their dessert in comfortable silence and watched as the sky eventually darkened into a gorgeous navy. A gentle wind swept past them, warm and sweet. Jamie closed his eyes, trying to hold on to the moment for as long as possible. A lot was going on in his mind—he had questions he wanted to ask and things he wanted to say, but he knew he didn't deserve it.

It had been ages since he had been able to talk with someone the way he talked to Olivia that night. He would never admit it to her, but nothing had been the same after she left. He couldn't even really say that he was able to love anyone else, because nothing felt remotely like the magic they once had.

It was just a simple dinner together to catch up, but it was at that moment that Jamie realized it had been a mistake. His dinner invitation had turned into an invitation to break his heart all over again, another invitation to regret all the ways he had messed things up for them.

She seemed happier without him, even if she would never admit it to his face.

Olivia was saying something to him now, but he couldn't make out the words as his thoughts drowned everything else out. She traced out patterns in the sky with her hands, oblivious to the fact that it was breaking Jamie's heart to realize that she still remembered all the constellations he taught her to recognize so long ago in Texas. His gaze trailed to her lips, and part of him ached to press his mouth against hers.

Jamie stood up suddenly. "You'll have to excuse me, Liv. I think I'm going to go downstairs for some water," he said, his words coming out quickly. "I'm gonna get us some water and then I'll be back. Just stay here, okay? I'll

CHAPTER 15

be back in a second."

"What? I can go down with you." Olivia stared up at him. "It's not a big deal."

"No, you should just stay here," he said, his eyes darting from her to the stairs. He licked his lips, which felt drier than his throat. "I'll be right back."

Without waiting for her reply, he went back down the stairs to his apartment. He went inside, shut the door, and leaned against it, planting his face in his hands in disbelief.

God, he was going to pass out. He was sure of it. He slid down to sit on the floor, his back still against the door.

He heard Olivia knock. "Jamie, are you okay?"

"Yeah!" he called back, brightening his tone. "I'll be back out in a sec. Just give me a moment."

There was a pause, then her voice drifted through again, a little quieter this time. "Jamie, please open the door. I know you're not in the kitchen getting water."

Raking in a breath, he reached up and unlocked the door, letting Olivia in at last. She stepped into his apartment and noticed him sitting on the floor with his back against the wall, the smile falling from her face as she searched his eyes, a concerned expression taking place instead.

"You're shaking," she commented, pointing to his hands. Joining him on the floor, she took his hands in hers and gave them a reassuring squeeze, worried that it was something she had said or done. "What's going on?"

"Nothing. I'm fine. I'm just a little dizzy," he lied. "I went on a long run in Central Park this morning and I think I overdid it."

"Let me get you some water. I don't want you to get up and—"

"No, it's okay," he interrupted, his hand shooting out to stop her. "I think I'd like it if we just sat for a minute. Can you do that?"

"Sure." Olivia sat back down, still staring at him. "I can do that."

A sense of dread sat in the pit of Jamie's stomach, embarrassed that he was making such a big deal out of nothing and making such a scene in front of the one person from his past that he still cared deeply for. He rested his forehead on his knees and closed his eyes, acutely aware of her presence and her touch and her *everything*.

Just moments ago, they were sitting together on the roof of his apartment building, eating cake and talking as if nothing had changed between them, but the truth was that everything had changed. The fact that he still felt the urge to kiss her and to spend time with her made it glaringly obvious to Jamie that he wasn't as over her as he thought he was.

But she was happier without him. The thought killed him, but it was true.

He should have called her more often, been more supportive and honest, and held her more closely—but the thing he regretted most was not having been a man of his word. If he had done more to show that he was serious about them ending up together, maybe they'd still be in love.

Maybe they'd be engaged or planning for a family or traveling the world together. Maybe she really had been the one for him, and he let her get away.

He felt Olivia's arms gently wrap around his shoulders, grounding him as the dull ache in his chest began to slowly fade away. It could have been a few minutes or a few hours that they sat there together on his living room floor, but Jamie was painfully aware of the fact that it was probably the only time she'd hold him like that again. And he almost didn't want it to stop.

He wanted so much more, but he knew that he didn't deserve it. Not anymore.

Softly, so softly that it was barely above a whisper, he said, "We were happy back then, Liv."

He felt Olivia stiffen, her arms resting around his shoulders heavy with hesitation. "What?"

"We were happy," he repeated. "A long time ago."

"It was a long time ago, but we were."

Jamie swallowed. "I know it doesn't matter anymore, but I sometimes wish that things were different between us."

"Different how?"

"Well, we wouldn't be strangers."

"We're not strangers."

Jamie laughed, but it sounded sad and broken. "Liv, we haven't talked in years. You didn't even tell me you were here in New York, though I can't

CHAPTER 15

blame you for that. We've both moved on with own lives while disappearing from the other person's. Wouldn't you call that being strangers?"

"Maybe, but that's what happens after a breakup. You move on." Olivia pulled back, studying him beside her. "Can you please look at me now?"

He finally pulled his face from his knees and looked at her, his lower lashes wet with tears.

"Are you okay?" she asked, still unsure about why he was suddenly so emotional over something that happened so long ago.

"Honestly? Not really. I hate the fact that I let you go so easily. I hate the fact that I messed things up." He looked away, his voice breaking. "When things ended, it felt like I was losing my best friend, my confidante, and my partner, all at once. I know I was an asshole about everything, and I'm just really sorry about all of it. I still feel responsible for things ending, and seeing you again just made me realize that I never got to tell you that."

"You're not the only one who messed things up. I should take responsibility too. It was easy for me to blame you for the way you made me feel in the end, but I put myself in a position to be hurt in the first place. I believed you even when there was no guarantee of things working out. I held onto that promise you made *so* hard, almost too hard. And when I realized that you weren't going to follow through with it, I just ran."

"I should've done more to keep it."

"Maybe, but neither of us was perfect when it came to dealing with the distance. At the end of the day, you chose to stay in New York and I chose to stay in Seattle. Neither one of us was willing to sacrifice the life we already built while apart, and that's just a consequence we're going to have to live with for the rest of our lives." It was strangely therapeutic to say that, so Olivia said it again, almost to herself this time. "What's done is done, and we're just going to have to live with it."

"Do you wish that things were different?"

"Sometimes," Olivia admitted. "Do you?"

Jamie faced her again, a pained expression on his face as he met her gaze. "Every day."

"Why didn't you say something? From the way you were acting after we broke up, it seemed like you were perfectly fine."

A laugh burst from Jamie's lips and he shook his head, embarrassed. "God, don't remind me. I acted like an asshole. I knew I couldn't give you what you needed at the time, so it felt pointless to reach out or explain myself. I just wanted to forget you and move on as quickly as possible because it hurt to think about you. I knew that I had fucked things up and I didn't know if I'd ever get a chance to make things right again, so I just *kept* fucking things up because it didn't seem to matter anymore. It wasn't like anything was going to bring you back to me."

"Well, I'm here now." Olivia looked at him, her expression unreadable. "I'm here with you."

It was so silent in his apartment that Jamie could hear his own breath and racing heart, a mixture of fear and courage simultaneously coursing through his veins. "I know. I just never got a chance to apologize for screwing things up so much, for all the things I said and did afterward. I know it won't make things right again, but I just need you to know that I mean it. You deserve that much."

"I forgive you, Jamie. Really, I do. I don't want this to weigh on you anymore," Olivia said, moving closer. "Promise me that you'll let it go?"

"I promise." Jamie paused, then let out a big laugh. "Here we go again with promises."

"Okay, no promises then. But just say you'll try."

"I'll try." He nodded at her, a smile finally returning to his face.

"What matters is us being happy now, in the present. And all I ever wanted back then was to know that you really loved me." She blinked, her eyes searching his for some confirmation that what they had in the past was just as special and beautiful to him as it was to her.

"Olivia," he said, "I never *stopped* loving you."

In the seconds that followed, the weight of all the time and love they had wasted in the past two years came crashing down on them all at once. The kiss that followed was a desperate attempt to make up for all the time that had slipped right through their fingers, one that somehow perfectly conveyed everything that words couldn't anymore.

CHAPTER 15

Neither of them wanted to be the first to break away, the kiss sweet and familiar in a way that only lovers knew. Jamie tangled his hands deep in her hair, holding her tightly to him, afraid to let go again.

Still kissing, they moved to Jamie's bedroom and she let him undress her, his impatient hands making quick work of the ties that kept her dress in place. She lay back on his sheets, watching as he pulled his shirt over his head and tossed it to the side of the bed, exposing his tan skin and taut muscles. Bending down to place gentle kisses along her neck, he asked if she was sure.

He was breathing a little hard, and his dark hair was falling into his eyes as he propped himself above her. Olivia reached up and smoothed his hair out of the way, her eyes sparkling as she looked up at him.

Instead of answering, she pressed her lips against his and pulled him down to her, holding on tight as he started moving against her with urgency, closing the space between their bodies at last.

* * *

It was a dream.

Olivia woke up the next morning and her first thought was that it had been some unhinged dream, that none of it had happened. But then she saw her dress on Jamie's floor and realized she was still in his bed, wrapped in his navy sheets.

There was no mistake about it—last night definitely happened.

Rubbing her eyes, she sat up in bed and looked around the room. Except for the little indent in the shape of Jamie's head on the pillow next to hers, there was no sign of him anywhere that morning. Slipping out of bed, she picked her dress up from the floor and pulled it on, the memory of how quickly it had come off just hours ago still fresh on her mind.

"Jamie?" She padded tentatively down the hallway into the living room, the hardwood floor cold against her bare feet. "Are you here?"

There was no reply.

She moved to the kitchen and found a note on the fridge saying he had to leave early for work that morning but would be back around three in the afternoon. He gave her the address to a coffee shop nearby and asked to meet there later—he had even drawn a little smiley face and left her the spare key to his apartment.

As Olivia poured herself a glass of water from a pitcher by the sink, she peered out the window at the bustling and bright city outside, their passionate and impulsive actions from last night finally sinking in. It was crazy what a dash of vulnerability and a whole lot of courage could do.

She stood by the sink for a long time, wondering what it was that kept pulling the two of them back together, her baffled reflection in the glass of water she was holding offering no answers either.

Grabbing her bag from the couch where she left it the night before, she took one last look around at the home that Jamie had built without her and left, knowing exactly what she had to do.

* * *

All day, despite having an overload of work and not much sleep to go on, Jamie could not get his mind off of Olivia.

He swore he could still see her face from last night as she slept soundly beside him, with her hair resting gently on the pillow and the steady rise and fall of her breath lulling them both into a dreamless sleep.

As Jamie went through his duties at the clinic and tried his best to focus, flashbacks of the way she fit in his arms and the smell of her skin nearly consumed him.

As soon as his shift was over, he left the clinic in a hurry and rushed back to his apartment to shower and change. He wasn't sure if Olivia saw his note about the coffee shop, but he was hoping that she was free and that he'd get to see her again for a little bit. It was stupid, but he didn't even think to ask for her number or the address of the hotel she was staying at.

Everything had happened so quickly last night and if she just happened to be free that afternoon to meet him, he wanted to make sure to keep his word and not keep her waiting any longer.

He opened the door to his apartment and saw that the note on the fridge

CHAPTER 15

had been removed and placed by the kitchen sink instead, so he knew she had seen it. Flipping it over, Jamie scanned the piece of paper to see if she had written back to him or responded in some way, but there was nothing.

He hopped into the shower to get ready anyway, scrubbing the day away under a stream of hot water while singing along to a Sinatra song. Ten minutes later, he stepped out of the shower and wrapped a towel around his waist, staring at his foggy reflection in the bathroom mirror. The lingering smell of the perfume that Olivia had worn last night was the only indication that she had ever been in his apartment. Although he felt stupid thinking it, the thought of her flying back to Seattle and the final remnants of her fading away into nothing once again made him inexplicably sad.

Seeing her again had given him more clarity, in some ways. He knew that he still loved her, even if their relationship had been far from perfect. It was still love and he still wanted to make it work. It felt crazy, but he couldn't shake the feeling that seeing her again was meant to be.

It had been so easy to make excuses for himself and his behavior back then because it was easier to avoid the issue and defend himself than face the very real possibility of losing her. He had been a coward, but he was done being scared.

Jamie rushed to the coffee shop and made it just in time, saving a small, cozy table for them near the back and keeping his eyes peeled for any sign of a brunette walking through the entrance for the next hour. It was starting to feel a little too warm in there, and he rubbed his perspiring palms down the front of his jeans, wondering if he had been presumptuous to think that she'd be there to meet him when she never said she would.

An hour and a half later, he went home. Olivia never showed up, not that he could blame her. It had been a strange night and he was pretty sure he had messed things up by being so candid and forward about everything. Maybe she was avoiding him that day and needed to think things through.

At home, he put on a show but barely paid attention to what was happening on the screen. As he sat alone on the living room couch, he caught sight of Olivia's book from the corner of his eye, the one she had gifted him just last night. He picked it up and thumbed through the first few pages, feeling like he was going through her journal in some way because of how personal and full of heart her writing was.

As he started to read, he swore he could almost hear her voice. There was a piece of her in every sentence, a part of Olivia that he was only now just seeing for the first time.

For two hours, Jamie sat there and read by himself, turning page after page and falling deeper into the fictional world she had created as reality faded away into the background. Maybe it was because the book was the only tangible thing of hers that he had left or the sheer adrenaline and curiosity coursing through his body, but he couldn't put the book down until he got to the very last page.

Pinching the bridge of his nose, he closed his eyes and fell back onto the couch cushions, his thoughts racing at a hundred miles an hour.

Olivia had written about *them*.

There were echoes of who they used to be, hidden behind the facade of new characters with different names and different settings. It was a romantic suspense novel with the main characters facing all kinds of otherworldly forces and situations, but there were threads of conversation and memories buried beneath them that Jamie already knew all too well, ones that had been tattooed on his heart from ages ago.

Their relationship came back to him in a burning, blazing red. Olivia had spent their time apart immortalizing what they had, cemented in dialogue and characters and worlds that only they knew. He could read between all the lines to see them for what it truly was—a love letter written for someone who didn't deserve it.

The main characters got the happy ending and the character development needed for the sequel, and it hit Jamie that he had been a complete idiot. Olivia had written the book to give herself closure, to give herself the perfect ending that she wanted and deserved—but never got—because he let her down when it mattered most.

Jamie leaned his head back against the couch cushions, blinking away the wetness gathering on his lashes.

The worst part of it all was that he couldn't even reach out to her to talk

CHAPTER 15

about it.

But as luck would have it, he heard three knocks on his apartment door an hour later. Jumping off the couch and nearly tripping over the coffee table in his flustered state, Jamie swung open the door and saw Olivia there, looking calm and collected with her hands in her blue jumpsuit pockets.

"Hi," he said, a little breathlessly.

"Hey."

"I'm glad you caught me. I wanted to reach you but realized I didn't have your number or anything."

"That's okay." Her lips pulled up in a polite smile, very different from the carefree grin she had been wearing when they were together just last night. "We should talk."

"You want to come in?"

"Actually, I was wondering if you'd want to take a walk with me instead." Olivia moved to the side of the entrance, allowing him to catch a glimpse of the taxi parked on the street. "I know you run around Central Park a lot and I'd love to visit before going back to Seattle." She offered him her hand. "Come with me? I know we need to figure out the state of us and where we stand."

* * *

It was gorgeous in Central Park that evening, with the summer heat taking a small break as the city drew closer to sunset.

The two of them walked side by side underneath the grove of American elms, the dappled light breaking through the canopy of green just enough to kiss their faces. Olivia looked up at the trees overhead, brushing her hair away from her flushed cheeks.

"It almost feels like you're in a cathedral, with the way the trees are bent like that over us. I bet it's even more beautiful in autumn," she noted, tilting her head up.

Jamie looked up at the trees too, the ones he had already seen hundreds of times, almost surprised to be seeing Central Park through Olivia's fresh eyes.

She had always been so curious and had an appreciation for the small details. Jamie tucked his hands into the pockets of his shorts, a small breeze ruffling the front of his linen shirt as he took another step beside her. "Yeah, it's one of those places that feels special every day of the year," he said. "I never get tired of it. I'm sorry I never brought you. Thinking back, I should've brought you here a long time ago."

Olivia laughed, dismissing his apology with an easy wave of her hand. "You're not a tour guide, Jamie. I was just happy to be able to see you and spend time with you in New York. It didn't matter where we went or what we did. All I ever wanted was to be with you. That's it. That's where my happy place was."

"I know, but I still should've taken you. You brought it up so many times back then and it always just slipped past me that you wanted to come here."

The two of them made their way over the iconic Bow Bridge, stopping right in the middle as Olivia gazed out at Central Park Lake, resting her hands on the marble railing. She turned to look at him, squinting her eyes a little in the sun. "It's all good. You don't have to apologize for every little thing, you know."

"Speaking of little things," he said, "what happened this afternoon? I left you a note about meeting for coffee, but I never heard back. You didn't show up either. Did I say or do something wrong the other night?"

"I had my book signing this afternoon." She cocked her head. "Remember? I told you over dinner."

"Shit." Jamie laughed, rubbing the back of his neck. "Sorry, I think I was so excited to see you again that it just slipped my mind. I'm sorry I'm making it a big deal. I should've remembered it since that's the whole reason you're here in New York again." He rested his arms on the railing as well, avoiding her gaze as he said the next sentence. "I read your book today, by the way. I had no idea you had been writing about us, Liv."

"To be honest, it wasn't my intention," she said. "I didn't even think anyone would be able to piece it together, but I just kept coming back to us. I guess it all had to come out one way or another. I just wanted the characters to have this gorgeous love story with an ending I felt proud of, that's all."

CHAPTER 15

"I know. Everything works out for them in the end."

"Yes, but I didn't make it easy for them. They really had to fight for it. That's what makes the ending so satisfying."

"You got me rooting for them." He lowered his voice so that only she could hear. "Since you showed up in New York, it's been really hard to think about anything else, and ever since the other night, it's been *impossible* to. I know this is going to sound like it's coming out of nowhere, but I've given it a lot of thought, Liv. I know we can't do anything to change the past and what happened has already happened, but I can't let you walk away again without telling you just how much you mean to me."

"What are you trying to say?"

"Liv, stay here with me." Jamie moved closer and took her hands in his. "I mean it."

"Stay with you?" she repeated.

"Yes, here in New York. With me. We're not kids anymore and surely the both of us being here and running into each other again counts for something, right? I know it's hard to believe, but I never stopped thinking about you since you left. I've got a lot to regret, but I don't want to add staying quiet about how I feel to that list." There was sincerity and hopefulness in his eyes that was unlike anything Olivia had ever seen from him before. "For what it's worth, I'm always going to be in love with you and I'm sorry if I messed it all up before, but stay here in New York with me and we can start over again. All you have to do is stay."

It felt somehow fated that they were standing on a bridge right then—a physical reminder of being in the middle between two very different outcomes.

Stay or go.

Seattle or New York.

Jamie or a future without him.

At that moment, Olivia realized it wasn't the distance, the waiting, or even the doubts that crumbled their relationship years ago—it was the fact that he needed to lose her in order to realize that he needed her and wanted to be with her.

And Olivia couldn't live with that.

She couldn't go on with someone who only saw her value when it was too late.

Everything that Jamie was saying was extremely distracting and heartfelt, but Olivia forced herself to stay true to the reason why she had asked him to meet her.

She wasn't used to standing up for herself or taking up space because she was so used to letting people like her dad, Landon Parker, and Lynn take over the narrative and make her feel inadequate or lacking in some way. She would just sit in her discomfort in the shadows, making sure everything and everyone around her was happy and in harmony, completely forgetting about what she wanted and deserved because deep down, she wasn't even sure if she was of value to the people around her.

But she wasn't that same person anymore. She wanted more for herself, to feel at peace with the decisions she was making for her future self.

Olivia let out a big breath and stared out into the distance. The sun was beginning to sink lower in the summer sky, painting the clouds and buildings around them in soft pink. If she had chosen differently after waking up in Jamie's apartment the other day, maybe they would be having a different conversation. Maybe they would be making plans or walking home together, ready to embark on a future together that was substantial and real.

But as much as she wanted that one night with him to turn into a lifetime, it was too late to try to fit their relationship back into their lives when it no longer had a place. It was something she was already aware of when she woke up in Jamie's apartment.

"I can't," she said at last, so softly that Jamie had to lean forward to catch it. "I can't stay here with you."

"Why not?" A flash of disappointment crossed his eyes. "Nothing is keeping us apart anymore."

"We don't get everything we want in life, Jamie." She took her hands away and moved away from the railing. "We make our choices and then we face the consequences. You weren't ready to give up your life in New York to build one with me and I've accepted that, but you don't get to stand here today

CHAPTER 15

asking me to do the same. I'd never be able to forgive myself if I did. I'm happy with the life I have back in Seattle, the one I learned to love without you."

"I thought you wrote us a happy ending because that was what you wanted. I thought it was your way of telling me." Jamie laughed humorlessly, a vacant look in his eyes. "I was stupid to assume that, wasn't I?"

"No, it's what I wanted for us at one point in time, too." A faint glimmer of a smile appeared on her lips as if going back in time to the highlight reel of their old relationship. "I really loved you."

"I loved you, too," he said. "But I don't understand why you won't give us another try."

"Because I don't think it's what we really want."

"What are you talking about? Of *course* I want this, Liv. I want to share my life with you."

"No, you want *easy*. You want me now when we already have everything in life exactly the way we want them to be. You want us together because there are no struggles or hard decisions to be made, but that's not what I want in a partner." Olivia's voice didn't waver, not even once, and she looked directly at him as she spoke. "I can't be with you knowing you only love and want me when things are easy and convenient for you." Jamie shook his head. "I never meant to hurt you."

"I know, but you did anyway."

"You can't hold that against me, Liv. I'm not the person I used to be."

"Neither am I," she countered. "The person I am now is someone who wants a partner that shows up when he says he will. I don't want to hold it against you either, but I'll always remember how it felt to lose you and give up on our future. I'm sorry, but I can't find it in myself to do it again, Jamie. I guess there are some things you can forgive but can't forget about."

Jamie nodded, the weight of her words heavy on his heart. "I understand."

The two of them crossed the bridge and kept walking through Central Park, but there was more space between them this time around.

"With that being said, I hope you can forgive me for turning our relationship into a bestseller," she chuckled, her eyes sparkling in the fading light as they walked. "Does that make me an opportunistic person?"

"No, not an opportunistic one." Jamie shoved his hands in his pockets and returned a small smile. "Just a creative one."

As much as he wanted to try to convince her to change her mind and stay, there was something about the way she said everything that made it clear she had thought about it for some time.

There was no turning back now.

They reached an empty park bench shrouded by trees and took a seat, both of them knowing full well it would be the last time they'd see each other again. It felt different this time around, knowing that whatever closure they got from those remaining few moments together would be the last of it forever. The future they could've had was just going to have to be water flowing under the bridge and out to sea for the rest of their lives.

They sat there for a long time on that bench, neither one of them wanting to give up their borrowed time together. Sooner or later, they would have to get up and go on with their lives, but right then, they had forever. And as much as he loved her, Jamie knew that it wasn't enough for their lives to always intersect and then ricochet in opposite directions. They were finally surrendering and closing the chapter, and there was a kind of peace that came with knowing they loved each other during a really special point in time—and that was going to have to be enough.

Jamie spoke eventually, his voice flecked with emotion. "I've got a lot to learn to live without, but I'm glad that it was you from day one. And—"

"And what?"

Jamie didn't answer right away, just looked at her with those brown eyes of his. "And thank you. For everything. For loving me, for trusting and believing in me even when I had nothing to show for it back then." He paused. "And for forgiving me even after everything that's happened between us. I'm glad that it was always you."

"I'm glad that it was always you, too. I'm glad it was *us*."

Olivia rested her head on Jamie's shoulder. There was nothing else to say, so neither of them looked for words. They stayed there on that park bench for a long time, allowing the last of the summer evening to envelope them in

CHAPTER 15

its warm embrace, grateful that the universe had brought them together one more time.

* * *

While stopped at a red light a few days later, Jamie's phone rang.

Pushing his sunglasses up, he squinted at the name on the screen, then punched the button with his knuckle to accept the call from Lynn. "Hey, what's up?"

"You probably already heard from Olivia that I was the one who got her in touch with you. I wanted to call to make sure you didn't put a hit on me or anything. Organized crime is not one of your strengths."

"I can sniff out your antics from a mile away, but don't worry, you're safe for now. My life would be a hundred times less interesting without your nose in my business all the time," he said, a touch of playful affection in his voice. "But yes, I saw Olivia."

"What happened? Where is she now?"

Jamie pressed his lips together. The summer heat created shimmery waves in the distance while a radio station buzzed loudly from the car next to him, the familiar crush of New York traffic somehow comforting in its predictability. "Nothing happened. She's back in Seattle."

There was a pause on the other end of the line. "No grand confessions? No getting back together? No impromptu proposal?"

Jamie laughed. "Not everything has to be grand and cinematic, okay?"

"I don't believe a word you're saying. If you're off work, let's meet for dinner so you can tell me what actually happened. I'm offering you free food here, J."

"I'm down for free food, but you're not going to get a word out of me. I'm warning you now."

"We'll see about that. I'll call you later." Lynn hung up.

Jamie turned up the music in his car again. It wasn't Billy Joel or Springsteen or Sinatra, but a new band that he just discovered that morning. It felt good to be listening to something new, something different.

As he nodded along to the first few notes coming through the speakers, he looked out his window at the green-and-gold bookstore he passed every day on his way home from work, recognizing a very familiar book cover. There was Olivia's novel standing front and center in the display window, their thinly-veiled love story spanning 188 pages out there for the rest of the world to have now.

The light turned green and the car behind him honked, but Jamie didn't move.

No one, not a single person in the world, would ever truly and fully understand it the way he did.

It was a final love letter meant just for him.

The ghost of what could've been materialized in the passenger seat beside him as some phantom version of Olivia. He could still hear her laugh over all the noise and her hand was just a few inches away from his, but just as suddenly as she had appeared, the illusion melted away into the rays of sunshine pouring through his car windows, leaving no trace of her behind.

The cacophony of New York traffic filled the space again in seconds and the driver behind him honked again, more impatiently this time.

He had a feeling it would be the last time he'd ever see her—real or imagined.

Jamie raised his hand in apology and stepped on the gas with reluctance.

He took a deep breath in, watching as the bookstore grew smaller and smaller behind him in the rear-view mirror until it disappeared completely.

About the Author

Elvira Chan was born and raised in Vancouver, British Columbia. She received her Bachelor of Arts in Communication from Simon Fraser University and is passionate about her work in mental health. She hopes to continue sharing stories and making an impact through her words for years to come. *The State of Us* is her first novel.

Manufactured by Amazon.ca
Bolton, ON